WHEN THE
WIND CRIES

WHEN THE WIND CRIES

CLAUDETTE NICOLE

CUTTING EDGE

ISBN-13: 978-1-957868-55-4

Published by
Cutting Edge Books
PO Box 8212
Calabasas, CA 91372
www.cuttingedgebooks.com

CHAPTER ONE

Once, evil was only a word. I heard it in church, during the sermon. Pastor Bourke often used it. Sometimes I heard it at home when the adults were in a heated conversation. Only a word.

But I was little, then.

Once, evil was a name for something bad, a term of contrast, the direct opposite of good.

But I was small, then.

Once, evil was a descriptive noun, a philosophic and religious concept, essentially abstract, though applied to human behavior.

But I was young, then.

I know differently, now: I know evil, now. I know the depth and breadth and terror of it. I have felt its touch, the silent clawing of it, the dark pursuit of it. I have felt it surrounding me, waiting, waiting with its infinite patience, refusing to be denied. I know evil, now, as it really is, no longer simply as a word, a descriptive noun, an abstraction. It's so much more than any of those things. It's a force, as real as any force you can see and touch and feel. It is a presence, a power in its own right. It is a raging demon of the soul and, like an incubus, it takes on a human form and shape and name. . . . It masquerades for me, cloaking itself, its vitally real presence, behind places, people, things, behind cheerful, earnest faces that bear names, Victor, Clay, Paul, Marie, behind the softly lush beauty of the Acadian country; it lies rooted in the very spirit of past loves.

No, it's not a word now, not an abstraction, but a terrible force, this presence called evil, along with its handmaiden, death. I know that pale rider now, and I know that somehow, in some way, I may have to ride him down again. I may have but one, final chance. I know only that. There is no way to know how or when he will come once more for me on his pale steed, galloping with silent hooves. I only know he's likely to come when the wind cries.

Tomorrow wears a veil to hide that final evening, and I must wait just a little longer. And, as I count off moments, I realize that I know only how it all began, how this came into being, this almost final point in a long chain of events. But even that gives me pause. We like to think we cut out our own paths, that we are what we are because of our own efforts. But are we, really? Such a confluence of forces make us what we are. I wonder how much we really choose and how much is begun for us, only waiting for our arrival. Certainly this moment had a beginning full of waiting aspects.

It was one of those bright, fall mornings when the world looks newly made. The outdoor Deven Horse show (American Horse Show Association, of course) was off to its usual snapping start, its ring-posts sporting the club colors—blue, yellow and gray—bright pennants fluttering over the grandstand seats, the grass a bright green carpeting underfoot. The ring was the focal point of all attention; to one side stood the saddling areas and, surrounding the show itself in, appropriately-enough, a horse-shoe shaped border, were rows of cars, trailers, horse vans and campers.

The crowd was, as usual, made up of people whose casual clothes were more perfectly tailored than the very best of most people's wardrobes. It was a special kind of world made of a special blend of elements; wealth was one. But wealth comfortably worn, a quiet presence never shouted. The appreciation of fine animals was there, of course, and the shine of polished tack and that particular, evocative smell of fine leather.

I'd grown up in that world, been part of it, ever since I was a little girl. I'd been an insider and yet an outsider, but I'd had the best of two possible worlds. Or it seemed so to me as I was growing up. The hood pick, dandy brush, curry comb, sweat scraper and stable rubber were as much a part of my household as a toothbrush and comb were to the average youngster. I grew up in a world of a special kind of talk, a special kind of companionship and a special kind of love. That last was the important thing, that special quality which separates the members of that world from those who only looked in on it. In that world, my world, there existed that love of horses, of all animals, that defies reasoned explanation. It is a kind of rapport which can never be successfully translated into words. It is a bond that is not, despite the pedestrian opinions of some behaviorists, an environmental, acquired matter. It is a mystical, magical communication that need not be explained to those who know it and cannot be to those who don't.

That had been my world always. I'd never minded the one part of that world which was not mine, the wealth, the comfort of real substance. Dad had always made a good living, though perhaps better than most men, and most material things were usually on hand for me as I grew into womanhood.

Once again part of that world, I was standing at ringside on that bright morning when it all began. I was watching Katie Elshermer on Trailblazer, a good, solid bay gelding. My pupils had gone first, second and first in the three equitation classes, and I was pleased. But not overly so. The competition had been quite ordinary and now I'd settled down to watch Katie in Open Hunters. She had just cleared the first post-and-rail and was heading for the second.

"Damn," I heard myself mutter. I always mutter when I watch, an occupational disease, my eye seeing so many things before they happen. The bay was getting his head up too high and I saw that Katie hadn't put the martingale on as I'd told her to do. Katie was stubborn and too easily pleased with herself. She was the second daughter of a Boston family who enjoyed the results of newly inherited money. I watched the gelding near the next jump, winced and uttered another "Damn." He had his head up much too high and she couldn't do much about it. I felt my lips draw back as the bay headed into the jump too fast, dislodged the top pole and came down heavily. She went on to the standard with poles and I almost turned away, the outcome of that as certain as the sun that flooded the field. She just barely maintained control of her horse as the two top poles went down and then I did turn away.

Katie Elshermer was more than stubborn. She had the hands of a stevedore. She would be a manufactured horsewoman, no matter how adept she might become with constant practice. Give me the natural rider, I murmured to myself as I crossed the grass. Regardless of inexperience, bad mannerisms or shortcomings, the natural rider automatically goes with the horse, automatically reacts properly. It was Katie Elshermer, and all the other young ladies and gentlemen like her, that made up the reasons why I'd had enough of the Bay State Riding Academy. And why old dreams were prodding and haunting with new insistence.

I'd paused to receive congratulations on my Equitation pupils from Robert Bendix, an old friend and competitor and had just started across the show grounds again when I heard a voice call my name. I turned.

"Miss Forester," the voice called again and then I saw the man walking toward me, a ramrod straight figure, tall enough to be impressive just for that, but it was his head that riveted me in its intensity. It was the head of an eagle, eyes that pierced, a large strong nose and a completely bald pate. His mouth was a straight, tight line across a high-cheekboned, angular face. He wore a gray and white hounds-tooth jacket and gray slacks and in his right hand, carried a gnarled, blackthorn walking stick.

"My name is Jeffries, Major Robert Jeffries," he said. His clipped intonation matched the imperious, chiseled features, I thought. "I've come here expressly to see you, Miss Forester," he said.

He managed to make the statement into a kind of command. It was probably meant as a compliment, I decided. He didn't seem the kind of a man who went out of his way to see anyone.

"Is there somewhere we can talk?" he asked.

I nodded and led the way to a row of round, metal tables placed near the judge's tent. I picked the last table in the line, slid into a chair and waited. Major Jeffries carefully folded himself into the chair opposite mine. He was, I saw, one of those people who look as though they're standing up when they're sitting down. His piercing eagle eyes moved over me, examining me with such intensity that I suddenly felt quite naked.

"You're not quite as I imagined you," he remarked.

"Is that important?" I asked.

"Not at all," he clipped out. The comment was not new to me. I wasn't the typical horsewoman, neither in face nor in figure. I had none of the average horsewoman's narrow-hipped, flat rear, small-busted, long, lean body, that particular kind of beauty put together of planes and angles that always seemed a human reflection of the thoroughbred and the fine saddle horse. Someone once said that I ought to ride quarter horses. I had a face that was not at all angular, my cheeks round and full, nose small and upturned and I had a deep bust, curved hips and a round little rear. Definitely not the typical horsewoman's figure, but then I wasn't the average horsewoman, either. I watched the hawk-faced man bring a small slip of paper from his pocket and begin to read from it.

"Gail Forester, twenty-six, five feet six inches, born in Lexington, Kentucky," he intoned. "National Equitation Championship winner at twelve, Grand Champion Open Jumpers at fifteen, Open Hunters at sixteen, winner of five gold medals at the Olympic meet in Munich, winner of the five-gaited saddle horse Championship at every major show in the United States. Became riding Instructor at Bay State Riding Academy three years ago. Youngest instructor ever to put five pupils into the winner's circle at Badminton. Attended University of Kentucky, majored in psychology, minored in English. Mother died when she was ten, raised by father, the noted racing and harness trainer, Dan Forester, now deceased."

He halted, looked up and the piercing, dark-blue eyes pinned me again as he put the slip of paper back into his pocket. His homework had been thorough but I felt more intrigued than flattered. "You have an advantage," I said. "I know nothing about Major Robert Jeffries."

"I shall be happy to tell you all you need to know, now. The rest you will learn after you work for me," he said.

"Work for you?" I blurted, surprise tumbling out in the words.

"Yes, that's what has brought me here from my home in Louisiana," the man said and caught the further surprise that touched my eyes. "I've traveled too much to have an accent left," he said quickly. "My ranch and experimental breeding farm is in the area called Acadiana, the Cajun country, the section west of Calcasieu lake."

I felt the interest surge up at once inside me, forced my voice to remain casual. Those eagle eyes missed very little, I'd already determined. "What kind of experimental breeding?" I asked mildly.

"Fine horses and cattle. I've a number of herds and strains I'm working with. The land is a mixed bag, bayou, marsh and good grass in places, some pasture land. I've the salt water of the Gulf if I need it and I go west to Texas only twenty miles away if I want real grazing room." He paused and the imperious visage didn't flicker as he slid the next sentence forward. "It's a fine opportunity for anyone interested in going into breeding," he remarked. I heard myself swear inwardly. The man either knew more than he had any right to know about me or he was a very shrewd, astute observer. Perhaps both, I decided as he replied to my next question.

"What makes you think I'm interested in breeding?" I asked. What may have been a smile touched his lips, a split-second relaxation of the facial muscles.

"A thought," he said. "You've gone as far as you can in your career as a rider and instructor. You'll look to other worlds to conquer."

I tried to match the expressionless mask of his chiseled face, knew I failed miserably and silently swore at myself. "Perhaps," I allowed. "Is that what you've come to see me about?"

"No indeed," Major Robert Jeffries answered quickly. "I've come here because I want you to teach someone to ride. It's to be a crash course—intensive, daily instruction. It must be done within three months at the longest. I want it done, I want her ready to ride in public in six weeks. I'm offering you a contract for five thousand dollars with another five if it can be done within six weeks."

"That's a good deal of money," I remarked, trying to see into the hawk-like face; I might have done better to try and see through a stone wall.

"I want the very best I can find. I want someone to devote their time wholly to this project. I'm willing to pay for that," he said.

"Who am I to teach to ride?" I asked.

"My daughter, Amanda," Major Jeffries replied.

"How old is Amanda?" I questioned.

"Eighteen," he said. "I've learned that your contract here is up for renewal so there's no question as to your availability."

The man had been thorough in his investigation and his eyes held mine, seeming to read the thoughts that danced through my mind. "The money is attractive but it's not all-important," he commented. "It wouldn't be to someone such as yourself."

Once again I had the feeling that this strange, dominant man knew me as well as I knew myself. "Is that why you mentioned your breeding farm?" I asked and his thin lips pushed forward.

"Perhaps. You'd have the opportunity to observe and learn. One can't teach riding all day and night," Major Jeffries said. He was thorough, acute, but I wondered if he knew how responsive a chord he had really touched. I'd grown up in my world, but riding and grooming had been most of it. I missed learning the hard, practical aspects of running a stable and breeding farm and that was what I needed to know.

"What kind of stock do you have?" I asked.

"In cattle, new strains and variations. I've crossed a variety of Texas longhorn and Brahmin, also Angus and Hereford with an outcross of Brahmin, the Hereford for beef, the Angus for bulk and physical stamina and the Brahmin for resistance to ticks, heat and other pests. I've also crossed Charolaise and longhorn with interesting results. In horses, I've concentrated on trying to build up foundation stock of some of the less known breeds as well as the Arabians, American Saddle and Standardbreds. I've three Shagya Arabs from Hungary and a half-dozen Knabstrups from Denmark. I'm particularly excited over the three Akhal Teké I have from Russia," Major Jeffries finished.

The excitement spiraling through me was beyond containing. "Akhal Teké?" I echoed. "How fantastic. How did you ever get hold of them? I understand the Russians just don't permit them out of the country."

"My wife's been dead for nearly ten years now but her family name still carries a lot of weight in the right circles. Wentley," he said. "Of Wentley Farms."

"Yes, of course," I murmured. The name appeared in the stud records of so many of the finest horses, one of the grand old names in the history of horse breeding here and in England.

"I traded on the name," the Major said evenly. "Old connections, old favors, old friends that still remember her father and his father. Past history still carries weight."

"Obviously. You got the horses," I remarked.

"I usually get what I want, Miss Forester," Major Jeffries said. The statement carried no hollow bragging in it, no smug triumphalism, only a cold certainty that made me shiver, suddenly. I met the hard, cold gaze of his eyes and felt very small. "I'll give you three days to think about my offer," he said, reaching into his pocket. He thrust an engraved card at me, his name in the center of it. *Darkwater Farms,* I read beneath the name, *Hackberry, Louisiana.* A phone number was in the lower right-hand corner of the card. "I'll be back there tomorrow morning. Call me and I'll have the contract and half the money sent to you immediately. I'll expect you down within a week after," he said.

He rose, an abrupt movement, now as an eagle exploding into flight, paused and looked down at me. He seemed to harbor not the slightest doubt that I would accept. Even more unexplainable to me was the fact that I wasn't angry. I always resented people making assumptions for or about me, and yet now, with this powerfully commanding man, I felt no irritation at all, only a tremendous interest. Of course, there were reasons for that, I told myself, reasons with their roots in other times and other wounds. And I always responded to the unusual, the challenging. I let myself be content with such rational explanations.

"Three days, Miss Forester," Major Jeffries said, turned and strode away, carrying but not using the blackthorn walking stick, I noted. It had been a strange meeting, the offer itself only the bare facts with obviously a lot left unsaid. He had been correct and polite but I had the feeling that it had been an effort, that correctness and politeness were invisible bars of a cage to him. I watched him until he disappeared from view in the crowd around the grandstand and then got to my feet. I heard the call for the three-gaited saddle horse class over the public address system and headed for the ring, putting aside thoughts of Major Robert Jeffries. Another of my students, Terry Kloster, was in the class. Terry had insisted on entering to show off for visiting relatives though I didn't feel her really ready yet. I had confidence in her, though. There were four entries but Terry had two important things going for her: her horse, a fine, bay gelding, a Morgan, with good manners and an enjoyment in showing; the other, her own relaxed personality. She wouldn't be uptight. That easy relaxation would communicate itself to her horse. They picked up your state of emotions quicker than a trained psychiatrist.

I took up a position at the corner of the ring, eyes narrowed, and concentrated on the scene before me. Terry did well in the trot and the walk and excelled in the canter, had her horse well collected, taking off with a right lead and letting him move into a good stride. With the bay's natural enthusiasm for showing, she took the blue. I threaded my way to the semi-circle of vans and cars. I wanted to avoid the endless round of congratulations and accolades. I found the van with Herb Egan leaning against it, a paper cup with bourbon and water in one hand. He held it out to me and I took a sip. Herb Egan was trainer and stable manager for Bay State Academy, had been so for over ten years. He was a good man, hardworking, sensitive enough, capable yet full of limitations. My father used to have a phrase for men such as Herb Egan. "You'll meet them all over," he'd say. "They're shadowed inside. They have all the good qualities yet their lives are always full of mediocrity. Inside themselves they fail, and so, of course, they fail outside. They usually find their best friend in a bottle."

Over the years, I'd met enough of them to know how right that was. Herb Egan was one, but he didn't miss much as he sipped his bourbon and water. "Who was the big man?" he tossed out quietly.

"A Major Robert Jeffries," I replied. "He offered me a very fat contract for a special job of instruction." Herb and I had exchanged confidences often enough. Besides, I wasn't the secretive type.

"You'll take it," Herb said, tossing away the paper cup. He went to the rear of the single-horse van we'd brought and opened the door as Jimmy, the stableboy, approached with the single filly we'd brought to the meet.

"Why do you say that?" I questioned.

"You're restless. You've been riding the edge for months, now," he answered. I felt my lips tighten.

"I didn't know it showed that much," I commented, annoyed with myself. He was right, of course, I mused as I climbed into the seat of the pick-up truck, listened to the sound of the filly being loaded into the van attached behind. The restlessness had been increasing, a quiet fire that consumed, all part of one thing. Herb Egan climbed into the truck, took the wheel and started to drive out of the show grounds. I sat silently with my thoughts on the way back and swung from the truck as he stopped for a moment in front of the house where I rented the second floor apartment, less than ten blocks from the Academy stables. I waved Herb away and went up the side stairway to my rooms, three small but neat, comfortable enough rooms in an old, white, framed house. I glanced at my watch. Tom Corbett was to call me at seven; plenty of time yet and I took off my slacks and blouse and stretched out across the bed at an angle. I closed my eyes, let thoughts begin to shift themselves into an orderly progression. It was time to take stock, to look backward once more before moving forward.

I thought about inner fires, back to the moment when they'd first flared into flame, a moment that had been seared into me. Some experiences are like brands, burned into us forever. It hadn't been that long ago, a handful of years, but a moment when I stopped being young. I had won the Olympic medals, plus a host of lesser awards, and I'd returned in time to attend the annual Maryland Conformation Ball, the yearly major social event of the horse set. The guest list was a catalog of every fine racing, show and harness stable in the country and everyone who was anyone in the horse world turned out for the night. I'd come back and received a special award at the Ball and the extra award of the pride in my father's eyes. He wasn't a big man, thin and slight of build, but he could radiate a quiet charm that made him very popular; Dan Forester had been trainer for only the finest farms in the country. I'd grown up well-known in that special world, always Dan Forester's girl, and that had been good. I'd enjoyed making my own mark and after the Gold Medals of the Olympics I felt I'd conquered everything, won a complete acceptance. It was a heady feeling, full of the näiveté of the young. It was later that night when it exploded in my face, that searing flame that was never to go out afterward.

I'd just come from the powder room, down the long side corridor of the ballroom in my off-the-shoulder light-pink gown, when I passed behind Mrs. Alistair Voorhis, owner of White Ridge Farms and the *grande dame* of the horse world, breeder of more racing greats and show champions than any other woman in the country. I paused as I heard her deep voice mention my name as she spoke to a small knot of friends.

"Dan Forester's girl? Oh, she's a really remarkable rider. Quite a bright little thing, too, it seems," I heard the woman say.

"You going to use her on your jumpers and hunters?" someone asked.

"I'd love to," Mrs. Alistair Voorhis said. "I'll always make a place for an excellent rider. I believe in utilizing every special skill."

"I understand she has a talent for teaching," someone else said.

"Really? That remains to be seen," Mrs. Alistair Voorhis pronounced and swept across the ballroom floor with her friends in tow.

I stayed riveted in place in the side corridor, the woman's words echoing. *Remarkable rider...quite a bright little thing, too.* Words, tone, phrasing, all coming together to say so much more than the actual words alone. I'd never known, till then, that one could be accepted and dismissed in one sweeping gesture. Silently, I heard Mrs. Alistair Voorhis again. *Always make a place…excellent rider…utilize every special skill.* Not even acceptance in those words but an assigning, an outlining of position. My accomplishments, my conquering of worlds, was suddenly a dry and hollow victory. Acceptance structured with limitations, like love with restrictions, I grimaced; no love at all and no acceptance at all. I was suddenly learning the distinction between recognition and acceptance and I rebelled at the lesson, refused the inequity of it. Furious, holding anger inside, I managed the remainder of the evening with mechanical sweetness, glad that the hour was already late. When the ball ended, I asked that my date, Phil Evans, take me directly home. Phil had been more a friend than a date, anyway, and he was gracious and not unhappy to comply.

Daddy and I were living in a comfortable old carriage house then and I saw the study lights on as I arrived. After saying goodnight to Phil, I went inside, pushed the study door open to see him in his favorite leather chair with a mug in his hand, his favorite way of sipping good whiskey on ice. He knew me too well, read the anger in my face at once and beckoned me in. Words exploded from me, a torrent of half-formed, too-new wounds. He listened and then, when I finally simmered down, replied. We spoke for a long time, and of all the things he said to me in those small, still hours, I remember a few words above all.

"You thought you'd opened all the doors, didn't you?" he said quietly. "But there are some doors that only open to special keys."

"Keys held by a bunch of snobs," I snapped.

He shook his head slowly. "No, not the way you mean it, Gail," he said. "It's a special kind of fraternity. Being the finest rider, the finest trainer, the finest judge of horseflesh, carries you up to the door but not inside it. People like Edith Voorhis, and it's a small club, have an earned right to that inner circle of theirs. They don't share it casually."

"How? What earned right?" I pressed.

"By being able to turn out, year after year, fine horses, consistent in quality, true-to-type, sound and capable of carrying on their line. That kind of breeding isn't luck. It's the heart of what makes fine animals. Not many people can do it. That's what makes that inner circle. The door to it will open when you show evidence that you can qualify. Fine riders come and go, my dear. Developing quality, consistent, true-to-type bloodlines is making yourself a part of tomorrow."

"I want to do that," I said quietly. "Someday I want to breed fine horses, my own stock, my own line. I know I can do it if I get the chance." His eyes studied me and his hand reached out, stroked my hair as I sat on the floor in front of his chair.

"Yes, I think you might be able to," he said thoughtfully. "I've watched you long enough. I certainly know you well enough. I've seen signs."

"What signs?" I asked quickly. "What does it take to breed and raise fine horses?"

His laugh was quiet and held ruefulness in it. "Breeding fine horses, fine dogs, fine anything, takes a lot of things. Yet none of them alone is enough."

"It takes money," I said with a certain grimness. He chuckled again.

"Yes, it takes money for good foundation stock, proper quarters, feed and care…but money isn't enough or any rich man could buy the finest stock around and go from there. I know people with a lot of money who've floundered through years of breeding without ever developing a fine animal, much less a great one," he said. "In the same way that it takes a knowledge of bloodlines, the working history of breeding, knowing what studs and dams have produced. But I can show you people who can quote chapter and verse about bloodlines, stud registries and pedigrees. They know exactly who sired what and the precise results of hundreds of breedings. Yet all that hasn't enabled them to breed a damn thing worthwhile."

"It take a knowledge of genetics," I interjected.

"Yes, but if that were the secret, one need only hire a professor of genetics, let him chart out a program and become a great breeder," he answered.

"It takes a good eye."

"That's important," he said. "It takes the eye of an artist, the ability to see line, beauty, anatomy, soundness. But that isn't enough or any good artist could breed fine horses and dogs."

"Then it takes all those things put together," I said.

"Yes, except all that isn't enough. It takes one thing more, that key element most people lack. Pilots speak of an ability they call being able to 'fly by the seat-of-your-pants.' It's a sensitivity, an innate, sixth sense, an intuitive ability. The good breeder must have a variation of that, an almost magical, intuitive sense, that quality that lets you look at a particular stud and a particular dam and say, 'Those two together.' It's a psychic matter, that seat-of-the-pants ability, but it's the extra dimension that makes the difference. Without it, I'm convinced, none of the rest is enough."

That night dissolved as I let yesterdays slide away and I found myself thinking about Major Robert Jeffries. The man had come at precisely the right time and only a part of that was the result of his careful investigation. The rest was something else, that confluence of forces, again. They determined what we conceitedly called our decisions. I wouldn't need three days to call him, I knew. I'd need only tomorrow morning.

I glanced at my watch and pulled myself up, swung from the bed. It was time to shower and change. I snapped off bra, stepped out of panties and went into the bathroom to stand under a hot shower. The Academy could get another instructor within the week, I knew. They'd be disappointed but not stranded. And Tom Corbett? I half-smiled as I stepped from the shower, dried myself. Tom would be upset but mostly because it'd mean a change in his routine and Tom was a person of routine. I'd met him over a year ago at one of the shows in Vermont and we'd hit it off well. Tom was a competent horseman, better than average, but his manners with a horse always bothered me. They were too studied, too precise, too careful. I put it up to poor early instructions until one night when I wound up in bed with him. Bed can be such a place of learning, you know. Tom made love with the same precise, competent manner, without that extra flair, that wildness that spelled the difference between pleasant-ness and pleasure, routine and rapture. Actually, we had a great deal more in common outside of bed than in it, shared interests, a common circle of friends, a kinship of pursuits, and so Tom became more a friend than a lover. I'd experienced the other, ecstacy in bed but very little outside of it and that, too, was an incomplete circle. I often wondered which of the two was the most unsatisfying. Men, I'd almost decided, were not unlike old jigsaw puzzles. Most were quite fascinating but there were always pieces missing.

I slipped into a gray skirt and deep-red sweater and was ready when he called, precisely at seven. We decided to meet at the restaurant, a sprawling inn some three miles from where I lived. I climbed into my little blue compact, was on the terrace sipping a stinger when he arrived. As usual, our initial conver-sation revolved around shows and horses. He'd been having trouble with his best three-gaited horse, a chestnut mare who kept developing windgalls. It wasn't till later, when we'd finished dinner, that I told him of the offer and my decision to take it. I kept my private smile inside as Tom's face lengthened. "Damn," he muttered. "I was counting on going to the Devon Meet with you as usual." Later, when I told him more about Major Jeffries and the offer, he frowned at me.

"Don't you think you ought to check this out a bit more? The money's damned inviting and all that but you don't know any-thing else about it," he protested.

"No, I might find some reason to turn it down," I laughed.

"His daughter might be an absolute little bitch," Tom said.

"I'll teach her to ride no matter what," I said. My lack of caution unnerved Tom. He'd never do anything like it, I knew. It seemed quite fitting to our last evening together, encapsulating the basic difference between us. And so the evening ended finally. He took me back to my place and we went through the motions that were no more than that for me, reaffirmations of their own. Then, afterwards, words that were no more than words. I was glad to be alone, finally. Hypocrisy came to mind but it was too strong a term. I settled for slightly shoddy. It was indeed a time for making new moves, for going on. That confluence of aspects was working for Major Robert Jeffries beyond his strongest expectations. I slid beneath the sheets, enjoyed their cool smoothness against my skin, reached out and set the alarm to wake early. Turning on my side, I slept quickly, soundly.

I didn't know how long I'd been asleep when I woke, eyes snapping open. I was sitting up, my skin cold, made of tiny little bumps and I was breathing hard. I'd been dreaming and the dream clung to me as I came awake. I'd been on a horse, racing through darkness, a void, jumping over unseen obstacles. I rode a wild steed through space and terror rode with me. I reached out, pulled the sheet up, my breasts suddenly cold. I was aware of the frown that dug into my brow. I was one of those people who never seemed to dream. And now I had only a vague memory of the dream, the wild horse racing, my face framed in fear, subliminal impressions of the subconscious and nothing more. Unusual, I muttered silently, terribly unusual for me.

I let myself fall back on the bed, let my breathing return to normalcy, my skin grow less cold. I lay still and tried to remember the last time I remembered dreaming about anything at all. The effort was unsuccessful and I closed my eyes, lay still and finally slept once again to wake only when the alarm went off in the bright light of morning.

CHAPTER TWO

M y little car was gray-blue under a heavy coat of road dust as I headed west from Plaquemine. I was in the heart of Acadiana, now, the Cajun country of Louisiana. As I'd driven the long distance, I conjured up a feeling of kinship with Longfellow's heroine, journeying from Massachusetts instead of Nova Scotia, uprooted by my own hand instead of Britishers'. Still, it was fun, seeing myself as a twentieth-century Evangeline, Longfellow's tragic heroine updated, moving on my own *grand derangement*. And the last few days in Wayland had been as hectic as if I had been uprooted.

First, of course, had been calling Major Robert Jeffries. "Very good," he'd said crisply. "I'll expect you within the week." The contract had arrived within a day, along with a check for five thousand dollars. I gave the Academy my notice and helped them find a replacement, a task that took more time than I'd anticipated. The next days were spent in packing and discarding. I always hate discarding. It entails throwing away part of yourself. After all, what are the things we cling to, the private things we keep, the personal mementoes, but little pieces of ourselves. But one wrestles, sometimes anguishes, and leaves things behind and, finally, I slid behind the wheel of my little blue car and headed south.

I rode the days down through New York, Pennsylvania, New Jersey, Virginia and Kentucky, then into the southland, Tennessee and Mississippi and I listened with my heart to the names that flashed past the windshield. These were names of but one land, carved-out names, I called them, that told of a people, a spirit and a life—Lone Oak, Hickory Flat, Guntown, Duck Hill, Scrabble Road, Indian Corner, Eagle Rock—names lean as a rifle, sinewy as a bootstrap. When I crossed into Louisiana, headed down into the Cajun country, names took on a new ring, softer sounds—Bayou Teche, Grand Coteau, Maringouin, Lore-auville, Mamou, Cote Blanche Bay, Chataignier—echoes of a people transplanted, a people taking their yesterdays into tomorrow. And everywhere, Evangeline, symbol of a tragedy that epitomized the larger pain of a people. As the names changed, so did the land.

I found myself driving along roads that skirted marsh and swamp and bayou and suddenly, unexpectedly, I came on a lush green field and glimpsed tall, stately mansions of white columns and red brick. They disappeared behind and I saw the narrow bayous again, waterways that all but disappear behind walls of willows, oaks hung with Spanish moss and giant cypresses that rose, ghost-like, from the bayous.

I hurried, kept a heavy foot on the accelerator as the day started to wind down. I didn't want to wander these unfamiliar roads by dark. I could already see the trees starting to take on strange shapes in pockets of deep, near-dark mysteriousness. I found a spot to pull to one side, halted and consulted my map again. As I checked out roads and crossings, I heard an unmistakable sound. My ears picked it up the way a foxhound picks up a scent and I looked up to see a small chaise drawn by a roan gelding coming toward me. Two young men occupied the chaise, slowed as they drew abreast of me. One was dark-skinned with even features, the other lighter of skin, his hair curly in contrast to the straight hair of the driver.

"Hello," I called out. "I'm looking for Darkwater Farms. Major Jeffries?" The driver of the chaise turned to the other and they spoke for a moment in Cajun patois. My French was pretty good but I could catch only a few words. Turning back to me, the darker skinned one pointed down the road.

"Go on till you see the two leaning oaks. Take the side road there," he said in English with a faint accent. "Don't tell him we told you the way."

"Why not?" I frowned.

"The Major, he does not take to visitors," the young man said.

"He expects me," I assured them. "Thank you." They nodded in unison, flicked the reins and moved on. I watched the chaise go down the road, its two-wheeled, delicate beauty a prettty sight to see. From the rear of the frame, I saw half-a-dozen brown pelts that looked like beaver, hanging down. The wagon disappeared around a curve and I put the car in gear, continued down the road. I'd gone a good distance and still not seen any sign of two leaning oaks and I pressed harder on the gas pedal, hurrying the car on, racing the oncoming darkness. Suddenly the road rounded a curve and I slammed on the brakes. A wooden pole stretched across the road, blocking it. Another roadway, much narrower, led off to the right. I swung the wheel as I braked, just managing to avoid crashing into the pole, and swung onto the detour.

I swore silently. A detour was not what I wanted now and I pressed hard on the gas pedal, gunning the car along the narrow pathway and short little curves, brushing low-hanging branches. I gunned the engine onto a straight section and suddenly there was no pathway at all in front of me, only the still water of the bayou. I crashed my foot against the brake pedal but I was going too fast to stop in time and the car skidded forward, the front end going down off the abrupt end of the roadway and into the water. I pushed the gear lever into reverse at once, felt the wheels spin, throw up dirt. Then they caught, enough to pull backward a little. I eased up on the gas, pressed gently and felt the wheels take hold, slowly pulling the car up from the water, finally backing onto the dry pathway.

My hands were wet with perspiration. I wiped them on the seat, got out of the car and examined the front end. It seemed all right except for some black mud clinging to the wheels and the bumper. I stared at the roadway. It just ended, without warning, dropping into the bayou. It was obviously a little side road to the dark waters, perhaps to carry boats. I climbed back into the car, found I had to back all the way out of the narrow pathway until I reached the spot where the main road had been closed off. Again, I found myself staring. The road wasn't closed off at all. No pole stretched across it. The road was open, wide open and I climbed from the car, examined the ground at this point. There was no pole there, nothing at all. I hadn't imagined it. My eyes hadn't played tricks on me. It had been there, I repeated silently as I slid behind the wheel.

"Damn," I swore aloud. The pole had been removed, the road opened just where I'd taken the little side path. A strange coincidence, to say the least, yet just possible. Or, had the two men in the chaise put up the pole for their own reasons, suddenly remembered and hurried back to remove it? That was also possible, and would have been just as unusual an occurrence. Dark thoughts slid across my mind and were quickly dispersed with reason. Certainly, it couldn't have been placed there to send me roaring into the bayou. No one knew I was coming except the Major. I decided on my first explanation. Workmen, perhaps, or even trappers, had come to reopen the road seconds after I'd swung onto the other pathway, an unhappy set of circumstances which hadn't turned out as unhappily as they might have. I was grateful for that much as I sent the car speeding onward

The road continued and I leaned sideways, looking for the two oaks; then, suddenly, I saw them just ahead of me, two tall trees that were bent into each other, branches intertwining, certainly easy enough to spot. A side road ran directly beneath them and I turned into it, glimpsed a bayou that paralleled the road. The trees made the road a cool, dark place and as it widened, circled, I saw a sign in gray-white wood with black lettering, hanging from a signpost close against another oak:

DARKWATER FARMS

The air became heavier, scented; I tried to identify the odors. I decided on mimosa and hyacinth and gave up on the others. The road widened again, suddenly became a lawn, and I watched the house rise up before me. Braking to a halt, I frowned as I stared at it.

Expectations have a life of their own. They form themselves secretly, whether we want them to or not, then lie silently for a moment to leap up, sometimes in mocking glee. Consciously, I'd formed no expectations, yet obviously they were quite well in place as I stared in shock at the house. I faced no tall colonnade of white Doric columns rising from an ample portico, no wrought-iron, second-story railing of graceful delicacy, no tranquil, southern beauty, graciousness materialized through an architect's magic. The house I stared at was almost castlelike, but without the massive grandeur of a castle. It was of unrelieved gray stone, thick-walled and thoroughly ungracious. Small windows and a steep roof made a squinty-eyed, glowering face of it and, over the gray stone walls, Spanish moss hung like a dark-green shroud.

The stone, wood, iron and glass of a house give it a body and a face. But those who live inside it form its character. It isn't just the architect who makes some houses open and bright, some quiet and reserved, some warm and others austere. Certainly, this gray-green house was a cloaked place, with something veiled and drawn about it, a malevolence in it that reached out. The emotions are puppeteers that pull on inner strings to make long-forgotten memories dance to life. Standing before the brooding house, I heard the childhood rhyme return to me.

> There was a crooked man, and he went
>   a crooked mile,
> He found a crooked sixpence against
>   a crooked stile;

He bought a crooked cat, which caught
a crooked mouse,
And they all lived together, in a
little crooked house.

Nonsense verse, it was, but touched with a hint of the aberrant and laced with gargoyle grimness. I felt a shudder go through me, grew annoyed at it and moved toward the front door of dark, heavy Spanish oak. I'd almost reached it when it swung open and Major Jeffries stepped out. He work dark slacks, riding boots and a checked jacket. The piercing eyes pinned me at once and the gray rock of the house seemed a perfect backdrop for the eagle-like imperiousness of the man.

"Welcome, Miss Forester," he said. He drew thin lips back in the motion of a smile.

"Hello," I said. "Won't you please call me Gail?"

"Perhaps in time," he returned. His face stayed severe. "It's not my custom to call people by their first names. We live in a too-familiar world."

The remark was given without further elaboration. Perhaps, I reflected, none was needed. A young man appeared in the doorway; straight black hair, features that were fine, dark eyes that were sullen. Major Jeffries nodded to him.

"Sami will bring in your bags," he said and I watched as the young man moved past me, saw the limp in his left leg. Major Jeffries held the door open wider in a gesture to me and I entered the house. "Sami grew up here," the man said. "He's French descent mixed with Indian. He's a kind of handyman."

I halted in the foyer, paneled with the dark, Spanish oak and the Major led me further into the house, through a library also oak paneled. The furniture was heavy, a stolid combination of primitive French with Spanish. I followed the Major into a living room, a large room with the same stolid furniture. A long side table took up one wall, definitely Provençal, but the legs carved with the Spanish foot. A pine Highboy had the usual cabriole leg with the Spanish foot added. The chairs were heavy Wing and Queen Anne.

"The house is yours to use," Major Jeffries said. I glimpsed another room to the right, a dark-wood desk taking up most of it, framed prints of horses and cattle on the walls. "My study. You'll find me there most of the time," Major Jeffries said. "There's another entrance from the main hall. I usually keep the door to the living room closed." He moved forward, pulled the door shut as if in affirmation. I turned as a woman appeared from the hallway, clothed in a floor-length, muslin dress, a brightly patterned kerchief almost hiding gray hair. She had Sami's face, with age added; the resemblance was unmistakable. "My housekeeper, Marie Opatu," Major Jeffries said. "Marie will show you to your room. Perhaps you'll still have time for a quick tour of the stables before it gets dark."

"Yes, I'd like that," I said. The woman turned and I followed as she started down a long, wood-paneled corridor. The young man passed, returning down the hallway, and I paused.

"Thank you," I said.

His eyes snapped hostilely. "For what?" he asked.

"For bringing in my things," I returned.

"Thanks are for the Major. I only do what I'm told," he said and strode away. I glanced at the woman. Her face was as in a mold.

"He resents," she said softly.

"He's your son, isn't he?" I said. "What does he resent?"

"The yesterdays he never had. The today he has," she said; she started down the corridor. I followed, decided that to question the remark further would be both out of order and fruitless. The woman had been cryptic out of a deep pain, her words carrying many years in them. She stopped at a door at the very end of the corridor. I glimpsed a narrow passageway that led to the other wing of the house, hardly wide enough for one person.

Marie Opatu pushed the door to the room and and I saw a large double-bed inside, the room spacious, brown drapes drawn at one end. The woman walked to them, pulled them open to reveal tall, French doors that looked out to a stretch of lawn and then a line of oaks that almost hid the bayou beyond. I moved to the windows and gazed out at a still land, gray-green and withdrawn.

"The house has two faces. One is turned to the bayou and the marshes, the other to the stables and pastures," Marie Opatu said. Only two faces, I found myself wondering. I turned, saw that my bags had been neatly placed along one wall. I looked in on a small bath off to the right, a somewhat antique shower over the tub. There were large closets, more than ample for everything I'd brought.

"Will there be anything more, now?" the woman asked and I shook my head. I left things packed and hurried out. I wanted a look at that part of Darkwater Farms that had really brought me here.

Major Jeffries emerged from the study as I reached the end of the corridor. "We'll go out the side door," he said and I noted that all his words were uttered with a tone of finality. Obviously, no one questioned the Major's words around here. He led me past a spotless kitchen, in which Marie Opatu was putting pans into a high, wooden cupboard, and out the left side of the house. As I stepped outside after him, I saw that the house did indeed have "two faces," the real import of the woman's words coming to me, now. This face looked out on open land, a lawn of green pasture, and the stables painted gleaming white with rust-color half-doors. I saw a good exercise ring, and a large oval track behind it with a half-dozen jumps spotted around it. Beyond stood corrals, subdivided into sections, post-and-rail fences for horses, stake-and-rider for the grazing cows. A herd of longhorn steers crowded around a feed trough in one corral.

As the Major approached the stables a man came out of the first door, a small, wiry figure, not any taller than I, wearing a blue work shirt and jeans. He had short-cropped, gray hair, bright, blue button eyes and a face that seemed made of old leather.

"This is Paul Agee, Miss Forester," Major Jeffries introduced. "He runs Darkwater Farms for me, general overseer of all of it. He'll show you the place." The big man paused, glanced at his watch with a quick flick of his eyes. "Marie is off this evening so dinner will not be as usual. She'll leave a cold platter in your room."

"That'll be fine," I smiled. Major Jeffries nodded, started to turn away.

"Your daughter, when will I meet her?" I asked and he paused as he turned, answered without looking back at me.

"When she arrives tomorrow," he said and strode away. I glanced at Paul Agee, met the little button eyes as they appraised me.

"The Major isn't a man to waste words, is he?" I smiled.

"The Major isn't a man to waste anything," Paul Agee said. His face was bland, expressionless, but the remark held a second meaning in it. I didn't press as the wiry little man's eyes grew softer as they held my glance.

"I read about you at the Olympics," he said. "I was proud of you."

"Thank you," I smiled.

"I was a pretty fair rider once," he remarked, his face softening. "I mean real fancy riding, dressage and all that. I never stayed with it though."

"Why not?" I asked.

"I got race fever. Followed the tracks all over. Slow horses and fast women and trying to stretch a dollar in between," he said and he chuckled. "But that's all behind me, now, too." He turned, pulled the stable door open. "Come on, I'll show you around," he said. I felt an instant warmth for Paul Agee, sensed a kinship of interests, probably of basic dispositions. Or perhaps I just felt at home around men like him.

"Tell me about Major Jeffries," I said and the small, wiry figure halted instantly. The button eyes grew serious, became small, cold dots.

"I'll tell you all you want to know about the stables and the livestock," Paul Agee said. "I talk about animals, not people."

I half-bowed. "I stand corrected," I apologized. He continued to regard me for a moment more, as if trying to decide if he should say anything further, then turned away and started into the stables. Loyalty, I wondered, or something else? I put the question aside, a little ashamed of it. Paul Agee waved a hand at a dozen stalls, each with a well-tended, good-looking saddle horse in it.

"These are the saddlers we supply to the dude ranches right across the Texas border. They need well-mannered mounts and we see that they get them. Sometimes we break-in trail horses for them," he said. He led me past another half-dozen stalls and I recognized the horses at once, all Morgans. "Some ranches have folks who do a good bit of riding and they want a good horse under them," he said. He went on and I followed, passed two empty stalls and then heard a gasp of excitement escape my lips. Before me were the three Akhal Teké from Russia, their coats gleaming with that special, unique color that was theirs alone, gold, but not the soft gold of a Palomino, a shimmering, metallic iridescent color. My eyes slowly traveled up, down and across each of the horses, noting their other distinguishing features, short manes and short tails.

"Two thousand five hundred years of pure breeding," I heard Paul Agee's voice say and nodded along with his words. "A strain as old as the Arab. The Turkmenians say older."

"Magnificent," I heard myself breath.

"They ride well, jump well, do everything well," he said. "The vet's coming in the morning to check the mare. We think she may be caught."

I followed him as he walked on, listening as he pointed out the Knabstrups, the Danish Appaloosa, the spots somewhat smaller and more evenly distributed. They were sturdy, intelligent-seeming horses with wide ears and a high forehead. They lacked elegance, I thought, as I went on. My eyes kept flicking back for another glimpse of the tall, rangy, gold-metal Akhal Tekés. It was only when I reached the last stables that I stopped looking back. Two really lovely Shagya Arabs were stabled alongside each other, a deep chestnut mare and a brown gelding. The last stall was a double stall with an extra high partition on it. I moved to stand in front of it and felt the breath drain from me for a brief instant, followed by a surging spiral of awe.

Standing in the double stall was a jet-black stallion, larger than the average Arabian, a stallion of absolute, breathtaking magnificence. I let my eyes roam across the powerful shoulders and hindquarters, the strength of his finely arched neck, the dish face and pronounced bulge of the forehead which the arabs called the *jibbah,* the short back and the delicate muzzle—this was an extraordinary stallion, even among Arab stallions. This was a tremendous animal of power and spirit that exuded from his every pore. I moved closer to the stall and his ears went up at once. The luminous, dark eyes took my measure, a proud, alert glance. I stepped forward further and his neck rose and he tossed his head. It was a gesture of warning, a statement of his throbbing, untamed spirit. Shakespeare's lines on the stallion in *Venus and Adonis* came to my mind: *His eye which scornfully glisters like fire, shows his hot courage and high desire.*

"That is Saladin," I heard Paul Agee say.

"Saladin," I echoed. "The name fits."

"Hardly anyone rides him," Paul said and I turned a glance at him. "He's not mean, not in the usual sense," the man said, picking up the question in my eyes. "It's something else I can't really put into words. The Major's ridden him, taken him out and come back sweating like a stuck pig. I tried him once, got off damn quick."

"Why?"

The man made a face. "Something. Just something," he said, paused, went on. "When you're on him, it's like you really oughtn't to be there and he knows it and you know it. I felt like I had hold of the wind, like I was touching some kind of wildness no one should touch."

He halted, looked embarrassed with that particular kind of uncomfortableness that comes to ordinary men when they realize they've revealed an inner poetic sensitivity. I glanced at the big, black stallion again and the wildness was in him standing still.

"I'd like to ride him," I said.

"Maybe you could," Paul Agee remarked. "But he's a dangerous horse."

"We'll see," I said and the wiry, thin frame lifted itself in a shrug, walked from the stables. I looked back again at Saladin as I followed, saw the horse watching me until I was out of his vision. Outside, Paul swept a hand to the corrals in front of me.

"You can't take care of all this alone," I protested.

"I hire local hands," he said. "Some for grooming, some for picking up, some for general cowhand chores. When the cattle are barned or coralled for the night, they leave. Sami helps me with anything that needs doing after dark. It works out. The local people get work and the Major keeps his privacy. He doesn't want a lot of hands hanging about the place."

He walked to a square stall built out from the nearest of the corrals, a gate closing it off from the corral itself. I came up to stand beside him and found I was staring in at a massive, long-horned bull, a heavily muscled animal of tremendous power, red-brown with meal-colored undersides. His small eyes glared at me but with none of the stallion's proud wildness, none of the great steed's beautiful abandon. These were mean eyes, full of cunning and with an implacable hate in them. He switched his tail and the small eyes seemed to grow smaller, meaner. I moved closer to the corral and though he made no overt move, I saw every muscle begin to gather itself, an inner spring preparing to explode.

"Never go into the corral if he's there," Paul Agee said. "That's one stinking, rotten, mean critter. He's a killer."

The man's words were not exaggeration, I knew. When you've been around animals long enough, you learn to sense certain creatures with the same, instinctive quality they sense you. Unlike humans, the really bad ones affect no cloak. That deep, inner meanness is there, seething openly all the time. The horse that has been made mean by mistreatment, the dog that has been brutalized and becomes vicious; they have their own kind of meanness—but with patience and time and care they can be reached. But, as in this bull before me, there's another kind of meanness, a kind of inner evil that is its own darkness of the spirit. It is beyond reaching because neither human nor fellow beast created it.

The big bull continued to return my stare with his malevolent eyes and I controlled the shudder that passed through me. "What do you call him?" I asked.

"Bastard," the man shot back. "That's the right name for him. Big Red Honey Island is his registered name. Believe me, he's bad business. We had a young fellow here, thought he could handle him and went against orders one day. He'll never walk again."

Paul Agee turned away from the bull, squinted at the last of the dusk as it drifter away. "You'll have more time for looking around tomorrow," he said. I turned back into the stables, stopped in front of the big, ebony stallion that glistened like black light.

"He'll get worse with no one riding him," I commented.

"Hah!" the farm manager grunted. "He doesn't need any stall courage. Besides, he's exercised in the ring every day, let loose to do whatever he wants."

"It's not the same as being ridden," I insisted and Paul Agee shrugged his agreement, went on and I followed. When we emerged from the stables at the other end again, he paused, gestured to the second story of the neat, frame building.

"This is as far as I go," he said. "My quarters are upstairs here."

"Can you tell me anything about the Major's daughter?" I asked.

"Tomorrow will be here soon enough," Paul Agee said. He was adamant—it showed in his face; his lips were drawn in tightly, uncomfortable little lines narrowed his eyes. I backed from the question.

"Is there a town nearby where I can do some personal shopping? One always forgets the little things," I asked cheerfully. Paul Agee cast aside the withdrawn veil, his features visibly relaxing.

"Santal," he said. "From the leaning oaks, it's about four miles west. It's not much of a town, like most towns here, but there's a general store, a Post Office and County Records Office."

"That ought to do for the things I'll need," I said. Paul Agee pointed past the house, beyond the first exercise ring. I saw a flat-roofed, long shed, open entirely across the front. Two cars stood inside it and there was room for three more.

"That's the car shed. Park your car inside it before you turn in. The Major doesn't like cars parked all over the place," he said.

"Will do," I smiled. "Thanks for the tour. See you in the morning."

I started to turn away, then waited as I noted his bright blue eyes still studying me. He seemed to be struggling with something held inside him, weighing words carefully before giving voice to them. I saw him swallow, let his lips open; his voice emerged as a strained half-whisper.

"Do what you came here to do and get out," he said. "Don't ask too much, don't want to know too much. Do your job and be on your way."

He spun on his heel, started to mount the outside stairway at the end of the structure. "Wait," I called, unwilling to let his cryptic remarks just hang in mid-air. He didn't look back but tossed his reply over his shoulder at me.

"No more. I'll say no more than that," he called, and quickly took the steps in twos. I watched him for a moment, turned away and felt the frown remain on my forehead as I walked back to the car. I slid in, slowly backed and wheeled around, then backed again and put the little compact in the car shed. I got out to see that the other two cars there were an open-topped Fiat sport model and a big, heavy limousine, a Lincoln I guessed to be at least fifteen years old. I walked over to it, took in the still-fresh paint, the solidity of the car. In tiny gold letters on the door of the driver's side, I saw the name: Major R. Jeffries.

I stepped from the car shed, walked back to the big, gray house. It seemed to watch me approach, glowering with its brooding, little-window eyes, not unlike a giant water-bug examining a potential victim. I went inside, paused at the study and saw it was empty. The Major's desk was a neat, ordered one with pencils in place, papers stacked in arranged piles. I strolled into the living room, swept it thoroughly with the same careful look. Next was the library and I scanned the desk there, too, and the shelves of books that lined the walls.

I returned to the corridor and began the long walk to the far end of my room. The house enveloped me in silence, a tomb-like, unnerving silence and the frown continued to crease my forehead. I wondered if I were not being over-imaginative, but it bothered me that neither in his personal study, in the library nor anywhere else had I seen a single picture of the Major's daughter. Most fathers kept numerous framed pictures of their children on their desks or somewhere in the house, certainly at least one. It was a little thing, I told myself, perhaps entirely unimportant, yet I was often bothered by little things and Paul Agee's strange, cryptic remarks clung to me.

I reached my room, pushed the door open and went inside. The drapes were still open and a small lamp had been turned on near the bed. A tray, covered with a linen cloth, had been set on the bureau. I lifted it off to see a platter of egg slices, tiny cubes of ham, centered with a circle of cold *chevrettes étoufées,* giant shrimp smelling of spices and touched with chili peppers and tabasco. Suddenly I realized I was hungry and I sat down to my own, private little feast. A decanter held what turned out to be a pleasant white wine and I made a mental note to thank Marie Opatu in the morning.

When I finished, I unpacked, hanging things in the spacious closets, standing my riding boots up in a corner. I hung two crops from a nail in one closet. I didn't believe in using a crop unless it was an absolute necessity. I'd considered using mine more on overamorous stableboys than on any horses with which I'd ever worked. After putting my things out, I opened the French doors and stepped outside. The warm, dank air swept over me instantly and once again I was conscious of how this face of the house encompassed a completely different world. This was a whispering place, slightly mocking, masked and uneasy. I walked toward the line of moss-covered oaks and the dark water that lay motionless. The air became thicker, cloyingly sweet with the scent of night-blooming jasmine.

I stood beneath the oaks and listened to the night sounds, the buzz of unseen wings, the click of cicadas, the steady noise of the swamp frogs interspersed with the deep call of the bullfrogs. I moved forward, to the water's edge. The thick-rooted cypresses rose from the bayou like guardians of some mysterious, forbidden realm. The sound came from my right, in the deep shadows, too soft and low to frighten but it did startle me; a single chord plucked on a guitar. I turned, peering through the dark, saw movement, a figure rising from the bank to stand up, tall, slender, moving toward me from the deep shadows. I watched the shape take form, become a young man holding a guitar in his right hand. I saw a shock of black, curly hair, a strikingly handsome face, angular yet soft. It would have been almost an ascetic face were it not for the sensuousness that radiated from it, the eyes deep and black, the lips full, almost a girl's lips, a face of sybaritic sensitivity and compelling magnetism.

"Sorry. I didn't mean to frighten you," he said in a soft voice.

"You didn't. You just took me by surprise," I answered. The dark eyes seemed to examine all of me, then my face and I saw that they were almost grave.

"You're Gail Forester," he said slowly, paused a moment as I nodded. "I'm Victor Jeffries."

I was never good at masking emotions and surprise flooded my face. I groped for the right thing to say and his smile was slow, full of understanding, almost rueful. "The Major didn't mention me," he remarked. I shrugged, felt a surge of embarrassment for him which he didn't seem to feel at all.

"I'm not here all that much," he said. "He doesn't always know if I'll be here or not."

"You don't live here?" I said.

"I was raised here. I can't escape that," Victor Jeffries smiled. "But I took a different turn. Music." He plucked the strings of the guitar and they vibrated into the night. "That's why I'm away so often."

"Are you part of a group?" I asked.

He shook his head. "Strictly a loner. Piano and guitar. I go off on my own one-nighters for as long as I like. That's my hiding place."

"You make it sound as if everyone has a hiding place," I smiled.

"Don't they?" He laughed but his eyes stayed grave. He raised the guitar, sent a chord dancing out across the bayou. Victor Jeffries had the same dark, mysterious magnetism of the bayous, I decided. His fingers moved on the guitar, picked out a dozen notes, minor, haunting and plaintive.

"I'd like to hear you play sometime," I said. His smile was sudden brilliance, whipping around me like a playful breeze.

"There's a music room on the other side of the house. We'll have a session there," he said.

"Wonderful," I smiled. "I'm looking forward to meeting your sister." There was no reply and I watched a kind of veil drop over his eyes. His features took on a fixed, mechanical quality. I sensed the same instant withdrawal there'd been with Paul Agee. His eyes fastened me again, the smile becoming soft once more.

"I didn't expect anyone as good-looking as you," Victor Jeffries said. "I'm glad for that."

The unsaid words, endemic here, it seemed. I decided to play.

"Just for that?" I smiled. His black eyes wore their instant mask again as he returned my smile.

"We'll see," he said softly. "Keep some time for me."

The admonition wasn't needed. The sensuousness of Victor Jeffries was as permeating, as strong as the scent of the night-blooming jasmine. I'd always heard there were men one could go to bed with simply because of their pure, animal magnetism. I'd never truly believed that. Until now.

He moved past me, went on to disappear around the side of the house. His presence here was one more small surprise, disquieting in its unexpectedness, another kind of unfinished statement. I stood for a moment, gazed across the still water of the bayou and suddenly realized it was not really still at all but moving with an unruffled smoothness. Everything here at Darkwater Farms seemed touched with the unsaid, deceptiveness. All except the great, black stallion and the other fine horses. Even the ugly killer bull stood openly. They were creatures uncloaked, wearing no masks, their beauty, power, danger there for anyone to see. I often thought that it was that quality, that unconcealed quiddity, that made me appreciate animals in contrast to humans.

Suddenly I was tired and I turned away from the deep night of the bayou. Fatigue always came to me that way, never gradually, a slow diminishing of energies, but always flinging itself onto me with a sudden fury for having been denied so long. I walked back to the house, closed the French doors behind me but left the drapes open. Turning the lamp out, I stripped off my clothes and slid into the bed, stretching out in the vastness of it. Sleep refused to settle as it had promised outside. My mind, suddenly awake, active, kept asking questions, prodding, pushing and I had no answers, only a growing uneasiness. The gray, glowering stone house contained so much that didn't fit, a man who made no mention of his son, who kept not a single picture of his daughter anywhere visible. It held a girl, brought up in a world of horses, who had to be taught, at eighteen, to ride. It was a place of unquestioned austerity. I heard Paul Agee again as I lay in the dark, *Do what you came here to do and get out.*

Friendly advice, I mused, a word about Major Jeffries' apparent passion for privacy? I turned away the explanation. The little man had had too much difficulty tearing the words loose. They held another message, perhaps a warning. A warning against what, I asked silently and had no answer; suddenly I was terribly tired again, fatigue starting to smother further speculation. I slept, finally, a deep, obliterating sleep.

We are creatures of vestigial senses, sudden flashes that cling from eons back, from a time when man sensed more than reasoned. I'd slept deep into the night when I snapped awake, conscious of not being alone. I lay still, gathering consciousness, focusing reactions into thoughts. Someone was watching me. I could feel it and I sat up, pulling the sheet up over my breasts, another automatic reaction, more conditioned than vestigial. My eyes went to the windows of the French doors where the night pressed against them like a black blanket. I could see nothing but I still felt the adrenalin surging through my heart. I waited, listened, then reached out to find the light, nylon robe I'd unpacked. I slipped it on as I swung from the bed, moving quickly to the French doors, pausing; I turned to the closet and took one of the crops I'd hung there.

I went to the windows then, peered out into the dark. There was nothing visible but the hanging outlines of the oaks and I put the latch onto the double doors and returned to bed. Under the sheets, I lay awake, listening further, but whoever it had been had fled. I knew that now as certainly as I'd known someone was watching me. I turned on my side, drew a deep breath and let the night fold itself around me again, happy to immerse myself in its protective silence.

CHAPTER THREE

Yellow fingers of sun painting the room woke me and I showered quickly, dressed in whipcord riding slacks and a cream
blouse with red stitching. Before going down the long hall, I
opened the French doors and stepped outside, knelt down on the
grass. It was soft soil made softer by the dampness of the night
and the sun hadn't time to dry it out yet. I searched carefully, and
found the marks just to the left of the windows; the grass was just
beginning to spring back—the footprints were definite in the soil
beneath. I frowned as I examined the prints, one deeper than
the other, uneven, the kind of print made by someone with an
uneven walk. Or a limp.

I rose, feeling a little smug and pleased with myself. I was
certain who my night visitor had been. Was Sami simply a nosey,
curious young man? Had he been prowling the night and simply paused to look into the windows? Or was he a quiet voyeur
desperate for opportunities? Or, was he checking up on me? The
latter made little sense and I discarded it, went back to the room
and out into the hallway. I hurried down its dim length, paused
at the study and saw that it was empty. I went on and almost
bumped into Marie Opatu carrying a tray of breakfast buns
into the dining room. I followed her in; a silver coffee pot surrounded by cups and saucers stood on the long, glistening table.
The woman wore the same long dress with a change of kerchief,
a bright yellow one this time.

"Thank you for last night. It was delicious," I said. Marie
Opatu moved to the big, silver coffee server, acknowledged my

thanks with a dip of her eyes as she poured steaming, black coffee for me.

"*Cafe noir*," she said. "Our breakfast here in Cajun country." I sipped the hot brew, absorbed the impact of it slowly. I'd half finished with my cup with the aid of a bun when Victor Jeffries appeared, in an open-necked shirt unbuttoned almost to his waist and dark slacks. The instant, sensuous magnetism of him was as real in the bright light of the morning as it had been in the night.

"Sleep well?" he asked with a wide smile.

"Yes," I answered. He sipped his coffee and I thought I detected a tension in him, a tightness to his smile, little lines of hardness rippling his jaw muscles between sips of the coffee. "Didn't you?" I asked blandly.

His glance was quick, sharp, and then he let a smile break into it. "No, frankly," he said. His smile widened. "I was thinking about you," he laughed. "How's that for the ego?"

"Wonderful, if I believed it," I answered. He laughed and his black-eyed, dark handsomeness pulled shamefully at me.

"We'll go riding as soon as there's time," he said.

"You do ride, then," I said.

"Self-preservation around here. Nothing like you, of course," Victor said. He tilted his head back, gulped down the rest of his coffee. "See you later," he said and his hand reached out to press my arm for a brief moment and then he was striding away. I watched him go, aware only of a surprise at his touch. It had been harder than I'd expected, a brusqueness in it. I half-laughed silently and my lips pressed tightly against each other. Touch, I mused inwardly, almost abstractly. I'd grown up knowing the vast depths of it, the subtle strengths it communicated. To the sensitive, it revealed so much more than most people ever realized. Ask any horse, any animal, I snorted silently.

I finished my coffee, put the cup down and walked from the room, crossed over to the "other face" of the house and stepped outside. The local hands were on the scene already, the stables, rings and corrals bustling with activity. In the two corrals at the far right, I saw Angus with their shining black coats and thick, deep-chested bodies and Charolaise, rangier, high in the rear with horns and ears in a straight line across the top of their skulls. In the big, oval ring, a dozen saddlers were being ridden and Paul Agee came up, caught the expression in my eyes at once, followed my gaze.

"Those yokels ride like they had quarter horses under them," I snapped. It wasn't exactly a mistreatment, more a mis-use and that was bad enough for me.

"They're just giving them manners," he said. "Nothing fancy."

"You'd do better to use quarters, then," I retorted.

"The Major's contract calls for saddlers. A heavy hand on them doesn't bother the Major," Paul Agee said. I absorbed the remark, wondered if the man knew the extent of its meaning to me and decided that he knew very well. I was going to say something more when a man came around a corner of the building. He wore a white lab coat with jeans under it. A square face looked at me from under sand-brown, unruly hair. It was an open face with clear, blue eyes, attractive in a pleasant, almost ingenuous way. He paused, looking at me for a brief moment, acknowledging me and then spoke to Paul.

"You were right. The calf isn't hanging properly. I'll need towels and warm water," he said.

Paul nodded, half-turned to me. "This is Doc Thedeaux, best vet in the county," he said. "Gail Forester, Doc."

The veterinary half-bowed, with a sudden, unexpected old-world courtliness and his smile was warm, inviting. "My pleasure," he said. "And don't listen to Paul. He exaggerates my talents."

"I'll meet you in the barn," Paul said, hurrying away.

"Trouble? A breech birth?" I inquired.

"Not really. Sort of semi-breech," he said.

"May I come along to watch?" I asked.

"Come on," he said, starting off at once. I half-skipped to catch up to him. He wasn't as tall as Victor Jeffries, his figure was more square and solid, but he walked with quick strides.

"I take it you do all the veterinary work for Major Jeffries, Doctor," I said.

"Pretty much. And the name is Clay," he smiled. I followed into the barn, to a box stall at the far end where Paul had arrived with a pail of water and towels. The cow was standing, restless and swollen, obviously ready to give birth. As her stomach muscles contracted, Clay Thedeaux knelt down at her side, positioned Paul at her head. He asked me to stand against her rib cage with a gentle pressure on her. I watched over his shoulders as he used both hands to push the calf back into the cow, press against it, slowly work to turn it, halt, then turn some more. The birth sac broke open suddenly and I saw the calf appear, forefeet first. The rest happened quickly, surprisingly so, with but one, solitary bellow from the cow, and in minutes, the new-born calf lay on the straw, wet and matted. Clay cleaned the cow with the warm water and the towels, finished and stood up. I moved from the stall as Paul cleaned it and Clay Thedeaux guided me out of the barn.

"Thanks for the help," he said affably.

"Some help," I retorted and his grin was again warm, quick.

"Everything helps," he said. "It was really pretty routine. I told Paul that though it's a little early to tell yet, I think the Akhal mare is caught."

"That's exciting," I said. "It'll be a first in this country, I think." I walked beside him to where he stopped beside a pickup truck, a flat back with stake sides and a flap tailgate, the cab bright red.

"My limousine," he said. "I never know when I might have to bring a patient back with me."

"You've a shelter near here?" I asked.

"A few miles beyond Santal," he said. "Mostly for small animals, though. He started to climb into the pick-up, held the door open and looked down at me from behind the wheel. "I was told you'd arrived," he said, his affable ingenuousness suddenly touched by a penetrating appraisal.

"Do I detect disapproval?" I returned.

"Not of you," he smiled and pulled the door shut, switched the ignition on. "I'll stop by tomorrow. Perhaps we'll have more time to talk, then," he said pleasantly. I watched the little truck roll away, held my frown inside. It had been one more unfinished remark and I turned toward the house to see Marie Opatu emerging with a bag of laundry.

"Have you seen Major Jeffries?" I asked with more sharpness than I'd intended. The woman met my question with round, grave eyes.

"He'll be back in an hour or so," she said.

"With Amanda, I take it," I snapped. The woman nodded, went on her way. I turned, impatience to meet my pupil combined with a moment's happiness at the delay. I walked to the end stable where Paul Agee leaned against a rail, watching the hands work the saddle horses.

"I'd like to ride Saladin," I announced. He turned, not at all surprised at my request.

"He's saddled up. The Major figured you'd want to take him out," the man said. I felt anger, resentment flare at once.

"Did he?" I shot back. "The Major assumes quite a bit, doesn't he?"

"Was he wrong?" Paul Agee returned, looking fully at me, his blue button eyes both bland and sharp. He didn't embarrass me by waiting for a reply, turned and disappeared into the stable. He was back in a moment, leading the big, jet stallion. Paul gave him a loose lead and the stallion shook himself. His head went up, ears alert at once as I started toward him. He snorted, pawed the ground with one foot and Paul shortened his grip on the reins.

The stallion moved sideways; Paul yanked him around. I got a foot in the stirrup, swung into the saddle, took the reins and felt Saladin begin to circle. I brought him around quickly, sharply, and he responded with no resistance. He knew at once, of course, that I knew my business. That wouldn't be the problem, anyway, I was certain, not with this steed. I swung him around again, and saw Sami standing by a corner of the stable, his eyes fastened on me. The sullen hostility was still in them, probably an inseparable part of him, I decided.

"You'll want plenty of riding room. Go past the main ring and keep on. You'll find good land, flat, and then woods," Paul said. I nodded, walked the big stallion past the exercise ring, conscious of the eyes on me. The horse walked as though he were on steel springs ready to snap. He arched his neck and I pulled him up, then let him have his head a bit. He broke into a canter as we reached the end of the big exercise ring and I let him go his way. The canter became a gallop and I tightened in on him and suddenly I was hearing Paul Agee's description of riding the big black horse. He did move like the wind, effortlessly, without straining. He eased up at command, went out again when I let him. He did all I asked of him and yet I felt he was humoring me. It was a strange sensation I'd never felt on a horse before. I was in command, it seemed, and yet I knew I wasn't at all. I let him out in a full gallop and he suddenly gathered himself, burst forward in power and speed; a quick, tremendous explosion that was frightening in its intensity.

I reined him in and it was as if I had hold of nothing but air; he tossed his head and thundered on. I yanked back hard and, as suddenly as he'd exploded, he came back under control. I slowed him to a walk, then a halt. He had obeyed me, and I'd used every trick I knew, but it had been different from the usual way in which a horse obeys its rider. Something, just something, Paul Agee had said. I knew now why the man hadn't been able to find words. I couldn't find any, either. I spurred Saladin into a trot, moved toward the line of the woods ahead. I saw three low hedges, one with a post-and-rails fence just back of it. I turned Saladin for the first hedge, let him go out. He soared easily over the jump and I again felt the tremendous power of him. He broke into a gallop as he went at the next hedge and I decided to stay with him; once again he was as if propelled into the air. He came down easily and I reined in. I wanted to see him take the next jump under tight control, collected and all in hand. He ignored me and I felt my lips draw back in a grimace as I fought him, using every bit of horsemanship I knew. We were nearly at the approach to the jump when he gave in, slowed, went into the approach under control, effected the take-off neatly and easily and landed smoothly to slow as I pulled him up.

I eased him into a walk, let a deep breath escape me and realized that I was perspiring profusely, the shirt sticking to my breasts as a wet leaf clings to a tree. I had dismissed Paul Agee's words about the stallion being a dangerous horse. I was reconsidering my smug disagreement. This was a horse unlike any I'd ever ridden and I'd jumped some tough customers. Saladin held a wild fury inside him that waited to explode at any chance. I'd shown him that I could stay with him, ride his throbbing power, but he'd shown me more. He'd shown me that he'd been broken to bridle and saddle by man and yet he was not tamed. He'd shown me that he would accommodate only the finest of riders, that one mistake, any kind of mistake, of skill, judgment, attitude, would be beyond repair, perhaps fatal. He did not hate with the ugliness of the bull, that implacable but thoroughly predictable hate. His hate was the proud fury of those captive but forever wild, the inner fire of the unconquered.

It was exhilarating, and terribly awesome, and I reached a hand down and ran it along the great muscles of his neck. I was trying to tell him something and I wasn't quite sure what. Perhaps only that I understood. I let him go in a slow trot back to Darkwater Farms. Paul Agee saw me as I passed the exercise rings, came out to take the big stallion as I halted, swung from the saddle. His blue, button-eyes were bright with questions.

"You could be right," I said and saw satisfaction come into his face. "But he's magnificent, anyway." The man grunted, led the big, jet stallion away. I started for the gray stone house and a man came out of the side door, white-haired, wearing a seersucker suit; he had a pleasant face that sported a small, white, neat beard. He paused, smiled at me.

" 'Morning," he said. "I'm Doc Thedeaux." I felt surprise vault into my eyes and he gave a low laugh. "Doctor Percy Thedeaux," he said. "You've obviously met my son."

"Yes," I returned. "I didn't expect two veterinaries in one morning."

"Clay treats the four-legged patients. I stick to the two-legged kind. Been doing it for fifty years now in Acadiana, twenty-five years around here. I'm supposed to be retired but it never works out that way in actuality. Somebody always needs a doctor and I'm about the only one around most times." He shook his head in mock exasperation. "The Major's inside waiting for you," he added.

"Thank you, Doctor. Nice to have met you," I said; his short, half-bow was courtly, his smile again genial. The resemblance to Clay was suddenly quite apparent. I went into the house using the side entrance. Sami crossed my path carrying a huge, earthenware cooking pot to the kitchen. His quick glance carried surprise and, I thought, a touch of disappointment in it. I wondered if he'd hoped I'd come back thrown, or possibly injured. I saw Major Jeffries fill the doorway to the living room, the penetrating eyes pinning me as I came up to him. He stepped aside and I went into the room to see the girl standing there; she had long, blond hair and a soft, glowing complexion, delicate cheekbones and a fine nose. Her large, round, light-blue eyes seemed to stare almost vacantly. She was really quite beautiful in a delicate, ethereal way, as though she might blow away at any moment.

"This is Amanda," I heard Major Jeffries say from beside me.

"Hello, Amanda," I smiled. "I've been looking forward to meeting you." She focussed on me, but the delicate face was expressionless. "Are you ready to start to learn to ride?" I smiled and once again there was no reply, no movement of the eyes, the face, not even an acknowledgement, a shrug. I shot a glance at Major Jeffries. The hawk-like, stern visage was fixed on the girl but he spoke to me.

"Amanda won't answer you," he said. "But she hears you and she understands you."

I looked back to the girl. She wore a loose, pink scoopnecked dress and remained absolutely motionless in it. Perhaps she's a mute, I thought, and just as quickly knew I was wrong. Mutes may not talk but they are not without animation, reaction, response. No, Amanda was other than mute. A woman appeared in the doorway, clad in a white, nurse's uniform. I caught Amanda's eyes flicker and she moved a step sideways, away from the woman. Major Jeffries motioned with his hand and the woman stepped back into the hallway. I looked at the Major.

"Why won't she answer me?" I asked. The Major's face showed nothing as he turned to me.

"Amanda hasn't talked to anyone in ten years, not since she was eight," he said. "I suggest we step into my study."

He turned abruptly and I looked at the girl again. She hadn't moved; her round eyes stared off into space. I followed the Major into the study and he stopped at the big, old desk, turned back to me as I waited.

"Amanda withdrew from the world when she was eight. She's been in Evangeline Sanatorium ever since," he said.

"Just like that? No reasons, no warning?" I asked.

"Oh, I suppose there may have been warnings, but one doesn't pay enough attention to those things until it's too late," the Major said. "She's been treated by dozens of psychiatrists at the sanatorium, given every kind of treatment. None of it has had any effect."

"Is she autistic?" I asked and saw his hard eyes narrow.

"You're familiar with the subject?" he speared quickly.

"Only from my college studies," I said. It was a partial truth. I had become very interested in the emotionally disturbed, especially children, and I'd had the chance to spend over a year working with Dr. Howard Haines, a leading authority in the field. Now, it seemed that it might be best to keep this secret, private knowledge. I suddenly had the chilled feeling that I would need my own weapons here.

"No one knows what made her break down?" I asked.

The man shrugged. "What makes anyone have a mental collapse? Emotional maladjustment? An inability to cope? Faulty ectoplasm? Some of her therapists felt that her mother's death, when she was eight, triggered her collapse. Why Amanda had a mental breakdown ten years ago is not important to your presence here, Miss Forester." He paused, his lips thinning. "Before bringing you here, I went over Amanda's capabilities very carefully with her therapists at the sanatorium. She can learn to ride!"

"Impossible," I snapped.

"No. She can ride and she will ride. When she was six, she was in the saddle. There's a residual knowledge inside her. What's more, she understands and takes instruction. That's been proven during the past ten years at the sanatorium."

"But no one's reached her. All they've done apparently is get her to respond to simple instructions. That isn't enough for her to learn to ride."

"She understands everything, they suspect. She responds to more than simple instruction. She can ride," the man said. My brows knitted together as I stared at Major Robert Jeffries.

"I doubt it very much," I said. "But why is it so important that she ride?"

He ignored my question. "You can teach her to ride, Miss Forester," he said. "You will teach her to ride Saladin."

I frowned.

"You're joking, of course," I said carefully. His eyes were blue ice.

"I have never been more serious," he said. "You will teach her to ride Saladin."

I felt emotions playing leap-frog inside me; incredulousness, disbelief, a gathering anger. "I can only think that you really have no concept of what you're saying," I replied. "That horse of all horses? Amanda could never ride him. Putting her on that stallion would be criminal. Without every bit of control possible, no one can ride him. Just go near him in the wrong way and you're finished."

"Saladin," he said. "You'll teach her to ride well enough for Saladin."

"He's a wild fury," I heard myself almost shout. "She'll be killed." The stern, eagle's head showed no emotion and his words rolled on as if I'd said nothing.

"The Acadiana Horse Show is an important part of the County Fair. That'll be in four weeks. I want her on Saladin for that show," he said and I felt a shocked, almost dazed sense of unreality.

"Why? Why, for God's sake?" I heard myself shout. The man's eyes flashed fire for an instant.

"That's not your concern, Miss Forester, but I'll answer it for you. In this county, everyone knows Darkwater Farms and everyone will be at the meet. I'm sick of people talking about my crazy daughter who will never be anything else. When they see her riding Saladin they'll shut up. These people will know what that means. It'll show them that Major Robert Jeffries' daughter isn't what they've been saying all these years. That's why it must be Saladin, not some rocking horse."

The incredulousness inside me took wing at the man's explanation, exploding into words. "You'll risk your own daughter's life for your ego, for your image? I never heard of anything so absolutely reprehensible," I answered.

"Your opinion in that area doesn't matter. You just see that she can ride Saladin," he snapped.

"I won't be a party to this," I said emphatically. The hawk face darkened and his hand came up, one finger moving in emphasis to his words.

"Yes, you will. You signed a contract and you'll live up to it. You are legally and ethically bound by that contract. You agreed to teach my daughter to ride. Your opinion of her capabilities aren't involved. Walk away from that contract and I'll have you blacklisted at every meet and with every stable in the country. You know I can do it and you know what it will mean. You won't get a job cleaning stalls when I'm finished with you."

The man's words were not idle threats. Contracts, agreements, reliability, these things were of special importance in the horse world where everything depended on the care, feeding and conditioning of living creatures. I'd seen, often enough, what being tagged as unreliable could do, yet I was too aghast at the man's total self-concern to accept his threats.

"I won't do it," I threw back at him. "Some things are more important than legalities."

His smile was cold, almost triumphant. "Indeed, and I'll give you one of those things. Amanda's going to be on Saladin at that meet. If you refuse to honor your contract, I'll get someone from around here to put her in the saddle. How does that sound to you, Miss Forester?"

My hands were clenched so tightly the nails dug into my palms. He knew exactly what that meant to me. The girl would have no chance at all in the hands of an ordinary instructor. If I refused to teach her I'd be sealing her doom, and this, he knew, I could not do. I stared at the piercing eyes in front of me with fury churning inside me, fury and utter helplessness. From that very first meeting, the things that had brought me here, to this morning when he gave me time to ride the big stallion, he had planned each move with the precision of a choreographer setting down the steps for his dancers.

"How can you do this?" I heard myself asking. "Just so people will stop talking about things you don't want to hear. How can you risk your own daughter's life this way? It's more than ruthless. It's … it's *evil*."

"With you training her, the risk is minimal," he said.

"No, dammit, it's nothing but risk. I'm no damn magician," I cried out.

"You're a riding instructor who signed a contract to do that. I suggest you go out for a walk and return prepared to start," the man said coldly. I felt my hands twitching. I wanted to strike out at that unyielding, unbending, tyrannical countenance, so full of icy certainty and callous disdain. Nothing he said held reason or judgment or even simple concern for his own daughter. Nothing made sense except on the basis of his all-consuming ego. I spun on my heel and stalked from the room, hurrying out into the daylight, feeling my body tremble in frustrated rage.

I strode through the activity outside, sights, smells and sounds I usually reveled in that now were suddenly disturbing, symbolic not of pleasure but of entrapment. I strode to my car, flung myself behind the wheel and sent the car roaring away. As I did so, I glimpsed Doctor Thedeaux in his neat, seersucker talking to the Major at the side of the house. I hurtled down the road paralleling the bayou, narrowly missed a huge snapping turtle crossing in front of me. At the larger road, I turned right and drove on, fast, aimlessly, along land that became marshy and then firm again. I saw a sign pointing to Santal and turned off from it down a narrow, bumpy road. I didn't want towns, now, not even tiny ones. My churning thoughts and the speed finally slowed together. Only my inability to accept such total selfishness stayed. That and the bitter realization that I was trapped, boxed in very carefully and very cleverly. Amanda had been thrust on me, made my responsibility. I knew that and I'd never stop knowing it. That was the single fact that gave Major Robert Jeffries his victory. If the girl had any chance to avoid being killed, or injured for life, that slim chance rested with me. I heard the short, harsh sound that burst from my lips. Obligations, responsibilities, honor, morality, all such big words for the simple act of being able to look in the mirror each morning.

I drove along a line of heavy, stooped oaks and slowed the car. The road curved and suddenly I was almost on top of the little pick-up truck pulled off under one of the oaks, the bright-red cab shining in the sun. Clay Thedeaux, in shirtsleeves, was sitting on the back of the truck, fishing into a lunchbox. He waved at me as I came up just behind him.

"Sorry you didn't get here sooner. I've finished just about everything," he said. "I usually bring lunch with me when I'm making my rounds. It saves time."

"I'm not hungry," I said, instantly sorry I sounded so cross. The genial face regarded me half-quizzically.

"You met Amanda, I take it, and were shocked," he said.

"Yes, but not as much as I was by Major Jeffries," I flared. "What is he, some kind of egomaniac?"

"He's a man of unusual power," Clay Thedeaux remarked thoughtfully.

"What kind of power?"

"He owns land but, more importantly, he owns people. He seems to have a talent for that," Clay said.

"Is he disliked?" I asked. Suddenly I wanted to know all I could about Major Robert Jeffries. I wanted some weapons of my own, certain I'd need them in time.

"Some dislike him, some don't, all respect him. He's a very private man," Clay said.

"He's a ruthless, unprincipled egotist. Frankly, I don't see how your father can be friends with such a man," I snapped. Clay's eyes held a quiet patience.

"A country doctor has to understand people. It's not as clinical as in big-city patient treatment out here," Clay said.

"Ask him how to understand a man who risks his disturbed daughter's life to satisfy his own ego and vanity, who cares more about what people say than a girl's life," I flung back. Clay Thedeaux's affable face took on a slow frown.

"I don't really understand all this, either," he admitted. "But people here in Cajun country have their own set of importances and behavior. If you want to understand the people, you have to understand their ways. That includes the Major."

I sniffed rejection at the remark. Major Jeffries was no Cajun farmer steeped in folk ways. If anything, he traded on those very attitudes.

"You're leaving, I expect," I heard Clay say.

"No. I have to stay. I have to try. It's her only chance. If I can work with her, teach her enough, she might get through it in one piece." Surprise colored his eyes.

"And if you can't?"

"I'll have tried," I said grimly.

"I'd go now, before you're deeper into it," he said and I tossed my head.

"I'm in too deep, now. The Major arranged that. He made sure I took the measure of Saladin before Amanda. He made sure I'd know what my decision would mean," I said. I half-turned to look past the pick-up truck as a wagon appeared coming down the road, one horse drawing it. As it neared, I saw the two men in it were the two I'd met yesterday on the way to Darkwater Farms, only today they had a spring wagon with a wooden dasher instead of the chaise. The back of the wagon was piled high with the beaver-like furs I'd seen hanging from the back of the chaise.

"*Bon jour, M'sieu* Doc," the one man called out, waving as they neared.

"What are those pelts?" I asked Clay.

"Nutria," he said. "The nutria is a cousin to the beaver, the core of the fur industry in Louisiana with well over a million pelts sold each year. The meat of the nutria is used for mink food.

The wagon halted and Clay smiled at the two men. "Hello, Marc. A good day's trapping, *hein?*" he called. Both men immediately grew solemn.

"Terrible, *M'sieu* Doc. This nutria, he grow so damn scarce he almost disappear. You can't hardly find him 'less you have eyes back of your head," the man answered.

"You keep trying, hear now?" Clay said and the two men nodded, drove on looking utterly despondent. I frowned at Clay Thedeaux.

"That wagon is almost overflowing. What do they call a good catch?" I protested. Clay laughed.

"The Cajun never brags about his catch or his luck. To do so would bring him bad luck, irritate the gods of fortune, a very bad move. To avoid any impression of doing that, he bends over backwards in the other direction," he said. "Understanding the ways of a people," he added.

"All of which the Major knows and understands," I sniffed disdainfully. Clay shrugged agreement. "That still leaves him a callous egomaniac in my book," I snapped. I turned, started for the car. I'd go back, now. Time was suddenly terribly important. Time and Amanda's chances were inextricably entwined. Clay leaned on the car door for a moment as I switched on the ignition.

"Tell me if I can help in any way," he said. "And let me know how it goes."

"I will. And thanks for letting me get rid of my temper. I'm really not always like this," I said.

"I'll look forward to finding that out," he smiled. He stepped back and I circled, started back down the road. Through my rearview mirror, I saw him climb into the little pick-up and then I rounded a curve and he was gone.

Major Jeffries was in his study when I arrived. Passing the living room, I saw Amanda, sitting on the very edge of a chair like a bird about to take flight from a branch. The nurse was filling a nearby chair, hands folded across her stomach. I confronted Major Jeffries as he looked up from behind his desk.

"Is there a room next to mine?" I asked and he nodded.

"I've already had it prepared for Amanda," he said. My lips tightened. Damn the man and his assumptions, I murmured silently.

"I want to talk to the nurse and then you can dismiss her," I said; I saw his piercing eyes reveal a touch of surprise and was glad for that. "If this is to work, I've got to reach Amanda in my own way with nobody undoing whatever I've been able to do," I said.

The man turned my words in his mind as his eyes bored into me. "All right,' he consented. "What do you want from the nurse? I can tell you whatever it is."

"What security measures were practiced at the sanatorium?" I queried. "Was Amanda locked in at night?"

"Never. She wouldn't venture outside," he said.

"Was she kept under watch all during the day?"

"No."

"Does she feed herself?"

"Yes."

"Dress herself?"

"Yes."

"Did she go on walks with the nurses and therapists?"

"Yes."

"Did she show any interest in anything?"

The man's face tightened. "No."

"She's said absolutely nothing ever since she was committed?"

"Only by signs, gestures, motions," he replied.

I nodded. I'd wanted only to know those few rudimentary things. The rest I'd learn with Amanda. "Do whatever you have to do with the nurse. I want to start working with Amanda right away."

He stood up, went to the door of the study, paused to turn back to me. "One thing you'll find out anyway," he said. "She has her mood swings, severe ones."

I felt myself grimace. "Wonderful," I bit out and he went on into the next room. I waited, heard his voice in conversation with the woman and then he returned.

"Amanda is waiting for you," he said. I brushed past him and went into the room with the girl. She was as I'd seen her, poised at the edge of the chair, her delicate beauty looking even more fragile.

"Hello, Amanda," I began brightly, sitting down opposite her. "Do you know what your father wants me to teach you?" The light-blue eyes didn't move. "To ride, Amanda. I hear you knew how to ride as a little girl," I went on. Nothing flickered in her eyes. "It'll be hard work but it'll be fun," I continued. "But you must do exactly as I say. You've got to do just what I tell you to do until you can go out on your own. It'll be sort of a game."

Amanda made no sign of understanding, nothing at all and I felt the anger knotting in my stomach. It'll never work, I murmured to myself. I stood up. "Let's take a walk, Amanda," I suggested. "Let's go down to the stables and look around." The girl made no move. I reached a hand out, slowly, gently, closed my fingers around hers. I felt more surprise than elation as she rose and began to go with me. She walked outside with me, her eyes as if blind, moving neither to the right nor the left. I led her slowly toward the stables and I caught her eyes moving, glancing out at the exercise rings and the horses being schooled there, at the corrals off to the other side. Her glances were quick, furtive, and her eyes showed no expression. Major Jeffries stepped from the side door of the house and the girl seemed to stare right through him as he crossed our path for a moment. He moved aside and we went on. I released our hands and she continued to walk beside me. We reached the stables and went inside. Paul Agee straightened up, his eyes on the girl, his leather face grave, almost sad. Most of the Morgans were in their stalls as were the Knabstrups and the Akhal Teké.

I started down along the stalls, casting a glimpse at the girl. She followed; her round eyes had, I thought, grown wider. I stopped in front of one of the Morgans, scratched his nose as he leaned out of the stall.

"Pet him, Amanda. Just as I'm doing," I said. The horse, a bay gelding, snorted. Amanda moved back and I saw what I thought was fear come into her face, a tightness, her eyes growing almost into blue saucers. I turned to Paul. "What've you got that's old and tired," I asked.

"An old mare," he answered. "She's a rocking horse. We keep her in the half-dozen stalls attached to the barn in the back."

I glanced at Amanda's dress. It was loose enough not to interfere in the preliminary things I wanted to try. "Saddle her and bring her out," I told Paul. "Oh, and is there an exercise ring away from all the others?"

"The small branding corral in the back," he said. "I'll bring the mare there."

He hurried off and I continued stroking the Morgan's nose, watching Amanda watch me. "Come, pet him," I urged. I took her hand, raised it gently, placed it against the gelding's snout. She let the hand stay exactly where I'd placed it, flat on the horse, and I saw an expression come into her eyes, a darkening of the pupils. Suddenly she pulled her hand away and stepped back, almost against the stable wall; under the loose dress, her breasts rose and fell in short, hard breaths. She stared at the horse and her eyes seemed to frown.

"He won't hurt you," I said quietly. "Here, watch." I opened the stall door and stepped inside. I patted the bay's smooth neck, ran a hand down along his forequarters, along his rib cage. I watched his ears; he enjoyed the attention. "Come here, Amanda," I called out. "Feel how strong and smooth he is."

I looked out the stall and there was no one there. Icicles instantly formed on my skin. I dashed from the stall, slamming the half-door shut. The girl was nowhere to be seen and I wavered between racing outside or down the line of stalls when, at the very end, at Saladin's box stall, I saw the door hanging open. I ran; horses moved restlessly in their stalls at once. Racing down the stable, I had visions of the stallion's hooves rearing up to come down with killing anger, of this fury smashing into this strange girl's body. I skidded to a halt in front of the box stall. Amanda was inside, standing absolutely still beside the big, black stallion. Saladin's ears were moving, uncertainty holding the horse. My throat felt dry as a dustbin and I watched Amanda move toward the stallion, reach out with both hands, place them against the horse's side. She stood silently, motionless, hands flat on the stallion. Saladin breathed in deeply and I started to move, tensed myself to yank the girl out of the stall. The stallion switched his tail and then stood still as a statue. Amanda's hands moved slowly over the horse and the stallion hardly breathed.

I found my voice, heard it as a hoarse whisper. "This is Saladin, Amanda," I said. I moved toward her, slowly, reached out, took her wrist gently. She turned, let her hands drop from the stallion. I guided her from the stall, swung the door shut and felt the breath drain from me. Nothing had happened. Luck? Pure and simple luck, I wondered? Or something more? I glanced at the girl. She was staring wide-eyed at nothing again. But she had rushed down to Saladin, the half-wild, unconquered stallion. She had gone into his stall, touched him. She had been drawn to him in some sudden way. Communication, I pondered, still another layer to its subtlety. I glanced back at Saladin. The big stallion's ears lay back and I saw a wildness in his eyes. I would not go into that stall now, I knew. Perhaps it had been only good luck after all. I led Amanda outside, around the stables to the rear and saw Paul standing in the corral with the old mare, gentle patience written all over her.

Leading Amanda to the horse, I released her wrist, let her watch me swing into the saddle. I dismounted, moved the old mare closer to the girl. "You mount her, Amanda, just as I did," I said. Amanda didn't move. I lifted her hand up to the pommel, placed her foot in the stirrup and suddenly she swung up, came into the saddle and sat there. Paul had put a simple bit on the mare and I took her by the side of the bridle, led her in a slow circle. Amanda kept her seat well, sitting straight in the saddle. I walked the mare across the corral and back again. The girl's eyes were expressionless but she made no move to dismount. I put the reins in her hands, had her hold them correctly, pushing her fingers apart to do so.

"That's it, Amanda. You're doing beautifully," I complimented. She held the reins in her hands lifelessly as I led the mare across the corral again. I let go of the halter and the horse followed placidly as I watched Amanda's reaction. She continued to hold the reins limply in her hands. I let the horse walk with her for fifteen minutes more, then stopped. It had been enough for this first day, a beginning, an introduction. How much more would really come of it, I wondered. I felt encouraged. Amanda did indeed understand and she could be helped to do things. There was an area in which she could be at least partially reached.

"You may dismount now," I said, waiting, watching. She sat motionless in the saddle and I stayed at the mare's head, equally motionless. Finally, the girl's round eyes turned to me, just the tiniest hint of expression in their depths. She extended one hand stiffly and I felt unashamedly victorious. I reached out, steadied her as she swung from the saddle. I pushed the mare off and took Amanda from the corral, feeling encouraged once again.

But it would be slow, I feared, too slow for Major Jeffries. I walked back to the house with Amanda beside me, silent as a stone, and I wondered about this lovely girl who refused to communicate but who understood words, instructions. Ten years of

WHEN THE WIND CRIES

the mind turned in on itself, I pondered. Irreparable? I let the question hang for a moment. I had seen others who lived in asylums more dead than alive, vegetating, those without all communication with the normal world. Some were children, some, like Amanda, admitted as children and grown into adults in their closed, isolated world. But the really severed, the minds gone beyond all reach, seemed not to understand. They neither spoke nor listened, heard nor understood, their very physical, bodily functions degenerated even beyond the animal level. They were, indeed, merely living organisms which no human, no battery of learned psychiatrists, no seekers armed with compassion, no one at all could reach. I had seen these and certainly Amanda was not one of them, not yet, at least. Her withdrawal was not a complete degeneration, I felt, but, nonetheless, no one had been able to reach her in ten years. No one had been able to penetrate beyond her obedience to simple instructions. Discouragement spiraled inside me and I grew angry again. I'd have to hold a tighter rein on my own mood swings, I told myself.

We reached the house, entered the side door and further speculation was cut off as, in the hallway, Amanda suddenly stopped. Her eyes slowly looked along the walls, up to the ceiling beams, back down to the doorway of the library, shifting to the connecting hall to the kitchen. She was visually caressing something very dear, something loved, and slowly savoring each moment. I watched her eyes move again; she gazed at the doorway of the living room and suddenly her delicate face grew red. Her lips opened, twisted and, like a runaway filly, Amanda bolted, raced from the house. Only my own responses, sharpened over the years to the unexpected things horses can do, enabled me to react quickly and reach the door just as she did. She tried to twist out of my grip, her strength surprising, but I managed to push her back against the door. I saw terror blazing in the round eyes. "Stop, Amanda, it's all right," I said. "There's nothing to be afraid of here."

Her eyes stared back at me in disbelief. Or was it disagreement, I suddenly wondered. I kept my grip on her, felt her begin to relax and finally the moment drained from her and I let go.

"Come, we'll go where you can be alone," I said soothingly, more calmly than I felt. She turned and went with me, walking beside me, quiet and docile as a lamb. But I had seen the sudden emotional explosion and been shaken by it. I reached the room just before mine, pushed the door open, saw it was small but not uncomfortably so, neat flowered wallpaper making it appear bright. A high window faced the bayous just as my room did. A suitcase was open on the single bed, two simple dresses and a pair of slacks in it. But the closet door hung wide; riding breeches and jeans, all obviously new, hung inside. Once again, the Major had thought of every detail.

"This will be your room now, Amanda," I said gently, watching the girl sit down in a high-backed wing chair. She folded her arms across her stomach, as if closing herself in. "I'll go out and see about dinner," I remarked. She lowered her head and seemed to become a small bird with its head tucked under its wing. Her entire mood had regressed since she'd tried to bolt from the house, and I felt grimness settling on me again. I thought back to how she'd exploded and groaned inwardly, my stomach knotting. That kind of thing when she was on Saladin and all hell would break loose. I swore softly under my breath and closed the door behind me.

The Major was in the study, standing near the desk. "Will Amanda be eating with us?" I asked.

"Not for a while," he said. "I think it's best not to push her too much, ask too many things of her. I want all her energies on her lessons. Marie has a tray ready for her."

"I'll bring it to her," I said and went into the kitchen. Marie Opatu was by an old, iron stove and I saw a tray of soup, chicken and salad waiting. I took the tray and returned to Amanda to find her in the exact same position as when I'd left her.

"Dinner," I called out cheerfully. The lowered head didn't lift, the small figure remained absolutely still. I set the tray down. "Enjoy everything. I'll be back later," I sang out. There was still no response and I left, went back down the hall with my lips drawn thin. I went to the dining room, saw that the table was set for only two and that Victor was waiting there. His slender, dark, sensuousness was again as real, as encompassing as it had been when I met him beside the bayou in the night.

"The Major?" I queried.

"He won't be joining us tonight," Victor said. "In fact, I've a club date later so I can't stay much after dinner." He pulled a chair out and I sat down, really quite satisfied not to have to go through a charade of politeness with the Major tonight. I was still seething inside at the man's callous, demanding machinations. Victor sat down at my right, poured a glass of white wine for me, a delicate Chardonnay. He wore a white, open-necked shirt under a black, silk jacket and his fingers, I noted, were unusually long and slender.

"I wondered whether you'd stay," he smiled at me, lifting his glass.

"What would you have told me to do?" I smiled back.

"Go," he answered without hesitation. I felt a moment of surprise.

"You don't think I can do it," I offered. His smile held wryness.

"Do you?" he countered and I felt my mouth tighten.

"You haven't tried to see your sister yet," I remarked and saw the line of tension pull at his jaw at once. "I'm sorry," I hastened to add. "That was unfeeling of me."

"Forget it. My own kind of withdrawal, I guess," Victor said. Sami came into the room carrying a casserole of chicken with shrimp, sauteed in a pungent sauce in which I tasted pepper and tabasco and something else I finally decided was mace. Sami brushed the table at one point and I saw his quick glance at

Victor, almost a sudden fear in it. I'd begun to think that Sami's eyes could only hold hostility and the fear surprised me. After he'd left, Victor's deep, black eyes turned to me.

"He resents the world because he was born that way," Victor said. "He gets no sympathy from me and that bothers him."

"Why no sympathy?" I asked.

Victor half-laughed. "Maybe because he wants it so much. I hate people who beg for things," he said. "Asking is one thing. Demanding is another. Begging is something else."

It was a kind of distinction I'd never thought much about and suddenly I heard Marie Opatu's voice outside in a sharp exchange with Sami. They spoke in the Cajun *patois* and I listened and understood hardly anything. Victor, watching me, laughed.

"Your French won't help too much," he said. "There's even a different rhythm and pronunciation to their French. The *patois* is their French with words of Portugeuse, Italian, Spanish and Choctaw Indian."

"I don't think I'll try to learn it," I sniffed. Victor poured more wine and we finished the meal talking about the romance of language.

"Voltaire said that speech was given to man to disguise his thoughts," Victor offered.

"How cynical," I returned. "It makes a masquerade out of everything." Victor Jeffries shrugged.

"Isn't that pretty much true?" he asked. I held words back with an effort. Maybe here, I wanted to say. His laugh, sudden and warm, dissipated the moment and he rose, took my hand in his to pull me up with him. His touch was warm, not at all hard this time.

"Come on, I feel like playing for you," he said. He led the way to the other side of the house, into a room I hadn't seen yet, a piano at one end, a tapestry of strolling, fifteenth-century musicians hanging from one wall, muted gray-brown colors that were nonetheless quietly warm. I saw the guitar against a chair as he circled, half-spun me into a soft cushioned chair near the piano. He sat down at the keyboard, his fingers rippling off a series of arpeggios and then he settled down, began to play, phrases that were haunting, all in a minor key. It was plaintive music, changing pace unexpectedly, shifting rhythm but not mood and his face became set, engrossed, it was as if I were not in the room at all. Suddenly the music became turbulent and I saw Victor's handsomeness grow hard, his eyes burning into the keys. The music became a progression of dark-hued chords and suddenly he broke off, whirled from the piano to spear me with brooding eyes. The moment vanished as he broke into a laugh, reaching out for me, his hands warm on my arm.

"You get caught up," I remarked. "It was exciting."

"Music soothes the savage breast," he said. He stood up, pulled me with him and his hand brushed hair back from my forehead, the touch soft as a butterfly wing. "I'll find more time for us," he said. "You'll deserve it."

The idea appealed, more than it should have. He left, then, walking away quickly, picking up the guitar as he passed. Alone in the room, I noticed that it had grown dark. I took the dishes into the kitchen, and found no one there. I left the plates and returned along the hall to Amanda's room. I half-started to knock, then decided it wouldn't be answered. I pushed the door open soundlessly, saw that the room was dark save for a small night light. I entered, moved toward the form on the bed, and listened to the sound of Amanda's breathing, regular and rhythmic. Satisfied that she was asleep, I left, closed the door quickly and went to my room. But I was restless and stared out at the bayou. I hesitated to go there, the veiled quality of it somehow forbidding. The unfamiliar, I told myself, was always frightening. Rationalization is such an obsequious force, always pushing forward to offer itself. I decided to venture beyond the other face of the house, and crossed the hallway to the other side. When

I stepped outside, a wind had blown up, surprising in its sud-denness and strength. I felt it catch at me, pull at my hair, wrap itself around me and I heard trees rustle in the distance. I walked down past the stables, listened to a horse neigh, another blow. I went past the shadows of the first barn, on to the second and the wind swirled around the corner like an invisible little boy play-ing tag.

I walked on, almost stumbled over the figure sitting in the straight-backed chair tilted backward against the barn, halting just in time. Marie Opatu turned to look at me, her face taking on form in the darkness at I peered at her.

"I'm sorry, I didn't mean to disturb you. I didn't think there'd be anyone out here," I said, casting about for words.

"No bother," the woman said, her voice soft.

"Taking in the night?" I offered.

"Listening," Maria Opatu answered.

"Listening?" I repeated.

"To the wind," she said.

"Yes, doesn't it sound lovely in the trees," I remarked.

"This way it sound nice, only this way," Marie Opatu said. My face questioned and the woman let the chair come down to rest on all four legs. "It whispers, now, blows some, pushes some," she said. "But sometimes the wind cries. You hear it cry when it does, wailing, sobbing. You hear it, all right, no mistake." She pressed her arms to her breasts and shivered. "When the wind cries there is death," she half-whispered. "When the wind cries, old man death is hunting, looking for someone ... when the wind cries."

She stopped, fastened her eyes on me for a long moment. "You don't believe," she said. "That only Cajun backwood talk, you say. But you wrong. It's true, damn real true. You take care when the wind cries."

She rose abruptly, stood very straight, then started toward the house. "But this just night wind, nothing to be 'fraid of, child," she threw back and stalked away. I watched her go, wondered how much more she knew than the lore of the wind. I walked slowly on, glad for the cool of the night, when, suddenly, from the square corral to my right, I heard a low, throaty sound. I turned; I was alongside the big, longhorn bull and he was moving along inside the corral with me, pacing my every step. I stopped and he stopped, the little eyes glinting. I moved a few steps and he moved with me. I stopped again and he did the same, lowered his head. I moved toward the corral and he came toward me at once. I could feel hatred in waves flowing from him. Absentmindedly, I leaned one arm on the top rail of the corral. He moved instantly, hooking upwards with one long, sharp horn. I jumped backward just as the point of the horn came up where my arm had been, smashing into the rail. I stood back and met the simmering, glowering eyes. He was too malevolent just to be called mean. Even Paul's name, Bastard, didn't do him justice. Evil, I murmured to myself, he epitomized evil. I turned away from the bull, wandered idly a while longer and then retraced my steps to the house. As I neared its gray stone bulk and narrow, small-eyed windows, it seemed as implacable and forbidding as the bull. And as thoroughly malevolent. Did it, too, epitomize the spirit of evil, I wondered. Did it harbor inner darknesses, an embodiment of those who lived their secrets within its walls?

I hurried inside, through tomb-like silence, to my room and, stripping off clothes, fell into bed. I left the window drapes open out of a kind of perverseness of my own. I wanted to fall asleep at once but sometimes the mind makes its own rules and I kept thinking about Major Robert Jeffries and his reasons for having Amanda ride the stallion. They didn't fit. At the time he gave them to me I'd been so shocked, so furious at his callous disregard for Amanda's life, that I'd accepted them. I'd even called his demands an ego trip, a personal obsession. He'd been quite willing to let me go along with that, I realized, now. But I'd been wrong, as wrong as his reasons were false. Major Robert Jeffries didn't give a damn about the approbation of his neighbors. He was too ruthless, too powerful for concern about their gossip and wagging tongues. There was more, I murmured silently. The man wanted Amanda on Saladin for all to see, but the real reasons were hidden away. Here, at Darkwater Farms, there were undercurrents that moved with the deep and dark stillness of the bayous.

Don't ask too much, don't want to know too much, Paul Agee had said, and now his words were steeped in new shadows. Everything here seemed shadowed, I reflected. I turned on my side, closed my eyes and felt a terrible uneasiness wrap itself around me.

CHAPTER FOUR

woke early, showered and dressed. If Sami had come in the night to peer into my window again, I hadn't sensed him this time. I left my room and crossed the few feet to Amanda's, pushed the door open. She was standing at the window, looking out, and her eyes turned to me as I entered, startled fright in them.

"Hello," I said quickly; the fright left her eyes to be replaced by an expressionless, dull quality. I went to the closet and pulled down riding breeches and a blouse. "Put these on for today," I smiled. "While I get you some breakfast." Amanda's face remained expressionless and she made no move toward the clothes. I left the room without glancing again at her, went down the hallway and found Marie Opatu in the kitchen, still another brightly-patterned kerchief on her head. She gave me a tray of cereal, milk and sugar and two cups of *cafe noir*. Amanda had put the riding breeches on and was just pulling the blouse over her shoulders as I entered. Now out of the loose, formless dress, she revealed a small, neat, well-shaped figure, a narrow waist and nice, girlish little breasts.

"Breakfast," I sang out cheerily. I poured the milk on the cereal, and motioned to the food but Amanda stared into space. I took my coffee, started from the room. "Be back in a few minutes," I said. I went into my room, sipped the strong, thick brew till I'd finished and then returned to the adjoining room. The cereal had been consumed along with the coffee and Amanda sat on the edge of one of the chairs. Like a wild creature that wouldn't eat in the presence of possible danger, I thought to myself, and felt suddenly sad. "Come on, we'll have a good lesson this morning," I said to her. "'I just know it."

I went to the door, waited, and Amanda rose, followed after me in mute silence. I watched her carefully as we went down the hall and neared the living room, ready to move quickly. But Amanda kept her eyes down, and let me guide her outside before she glanced up. Paul stood at a corner of the house; he waved at me. "The mare's waiting for you in the corral," he called. I led Amanda past the activity of the exercise rings; horses were being ridden inside each ring. Her eyes cast quick, almost furtive glances and then I caught sight of the red cab of Clay's pick-up truck. He was making a post-natal visit to the heifer and calf, obviously.

I'd just passed the little pick-up truck when everything seemed to happen at once. In the distance, crossing toward the house, Victor was carrying his guitar case, looking tired, obviously returning from the night. He glanced up, saw me and I waved a hand at him when I felt the sudden, sharp movement beside me. I whirled but Amanda had already spun around, was racing away, heading for the nearest door to the stables. I made a leaping dive for her that was a mistake. My right foot came down on a piece of soft ground, half-mud, went out from under me and I catapulted sideways. I hit the ground in a twisting slide, unhurt, but precious seconds had flown and Amanda was in the stables already.

"Damn," I muttered as I regained my feet. I knew the sinking feeling of fear as I began to run again. I caught hold of the stable door, and used it to swing myself inside without slowing down. At the big box stall the gate was hanging open. I ran again, and skidded to a halt to see Amanda in the stall, leaning against the big, black stallion. She was almost clinging to him, her hands outspread, pressed against his shining, jet-black coat. She turned her head and looked at me with eyes that held emotions I couldn't define. I started into the stall with mixed emotions of my own, relieved to see she wasn't under the horse's hooves, and angry at this second explosion on her part. I'd just put one foot in the box stall when the stallion snorted; the sound was unmistakable, there was warning in it. I glanced up at him; his ears were laid back, his eyes widening. He snorted again, struck one forefoot against the flooring and I felt my throat going dry. I glanced at Amanda. She hadn't moved and I saw Saladin's agitation mounting. I backed from the stall, the stallion tossed his head and I caught the whites of his eyes.

Just outside the box stall, I forced my voice to stay calm. "Amanda, come out of there," I said. "Now, Amanda, right now. Move very slowly."

The stallion swung his hindquarters to the right and his ears still lay flat. His movement made Amanda's hands come down along the sides of his forequarters. "Amanda, come out of there," I said again. "Now, Amanda, right now."

She stepped back and I saw Saladin stretch his neck, start to move backward, gathering himself. *Oh, God,* I groaned inwardly. Amanda was backing toward me, finally close enough. I reached, grabbed her wrist and yanked her out of the stall as I slammed the half-door shut. The stallion half-charged then, an angry, wild snort exploding from him and then he stopped, moved in an agitated trot around the edges of the box stall. Amanda watched him and I felt little drops of perspiration run down between my breasts. Clay Thedeaux stood just by the other doorway, frowning.

"I saw you fall, and knew there was trouble. I got to a window just as you reached the stall," he said.

"Then you saw," I said, and he nodded. "That's the second time she's been lucky. Only this time she was really lucky," I said.

"I'm not sure," Clay Thedeaux said carefully. I felt a frown press into my forehead, gestured to the stallion.

"Good God, didn't you see him starting to go? His ears were so flat they all but disappeared," I said.

"Yes, I saw that. But it happened when you started in after Amanda," Clay said slowly.

"That could have been plain coincidence," I said.

"Maybe," he agreed. "But maybe not. She did run to him, for the second time, you say. Something drew her to him." He paused, let his lips purse for a moment. "Affinities, attraction, psychic communication. We think we know so much when we know so little. We draw such pedestrian conclusions from our pedestrian studies."

I cast a quick glance at Amanda. She showed nothing but I could feel her listening. "I'd like to talk to you more on this," I said to Clay and his smile held understanding in it.

"Anytime. Tonight, if you like. I'll call you later," he said, and I nodded agreement. I turned to Amanda, took her by the elbow. "Let's go, Amanda," I said gently. "We have work to do." Her eyes went to the black stallion and I saw that he stood at the door of the stall, still agitated. *Coincidence,* I murmured to myself, more out of stubbornness than conviction. It had all happened so damn quickly. Amanda had seen Victor, of course, just as I had. Had that made her bolt, I wondered. Or had she been waiting for a moment, taken that one and run off with it? She walked quietly now, alongside the corral, past the bull who turned to eye me as I led her past. The old mare waited in the corral and Amanda went up to the horse, ran her hands across its neck, down the forequarters, then past the saddle and along the flanks, moving her hand as a blind person would, carefully, seeing through the fingers.

"Mount up," I said. "One hand on the pommel." Amanda swung into the saddle with surprising ease and sat there. I put the reins into her hands. "Move her, Amanda. Use your legs, a little squeeze," I said. Amanda pressed with her thighs and the mare ambled into a slow walk. I'd already decided that time wouldn't allow teaching her many of the usual steps such as saddling, bridling, adjusting stirrups. I'd concentrate on control and riding. I watched the mare halt at the corral fence.

"Wheel her around, Amanda. Right rein, the way I showed you yesterday," I called. "Pressure with your inside leg, that's it." The mare turned, taking her time and headed for me. I let her go by, helped the girl turn her to the left, walk her in a slow circle. "Don't slump," I called, "Straight in the saddle. Keep your hands down, elbows in."

Amanda obeyed, more quickly, more responsively, than I'd dared hope and I decided to let her trot. She did well though I had to keep at her about her hands. Whenever I called a moment's break, she rested her hand along the mare's neck, not stroking but just laying her hands there as if she were trying to absorb the feel of the horse. I kept working with her, taking advantage of what seemed a positive mood on the girl's part until I saw her begin to wilt. I called a halt, and checked my watch to see that we had worked longer than I'd realized. "Dismount, please," I said and the girl swung from the saddle. She walked from the corral with me and I felt more than satisfied. Paul Agee was standing near and Amanda drew back at once as we approached him. I took her arm, the eruption earlier in the day all too fresh in my mind. "There's nothing to be afraid about," I said soothingly and she came along. It was as we reached the stables that she stopped, turned toward the open door.

I tried to urge her along but she was as stiff and unyielding as a statue. I relaxed my hold on her arm; she moved into the stable and I was close behind her. She went to the box stall and I saw Saladin move toward the door at once, halt a foot or so away from the girl; they stared at each other. He swished his tail, struck a hoof against the floor and I grew apprehensive at once. I took Amanda by the arm, pulled her back gently and she came, turned and went with me down the corridor of the stables. I took a deep breath. It was time for another lesson, perhaps the most important one for Amanda. For anyone, perhaps. I wondered if she could absorb it as easily as she had instructions that dealt with relatively mechanistic, physical responses.

"How you feel is very important when you work with horses, Amanda, or any animal," I began. "If you're nervous, your horse will become nervous. If you're excited or upset, he'll become upset. That's why you should stay away from Saladin, or any horse, if you're upset."

I searched the girl's face, found nothing, but I'd quickly become accustomed to that. I only hoped she understood inner as well as outer matters. I crossed the yard with her, went into the side entrance of the house and took her to her room. She walked with head down inside the house, again. "I'll get you some delayed lunch," I said. "Take your things off and lie down and rest for a while."

In the kitchen, I found a large platter of sandwiches, egg and tuna and crabmeat, along with a large pitcher of ice tea. I made a small plate, poured some tea and took it all to Amanda. She had taken off her blouse, lay across the bed and didn't move as I set the plate down. "You did very well today," I said, searching her face for some sign of response; I found none. "Have some lunch," I said as I closed the door and started down the hall. Paul Agee was in the kitchen, munching on one of the sandwiches and Sami passed the door, carrying a net and a small knapsack. Marie Opatu appeared, to stand in the doorway and look after her son.

"Sami's going crabbing," Paul remarked.

"You take care," the woman called out. "You look out for *Congo*." I turned a questioning glance at Paul.

"Cajun name for the cottonmouth water moccasin," he said between bites. A language of other languages, I thought, taking up a sandwich. Marie came into the kitchen.

"I believe I'll make a sillabub today, Paul. How does that come to you?" the woman said.

"It comes to me real fine," Paul said. "A lemon sillabub?" Marie Opatu nodded, glanced at me.

"You ever make a sillabub, child?" she asked; I shugged helplessly and felt quite unlettered.

"A good sillabub depends on how you put it together as much as what you use," the woman said, almost to herself. "The rind of three lemons, grated fine, then the juice. One and a quarter pints of cream, a pint of white wine and then a little more, then the sugar, enough for your own taste. Then you stand it for a time, let it all come together and then the whipping, real hard whipping till you have a real froth. You put the froth in a sieve and the rest into the glasses, then you lay on the froth."

"It's something special, all right," Paul said. The hint of a smile touched Marie's face. I saw Paul start to move toward the door.

"Amanda's done enough for one day. Mind if I go along with you?" I asked.

"Want to get the feel of running a place like this, do you?" Paul laughed and I nodded honestly. "Sure, come along. It's not all that different from any good horse farm." I hurried along with him, and spent the rest of the day at his side, taking in all the little details that are never insignificant. He drove into the fields, west toward Texas where the land became drier, and checked on the young calves that had been turned loose with the herd, mostly longhorn and angus crosses. Returning, he went over the new colt that had been born a few weeks earlier. He took a long time going over the colt's legs, saw the questions in my eyes.

"His grandfather threw leg problems," Paul grunted. "I keep a close watch for any sign."

"This early?" I asked.

"It shows up early, then seems to disappear until they're older when it really comes out. By then you're in trouble. I like to catch it early if I can. If I see it, I'll sell him off for ordinary stock." From the colt, he went on to check feed and I found out that the farm had its own oat crusher.

"Saves me from worrying about some dealer giving me an order of poor oats. It's hard to tell that once they're crushed. Good oats are sweet, long and kind-of-plump before being crushed,"

Paul said. I watched as he checked the storage bins, peering into each, sifting with a long-handled shovel. "Checking for dust or mold," he said. "Those things'll give you colic and fodder poisoning sure as all hell."

"Do you supplement with bran?" I asked.

"Definitely, along with linseed meal. But not too much linseed," he cautioned. "And the main bulk of the diet is hay, of course, good hay, clover or timothy." He paused to watch one of the hired hands starting to fill a feed rack in a stall. "The grain at the bottom, dammit. Then the hay on top," I heard him bark. "How many times must I tell you damfools that?"

The man quickly emptied the rack and changed the order of the feed as Paul went on with me. "Most horses are greedy, especially after a day's work. They'll gulp down the grain too fast. A few bites of hay, which is chewier, slows them down and takes the edge off their appetites," he explained. I made more mental notes as the afternoon drew to an end and Paul became busy with the local hands. I returned to the house, then, glimpsed Sami in the kitchen, sitting at the table with a bucket of crabs at his feet. He looked up as I passed and I thought I detected a smug, self-satisfied light in his eyes. I went on to Amanda's room, knocked once and opened the door. She was on the bed, curled up in a fetal position, her eyes staring openly. I hurried to her, felt apprehension at once sweeping over me.

"Amanda, what is it?" I asked, reaching out for her. She twisted, kicked out at me, half-leaped from the bed. She seized an ash-tray from the top of the bureau, and threw it in rage; I ducked. "Amanda, stop it," I cried out. She was shaking in rage or fear or a combination of both. I saw her glance about wildly, focus on a set of books and dive for them. I reached them just as she did, knocking the one she'd seized from her hands. She backed away, turned and flung herself onto the bed to lie there, her body shaking, heaving, hardly a sound coming from her; the sobs were all turned inward. I move to her, edged down on the bed.

"Amanda, Amanda, what it is?" I asked softly, and felt my own stomach become knotted. She had done so well in the morning, and she'd been fine when I left her; I grimaced. And now everything was shattered. I put a hand on her back, gently, and spoke to her again.

"Amanda, please, what happened? What it is?" I asked, but her face stayed buried in the bedcover. I felt torn apart, betrayed, and knew that was my own fault. I'd wanted so hard to see Amanda in positive, explainable terms. But she was obviously far more unpredictable than I'd allowed myself to admit, far more irrational. I pressed my hand against her back and finally her body quieted. I rose, a terrible disappointment stabbing into me. It was only when I turned that I saw the photograph on the floor, just inside the door. I hadn't seen it as I'd rushed into the room and now I bent down, picked it up. It was a five-by-seven studio portrait of a woman, her name written across the bottom of the photo. Edith Wentley Jeffries, I read; Amanda's mother. She'd probably been twenty-five years old, I guessed, from the coiffure on the woman, and the resemblance to Amanda in the delicate facial structure. But the presence of the photo on the floor burned into me now with a wild flame, exploding everything I'd so quickly assumed; Amanda's irrationality was perhaps not so exaggerated at all.

I glanced at Amanda; she had turned her face enough to watch me. It was all so clear suddenly. The picture had been slipped under the door for her to see, the past pushed at her. Whoever did it probably felt certain of the effect it would have, wanted to send her into an emotional tail-spin. With Amanda still watching me, I very deliberately turned the picture face down in my hands and walked out of the room with it, closing the door behind me. I marched down to the study; I wrote a note saying that I'd found the photo in Amanda's room and left the photo there. Then I returned to my own room to sink down on the edge of the bed. It wouldn't have been done by Major Jeffries. He'd be all too aware of how that would affect Amanda. Certainly, if her mother's death had been the triggering factor in her emotional collapse, the photo would be brutally shattering.

Then who had slipped it into her room? And why? To see that Amanda didn't ride at the meet? Why was that important to anyone? (Why *was* her riding in it such an obsession with the Major?) Had it been done to simply strike at the Major, to foil his plans? Perhaps someone had seen it as a way to hurt him. But what a brutal, totally callous disregard of Amanda. It matched the Major's callousness toward the girl's safety. Who, I asked again, and suddenly I saw Sami's face as I'd passed him on the way in, that tiny, smug, self-satisfied light in his eyes that I'd never seen before. There'd been only glowering hostility before. I'd assumed he was reflecting his satisfaction with his day's crabbing. Perhaps I'd been very wrong. He hated with a deep, brooding hatred. It was in his eyes, hardly masked.

I heard the faint sound of the phone ringing and broke off thinking. I could only speculate, now. But I'd try to find out, I told myself angrily. Amanda was not the only one being made into some kind of pawn here. I rose, went outside and met Marie as she started to emerge from the living room. "Doc Clay, for you," she said.

"How about driving down to my office in Santal?" Clay asked. "At the far end of town, about seven?"

"All right, I'll be there," I said. "See you then." I hung up, undecided whether to tell him anything about the photo yet. I started back to my room to find Sami carrying his crabbing bucket from the house. He paused to meet my hard glance and now the brooding resentment was back in his eyes. My own anger pushed words from my lips.

"Why do you resent my being here?" I blurted out. He was taken off-guard by the remark and the hostile eyes blinked back at me.

"Who says that?" he returned after a moment.

"I say it. Your eyes say it," I snapped.

There was another moment of silence and then he shrugged. "The Major brought you here. You do what he tells you to do. Why should I care?" Sami said, and he went off, the left leg dragging after him. His disclaimers had revealed more than he thought; each word, as with everything else I'd heard him say, was coated with hatred for Major Jeffries. I was here to serve the Major, to do his bidding, Sami had in effect said. Therefore, I was included in the circle of his hatred, a hatred possibly deep enough for any act. Certainly it was deep enough for him to have slipped the picture under the door. Hate, I pondered, turning the word in my mind. It was probably the most simple, the most direct of human emotions.

I started back up the hallway and wondered again why Sami hated so deeply. General, amorphous resentment of the world as Victor had characterized it, was not enough. Nor was Marie's explanation of an introspective resentment. I opened Amanda's door and peered in. She was on the bed, curled up in a fetal position again, her eyes shut. I closed the door and went to my room feeling bitterly disappointed. The undercurrents of Darkwater Farms were more subtle and devious than I'd imagined. The place was well named.

I shed my clothes, and let the lukewarm shower water play a tattoo over my body until I felt refreshed. I put on a print dress, suddenly feeling the inner need to be feminine. A touch of cologne and a simple, gold necklace was enough. I glanced at my watch. I had time for a leisurely drive to meet Clay and I wanted it that way. I'd had enough turmoil for one day. I went down the hallway, and had reached the front door when I heard the Major's voice call. He stood at the library doorway. He had my note and the photo in his hand; his stern face revealed shadowed planes that heightened the severity of it. He came forward.

"How is she, Miss Forester?" he asked.

"Not good," I answered grimly.

"A night's sleep will help," he said.

"I wouldn't count on it," I replied. "Who would do that?" I questioned. His face remained immobile but his eyes narrowed a fraction and he lifted the photo, looked down at it for a moment.

"It was in the top drawer of my desk, along with some others," he said. "Anybody passing in and out of the house could have taken it. Even some of the hired help. They go into the kitchen and sometimes down to the cellar for things."

"Anybody?" I questioned. "It had to be somebody who wanted to get at you. Apparently the list is fairly long."

I wasn't ashamed of the remark. The man didn't need carefully chosen words. His imperiousness forbade him that courtesy. His piercing eyes fastened on me for a long moment.

"A word of advice, Miss Forester," he said. "This incident changes nothing. You are to prepare her to ride Saladin, no matter what happens. You have her in the riding ring tomorrow morning if you have to lift her into the saddle."

I wanted to find words draped in acid, hurtful, stinging, to hurl back at the stern, unyielding countenance but I could only stare at him totally overwhelmed by the absolute insensibility of the man. I waited a moment, felt myself turn away and walk from the house in a kind of shocked daze. I slid behind the wheel of the car, sat there for another moment and gathered myself. Amanda was his daughter. He'd supported her all these years in a sanatorium. How could he have such utter disregard for her now, I asked myself. How could he be so obsessed with one, single event? No egomania, I heard myself saying again. Something more, something else.

I drove from Darkwater Farms as dusk began to settle itself. I heard a cow bellow in the distance, a strangely comforting sound, an uncomplicated, direct sound of the earth, simple, eternal. I turned down the narrow road, shaking off my exchange with the Major as best as I could, concentrating on the driving. It was just turning dark when I reached the town, a wide, clean main street bordered on both sides by shops; a general store, a hardware store, a barbershop, a furniture store and an icecream parlor. I noted a hairdresser's and a bowling alley alongside a bar and an Elk's lodge and dance hall. A square, low, whitewashed stone building, more official looking than the others, bore the sign COUNTY RECORDS OFFICE—POST OFFICE outside it. The people were neat, men in pressed shirts and trousers, some in overalls, the women in simple dresses, the teen-agers much the same as others anywhere else. I'd reached the end of Santal when I saw the pick-up truck outside a low, rambling one-story building painted a light yellow.

I drew up in front of it and heard barks, chirps and bellows coming from behind it. Clay emerged almost at once in a dark-blue jacket and white slacks. His affable, pleasant face was what I needed tonight, I decided at once and he slid in beside me.

"Just keep going on this road. There's a little place a few miles on," he said. His glance had seemed casual but I found out it hadn't been at all. "What happened?" he asked.

"What makes you think something happened?" I queried in surprise.

"Your face is still carrying it. Little tension lines around the mouth," he smiled. I drew a deep breath, his perceptiveness somehow relaxing to me, and I told him, first about the photo and Amanda's reaction and then of my exchange with Major Jeffries. We'd reached the restaurant when I finished and he said nothing as we got out of the car. It was a dark-wood, modest place with a screened terrace that looked over a small lake, a low candle on each wooden table. Clay took a table in a corner and ordered drinks. I decided on a whiskey sour and looked out at the lake, a dark irregular shape among the still-darker oaks, cypresses and willows.

"Sorry the day turned out so poorly," Clay said as the drinks came, his a gin and tonic.

"*Why* is he so obsessed with her riding that stallion?" I asked almost angrily, flinging the question out.

"I don't know," Clay answered.

"It's more than just his ego," I snapped. "It has to be more."

"Not necessarily. Men such as the Major have very large egos. And then, the ego grows like a weed. It can assume dominance," Clay answered. I heard the reasonableness of his answer, but shook it off inwardly. There was more, I was certain.

"You said he owns people," I remarked. "How?"

"He always seems to be around when people are in trouble. He helps them but his help often carries a high price-tag. Somehow, he gets into their private lives and holds onto them. He owns a lot of people in the county that way. He knows private things about a number of lives and that's a very real kind of power," Clay said. "Frankly, I doubt that my father, who's been doctoring here all his life, knows as many secrets about people as does Major Jeffries."

"He's an octopus," I said angrily. "But he has his own dark places, too. I'm convinced of that, now."

"You don't mean Amanda, I hope. She's no secret from people in the county. He was right when he told you that people talk about her."

"No, not Amanda herself, but whatever surrounds her being what she is. Those are the Major's private darknesses, I'm sure," I said.

"Maybe," Clay shrugged. "I know that he's visiting my father at the house, tonight. That's unusual in itself. People usually go to visit the Major."

"Any special reason for the visit?" I asked.

"I suspect he wants my father's medical opinions regarding Amanda," Clay said. "But Dad's no psychiatrist. He can't contribute much of a specialized opinion on her."

The waitress appeared to hand us menus. Clay ordered another round of drinks and I studied the menu with no idea what to order. "Everything sounds enticing," I said.

"Try the gumbo, if you like seafood," Clay said. "It's fantastic. Everything you can think of and more is in it. I only know some of what they put in, a little chicken, a lot of fresh crab and young mullet, onions, tabasco, bay leaf, vegetables."

"Wonderful," I agreed and Clay finished ordering. When the waitress left us the second round of drinks, he leaned forward.

"You didn't come here to talk about the Major," he said.

"No, but everything touches on everything else," I agreed. "I came to hear more about the things you said this morning."

"Animals and the disturbed," Clay said thoughtfully. "Or perhaps I should say non-humans and the disturbed. When I was still a student, I got into a side road concerning animals and the disturbed. It concerned mostly dogs, then. There was a sanatorium for disturbed children near the university and I became friendly with the head of it. Some of the kids were only socially maladjusted, others were very severely disturbed. First, quite by accident, the chief psychiatrist became fascinated by the reaction of one little boy to the doctor's pet collie. The results so astounded the man that he brought in other dogs and set it up so that some of the most severely disturbed children could have access to dogs. What happened was staggering. Children, and young adults, whom they hadn't been able to reach in any way, began to change. They began to respond to the dogs, at first, then later, partially to the therapists. It was obvious that a kind of communication took place between the children and animals that didn't exist anywhere else."

"The children didn't feel threatened," I offered and Clay shrugged.

"That was the primary conclusion drawn but the explanation was too simplistic for me. Remember, some of the disturbed were really adults whom no one had been able to get to for many years, patients with whom they'd tried every other kind of therapy. In connection with this business of responses, I should mention the learning machine constructed by a team of doctors working out of Princeton's Advanced Institute of Sciences. Patients could manipulate this machine, talk into it, get answers from it, be corrected and praised. This machine also has had amazing results. Children with whom no one had been able to establish contact responded to the machine."

"The machine wasn't threatening, either," I offered. Clay shook off my answer.

"That may be part of it. I can't believe it's all of it," he said. "Was every human threatening? In ten, fifteen years, couldn't one person have seemed non-threatening?"

"Maybe not," I said.

"I think there's more, a lot more. The disturbed patient enters into some kind of psychic communication we don't understand yet," Clay said.

"With a machine?"

"The machine can act as a substitution mechanism if the essential elements are there, those elements the animals brought to the fore with the children. I mean a level of contact that is made up of completely non-thinking, nonintellectual sensitivities. The animal acts as both an emotional conductor and receiver for those sensitivities. There may be entire levels of communication between man and animal which we know nothing about yet because we, the average, undisturbed, so-called rational man, are incapable of surmounting our own truncated sensitivities. The disturbed may well be able to recognize those channels, to respond and relate to them."

"Because the disturbed have regressed to basic, animal responses or because their emotional disturbances involve added sensitivity?" I asked.

"I can't answer that one," Clay said. "But we explain animal behavior, or the powers of animals, on our own empirical terms, just as we interpret our own behavior. An animal reacts in a way we cannot because it has keener hearing, better eyesight, a special antennae of some sort. We see everything as a continuum of our own faculties. This attitude is related to our impatience with the psychic phenomena we can't explain on our scientific, empirical terms. Just look at how superficially we explain away some people's love of their dogs, cats, horses. We cannot face the fact of a special rapport, a channel that eludes our defining, so we define away with ridiculous explanations. The communications between the disturbed and animals, and yes, the disturbed and the machine, may one day explain a lot more about all human-animal relationships, perhaps even the need to hunt when there is no need."

Clay paused, turned his thoughts about in his mind before going on. "There is a special communication here. It's worked with many people who've been given up as unreachable. As long as they retain the ability to relate, respond, they will do so when the proper emotional communication is present," he concluded.

"You think Amanda has some form of this with Saladin?" I said.

"Something draws her to the stallion," Clay said.

"I've been afraid for her near him. Am I wrong in that?"

"No, there's a danger despite her communication with him. His reactions will be instinctive and automatic. She is unstable; he could react unpredictably. That danger will always be there with an animal such as Saladin. We don't really know a damn thing about the basic nature of this special communication, its character, depth." Clay paused, leaned forward and concern as well as sincerity showed in his eyes. "And maybe there's danger to you, too. You don't know the real depth or character of Amanda's disturbance."

"No, but I suppose a report on that is at the sanatorium," I said. Clay's genial face creased.

"Evangeline Sanatorium is no first-class psychiatric institution. It's a place for the rich to put away their personal embarrassments, an expensive closet for living family skeletons. The care is excellent. But modern treatment is minimal," he said.

The gumbo arrived wheeled to the table in a huge casserole on a cart. It was delicious and I dipped into it eagerly as I turned Clay's last remarks over in my mind. "Amanda's mental collapse came right after her mother's death. The connection would seem obvious," I ventured. "How did her mother die?"

"Suicide. Gunshot," Clay answered and I felt a wave of shock go through me.

"My God," I murmured. "Of course they connect. It shattered the child."

"Probably," Clay said.

"Why only probably?" I shot back.

"You're being a causist," he said. "One overt act causes another. That kind of simple environmentalism fails to take into account a lot of other possibilities."

"Such as?"

"The presence of emotional problems to begin with," he said. "Other children have deep, upsetting, traumatic experiences. They don't all go into emotional and mental collapse."

"That's immaterial. Some of us feel pain more than others. Some of us bleed more and some of us love more deeply than others," I returned.

"True enough, but I think most people have a kind of built-in emotional shock absorber for the traumatic experiences of life. It's part of our emotional protective equipment," Clay said.

"And those who don't?"

He shrugged. "Incomplete, perhaps. Flawed, if you like; a necessary part of the organism missing."

"I think she's blocking," I announced, an inner feeling more than any proper evaluation. "Canceling out painful experiences. Withdrawal is often just blocking on a massive scale, shutting out the world because it's too painful."

Clay lifted one eyebrow. "It's possible she's blocking. Nevertheless, no one's been able to penetrate that for ten years," he reminded.

"Maybe there's a chance now, with that special communication of yours helping," I said and he shrugged again.

"Maybe. It's all made of maybe," he answered and he was right, of course. Dinner had passed quickly and, after coffee, I realized how late it had become. Clay, seeing me glance at my watch, nodded in agreement. "I've an early day tomorrow, too," he said.

"It was a lovely dinner. And you've given me a lot more to think about," I said.

"Then let's do it again soon," he replied. "I'd like to know more about Gail Forester."

"Agreed," I laughed and he rose with me, walked back to the car in silence. He didn't make small talk and I was grateful for that. Clay Thedeaux was a comfortable person to be with, I decided. When we reached his place and he got out, he came around to the driver's side to pause at the window.

"Teach her to ride. That'll be consuming enough. Don't make Amanda's problems yours," he said.

"Don't ask too much," I echoed. "That advice is given by everyone here. But thanks, anyway."

I drove home thinking about the pleasantness of the evening but mostly about Clay's last admonition. Did I have a choice as to Amanda's emotional problems? Hadn't they been flung over me, inseparable from what I was to do with her? I still couldn't accept the Major's reasons as pure egomania, and Clay was willing to do that. Perhaps he was too tolerant of personal drives and the idiosyncratic customs of the Cajun world. Perhaps he was willing to understand too much. Perhaps, I reflected, I was too unwilling to understand. I let thoughts dance around my mind as I steered the black, backwood roads and only one certainty continued to persist. The Major's obsession to have Amanda appear at the meet on Saladin was more than egomania. I couldn't turn aside from that conviction and I found myself thinking about Sami, wondering if he had indeed put the photo under the door of Amanda's room.

I wished I could cut away that darkness as my headlights illuminated the night. Suddenly the lights picked out something on the road: my foot reached for the brake automatically.

I slowed, and braked almost to a halt as I neared the object, a huge snapping turtle, its tremendous jaws locked around the hind leg of a 'possum as it dragged the animal slowly across the road toward the bushes on the other side. The 'possum struggled wildly, twisting and straining, but he was absolutely helpless in the grip of the big snapper. I could only watch the gruesome, raw enaction of the macabre tableau and, in the 'possum's frantic struggles, it was plain that he, too, was aware of the inexorable approach of death. I thought for an instant of getting out and trying to free the 'possum but I knew it would be impossible. The giant turtle would disdain any blows I could rain on him and so I could only sit and wait. And watch, with stomach knotted.

Behind the turtle, a big willow dipped gracefully and moss-covered oaks arched. The grim mercilessness of the scene in front of me formed a jarring counterpoint to the background. The jasmine-and-cypress softness of this land hid a fierce savagery; everything was veiled, just as at Darkwater Farms, where everything cloaked strains and tensions. Even Amanda, herself, I reflected, was hidden in her own, inner ferment. The turtle finally crawled his slow path to the other side of the road and I stepped on the gas pedal at once, unwilling to watch him disappear into the bushes. I hurried away before that final closing, while I could still cling to the thought that somehow, someway, at the very last moment, the 'possum might escape. Self-delusion, of course, I knew. But I was in the mood for self-delusion. Sometimes it is the only comfort.

I hurried through the darkness and finally drew up in front of the house. I entered quickly, refusing to look at its squinty-eyed face that would, I felt sure, wear an expression of cold satisfaction. I opened Amanda's door noiselessly. The girl had undressed, left her clothes on the floor beside the bed. She lay in a long nightgown on top of the bed, asleep. I closed the door and uttered a silent prayer that she would forget the day's trauma in the morning. I went into my room and put on light, red-and-white polka dot pajamas. In the darkness, I clambered into the bed, stretched out, and waited for sleep. A sound drifted through the French doors, soft chords strummed on the guitar, vibrant yet quiet, notes that were more than notes, a summoning. I swung from the bed, put on a robe, and opened the French doors to step outside, the grass cool and wet underfoot.

I saw Victor's thin figure rise from the edge of the bayou and walked toward him. His smile was slow, sinuous as a snake as it wrapped itself around me and I instantly felt the pulsating magnetism of the man. "I've been waiting for you," he said, and I wondered if there wasn't the hint of reproach in his tone.

"No job tonight?" I asked, and he shook his head.

"How's Amanda? Were you able to calm her down this morning?"

"Yes," I said, deciding to say nothing about the picture as he obviously knew nothing about it. "Do you think that seeing you this morning sparked a reaction?" I queried.

"I don't know. I haven't seen her in ten years, not since they put her away," Victor said, and I felt my eyebrows lift. "The Major felt that anything that reminded her of home would be upsetting and I guess the doctors agreed with him. That was at first, and then, in later years, there just didn't seem any point in visiting her. There was always the chance that it might upset her. I guess maybe they were right, from this morning."

"Maybe," I mused aloud. Victor looked at me with affection. His hands struck a vibrant chord that shimmered in the air.

"Very beautiful," he commented. "Beauty is its own excuse, Emerson said."

"Did he?" I smiled.

"I don't need an excuse to do something if it feels right, if it pleases me."

"You're a hedonist," I laughed. He shrugged, and stepped closer, he leaned forward and his lips were pressing mine, soft yet vibrant, electric, and his hand caressed my shoulder. I didn't pull away. I didn't want to pull away, I realized with some surprise. It was Victor who took his lips away first. His deep eyes held tiny lights, danced with a private amusement.

"See, that needed no reason except itself," he said. Inwardly, I felt myself agreeing. Outwardly, I fell back on caution.

"I don't think my stay here needs further complicating," I remarked.

"No complications," Victor smiled. "Just pleasure. They don't have to be one and the same." He half-turned me toward the bayou, pointed to a slender shape drawn up onto the shoreline, a wooden craft. "We'll go out in that pirogue tomorrow night. I'll show you the bayou," he said. I nodded, suddenly filled with unwarranted anticipation. Victor Jeffries could weave a web of pulsating vibrancy with entirely too much ease. He stepped back and half-bowed. "Till tomorrow night," he said, turning quickly and walking across the grass, around the corner of the house.

I waited a moment, then started back to the French doors to my room. I'd glanced only casually to the left, at the window of Amanda's room, when I froze in place. The window was opened wide, the curtain skirling out in the night breeze. Running, I reached the window, and peered in. The bed was empty and, my breath catching, I spun away, and began to run down alongside the house till I reached the front. There, I raced across to the other side and down toward the stables. I slowed only as I neared the last door, at the far end of the stables, that opened in front of the box stall. I forced myself to move carefully, noiselessly, and peered around the edge of the door. The night light made soft-edged shadows along the floor. The box stall was open and I saw Amanda inside in her nightgown. She stood silently against the stallion, her head pressed into the horse's body, her hands upraised, against his hide. Saladin stood absolutely motionless, as if he were a statue carved there in the stall. Suddenly, I saw his ears move and his head lifted to peer forward. He'd caught my presence. I moved back at once, flattened myself against the outside of the stables and hardly breathed.

Listening, straining for any sound, I heard nothing, and then, after a few moments, the sound of a soft snort of breath from the stallion. I leaned forward, peered against the door again. Amanda was still in the stall but now she had her head against the stallion's neck and she stood alongside him, leaning against his black beauty. I moved very slowly into the open and stood quietly to let her see me. The stallion's ears were up instantly and alertness gathered in every muscle of his huge frame. Amanda's eyes had turned to me, and I spoke very quietly.

"Let's go back now, Amanda," I said. I took a step forward, close enough to reach the stall door. "Please, Amanda." The girl's hands slid down the stallion's neck; she turned and came toward me. As she emerged I pushed the stall door closed, heard the stallion's lips blow. Amanda walked from the stables and I went with her, let her go back alongside the house to her window. She swung over the sill and went inside. I followed the same way and watched her sink down on the edge of the bed. Clay's special communication was no longer a theory but very much a fact and suddenly, boldly, I wanted to make use of it if I could.

"Would you like to ride Saladin someday, Amanda?" I asked. The question had been put to help overcome her reaction to the photo, to stir anticipation and make her want to return to the ring in the morning. Amanda's light-blue eyes stared at me and, in disbelief, I saw her lips move, heard the single word as she formed it. "Yes," she said and I stared back at her, transfixed, my very breathing suspended. Amanda then swung her legs up on the bed and lay down with her back to me.

I walked from the room in a kind of trance. Ten years, I kept thinking. In ten years not a word to anyone. In my room, I shut the French doors and sprawled across the big bed. I could think only of Amanda and her single word, and, of course, the big stallion. Strange, mysterious emotional depths had been touched, the unknown reaches of a mind and psyche had been stirred. I understood now what Clay had referred to as explanations which were too surface. All the quick answers that came to my mind were wildly incomplete, entirely too simplistic. All that remained unquestioned was that a force, a non-human essence, had been able to achieve a communication no person had in ten years.

But why this half-wild, fiery stallion? Why Saladin instead of the gentle old mare? Because he, too, suffered an imprisonment of body and soul? The old mare accepted her state, as did most horses. But not the stallion. Acceptance for him was never complete. Was that the spark that brought her to Saladin, I pondered. The wild in mind and the wild in spirit, I mused; was that the spark that connected her and the stallion? But Amanda had spoken and the excitement of that single word reverberated inside me. I wanted to rush out and shout the news for all to hear, but I remained quiet, held it close to me. There were strange forces here, obsessions that had roots in dark places. News of Amanda's achievement would perhaps be more than unwelcome.

I turned on my side. The event would stay a secret for now, Amanda's and mine. But she had spoken; a wall had been pierced. I would not let it close again if I could prevent it. My eyelids dropped in weariness, I pushed aside further thoughts and suddenly slept.

CHAPTER FIVE

In the morning, I brought breakfast to Amanda; milk, pears with honey and coffee. Marie had given me the trays, and questions were just back of her quick glances. "She's coming along slowly," I said, and the woman accepted the comment without reply, a guardedness coming over her face. Amanda was dressed when I entered with the trays; she ate silently. I tried a few unimportant questions and got no response, finished my coffee and opened the door. Amanda rose and went down the hall with me and I breathed a deep sigh of relief. The photograph incident seemed to have been taken in stride, perhaps a more exciting sign than I realized. As we neared the living room, Amanda started to tense, the lines around her mouth pulling deeply. She lowered her head, half-closed her eyes and I took her arm, felt the rigidness of her body. I held onto her until we reached the side door and stepped outside.

The outside was another world; Amanda's gaze lifted and I released my grip on her arm. We walked down the path near the stables but she made no move to enter. The big bull had been let loose in the corral attached to his box stall. He moved back and forth in a trotting gait, a tremendous living vessel of contained fury. As we neared the corner of the stall, he swerved and came toward us, his small eyes glaring with stolid viciousness. Amanda stopped to stare at the bull and, with a sudden, explosive burst of motion, he charged forward, and slammed into the corral fence so that the ground shook beneath our feet. I jumped, an automatic reaction, but Amanda remained absolutely motionless. She simply stared at the bull and I watched as he backed, then tried to hook up through the opening between the fence rails with his horn. I yanked Amanda back. She turned, and came along with me; there was no expression on her face at all.

In the end ring, where the old mare waited, I started the day's lesson. She took command of the horse so much more completely than I'd expected that by afternoon I decided it was time for her to go on one of the saddle horses. I let her finish off the session riding around the edges of the ring on her own, turning and wheeling the mare as she wanted, with only an occasional admonition of "thighs close to the saddle, toes up." At one point Doctor Thedeaux stood by the ring, his white hair glistening in the sun, and I strolled over to him.

"I've been watching," he said. "Remarkable, really remarkable. My compliments."

"Thank you. You go along with the Major that she can ride Saladin?" I fished.

"I can't say that I did, but perhaps he's right. You're doing splendidly with her," Doctor Thedeaux said. It was a slightly guarded answer and I wondered if he'd been watching to see for himself, or to give a report to Major Jeffries. "My son told me he'd had dinner with you and that you know a good deal more than how to ride a horse," the man said.

"Clay is a kind person," I laughed.

"Hardly," Doctor Thedeaux answered. "Keep up the good work." He gave a courtly bow and turned, went back toward the house. I had Amanda dismount and started back to the house with her. The bull had been put back in his box stall where he stood in the center, implacably exuding fury, his tail swinging from side to side impatiently. Amanda turned toward the stables as we neared them and I let her stop at Saladin's stall. This time she didn't touch the horse but stood silently in front of him. He moved toward her at once, halted only inches from her and matched her motionless stare. Finally, turning away, she went on with me but I knew that I had witnessed a silent exchange. As we entered the house, I decided that if I were to keep that wall pierced, I couldn't turn away from anything.

"We'll be at the living room door in a moment," I said evenly. "It's time you stopped looking away as we pass the doorway, Amanda. You have to stop that sort of thing if you want to ride Saladin."

She made no response and I expected none. "To control Saladin, you have to be in control of yourself," I added. She walked on, lowered her eyes as we passed the living room but kept her head up. I was satisfied. My years of working with horses were a help. I knew the meaning of small successes. In her room, Amanda collapsed onto the bad, worn out, and I brought her rice pudding and a carbonated drink, left them and sought out Paul Agee again. "I expected you," he laughed, and I followed him on his rounds. I glimpsed Major Jeffries talking to three men Paul said were horse buyers from the Texas dude ranches. I stayed with Paul, a helpful shadow, listening and absorbing and finally the day came to an end. I went back to the house, and found Marie in the kitchen.

"I'd like a hotplate for Amanda and myself," I said. "I'm going to eat with her in her room, perhaps every night for a while."

Marie Opatu nodded and once again, in her eyes, a faint hint of private wisdom appeared. I went to my room, changed and when I came back to the kitchen, the two trays were ready. I took them both to Amanda's room and set hers down on a small table, mine on my lap. She ate silently, almost gulping her food and when we were finished, I put the trays on top of the dresser, relaxed in the wing chair.

"The Major wants you to ride Saladin at the County Fair meet," I said. "But you don't want to stop after that one time, do you?" There was no reply but Amanda's eyes looked up at me in a direct, expressionless stare. "I want you to ride Saladin after that, as often as you want," I went on. "But that means you have to step into tomorrow." Amanda's eyes continued to stare. I felt my hands gripping the edge of the chair, growing tight, and forced them to relax. "Tomorrow's are made of yesterdays. No yesterday, no tomorrow. To step into tomorrow, you must face yesterday, Amanda."

I saw fear gathering in the round, light-blue eyes and I went to her, put my hands on her shoulders. "There's nothing to be afraid of, now. There's just facing yesterday, remembering," I said. She shook her head, vigorously, tossing her hair back and forth. "It's the only way into tomorrow, Amanda. Every evening we'll remember a piece of yesterday," I said. She continued to shake her head and I saw her hands, gripping the chair, turn white; I stepped back. "All right; not now, Amanda. Only when you're ready," I soothed. "But there's no other way, Amanda. If you shut out yesterday you shut out tomorrow."

I stood watching her; she stopped shaking her head, the fingers of her hands relaxed slowly, and then she looked up at me for a long moment, almost with accusation in her eyes and she rose, went to the bed and lay down on it, her back to me. It was a dismissal and I honored it, gathered the trays and left. Only when I walked back to the kitchen did I realize how shaken I was. The course was pitted with danger, yet I was convinced, now more than ever, that she was blocking. To help her unblock, face reality, relive what had emotionally shattered her, was perhaps her one chance for real recovery. Now, with that strange, special communication working inside her, a form of inner release, I had to try.

I returned to my room, took off my sandals and stretched out in the darkness. The session with Amanda had made me tense, partially because, with Amanda, everything was unfinished, left dangling for next time and I always hated the unfinished. I'd just turned restlessly on the bed when I heard the guitar strummed again, a low chord. Swinging from the bed, I opened the French doors and stepped outside. Victor was there.

"Just a little moon tonight," he said. "A good night for the bayou." He held a big flashlight in one hand and he put his arm out for me to take, led me down to the bayou. The moon was indeed a sliver, barely glimpsed through the trees. Victor guided me to where the pirogue lay partially on the bank and I climbed in, first; the narrow craft was more stable than it appeared to be. He pushed it from the bank, and stepped in to sit behind me, his knees just touching my back. With his paddle, he sent the boat silently out into the bayou, moving from the shore to midstream, skirting a cypress that rose out of the water like a creature from another world. The simile was apt, I decided, for this seemed another world indeed, a strangely silent, peaceful, shadowed world, a nether region. The night sounds were soft, the air cloying and heavy and Victor sent the pirogue gliding along past numbers of cypresses that reached out of the water with gnarled, knobby roots. A particularly wide tree loomed up to the right; the water seemed turbulent near the trunk. Victor snapped a light onto the tree. A snake pulled itself from the water onto one of the thick roots.

"Congo," he said and I shuddered involuntarily. I wasn't afraid of snakes. Years ago I'd had a collection of garter snakes and another of com and black snakes. But this deadly reptile personified danger, its flat, triangular head venomous, raised and ready to strike. In the glare of the flashlight, the heat pits of the viper were clearly visible between the eyes and nostrils. Victor snapped the light off. "They like the bayous at night," he said. "Good hunting at night for them."

We moved on and Victor slowed the pirogue as we skirted another tree. Two orange-yellow objects loomed to my right, looking not unlike small, yellow flashlights. " 'Gators," Victor commented. "Only the very tops of their heads are surfaced." I stared at the orange-yellow circles; another pair of yellow-orange bulbs appeared and then still another set farther on.

"They're not vicious, like crocodiles, I've been told," I said somewhat hopefully.

"No, but they're dangerous enough, especially at night. They don't look too hard at whatever swims in front of them. They grab first and maybe spit it out afterwards, but that doesn't do much good then," Victor said. The bayous widened suddenly as Victor moved the pirogue around a curve and suddenly the water seemed to be lighted with a cold, bluish fire. Fish moved through the water looking like trails of glowing flame. "Ghost fire," Victor said.

"What is it?" I asked.

"A kind of phosphorescent plankton," he said. "Put your hand in the water and pull it out."

I did, and saw my fingers aglow with the blue fire that, when I shook my hand, became a small shower of fireworks. "Is it always here?" I asked.

"It changes in intensity a good deal," he answered. He steered the craft through the glowing water to a little island that rose up in front of us; the ghost fire seemed entirely appropriate in this otherworldly place. The pirogue bumped gently against the island, slid partially up on the moss-covered soil and I stepped out of the boat. Victor followed. Then he stretched out on the soft moss. I sat down beside him and looked down the bayou. It was a dark tunnel of an unearthly shadow land, the scent of mimosa clinging to the heavy air.

"I like the bayou. I often come here," Victor said. "It's a place for thinking. It keeps its own aloneness."

I looked at Victor's dark handsomeness, that pulsating animal vibrancy of his, heightened here in this silent, sensuous place. He was indeed home here, I thought, and then, suddenly, he pulled me down, half on top of him. Victor's lips reached up, found mine, and his hands moved along my shoulders, his mouth hot, demanding, and I felt his fingers circling my breast. I thought of his statement about pleasure needing no other excuse for being and the tensions that had gathered inside me suddenly demanded release. Or were they just willing to serve as an excuse for my own desire to taste of this wantonly attractive man? Victor's touch was caressing, exciting, and then suddenly commanding, triggering a hunger never too far from the surface. As he made love to me, a kind of demanding fierceness came over him at which I might have rebelled in another time or place. I wondered only if Victor was instinctively wiser than I.

Later, when I sat up and straightened out my clothing, I realized that though it had been quite consuming, exciting, in a strange way, it had been unfulfilling. It was as if it had happened too soon. Victor's pure animal magnetism had cut into my wanting, and yet it hadn't been what it should have been. Or might be, I wondered? First times were hardly ever the best. I put it down to that. Victor sat up on one elbow, ran a finger down along my side, then up around my shoulder.

"You're thinking hard," he said idly.

"Sorry about that," I smiled, quite willing to put aside my thoughts.

"You know, you can count on me if you want to cut out of here," he said, and I turned to face him.

"Meaning what, exactly?" I asked.

"This thing my father is doing with Amanda; I don't see it, myself. If it doesn't go well and you want to get away, I'll help you," he said.

"Don't you think I could just leave then?"

"I'm not sure. Not if he thought you should stay. He sees that people do what he wants, one way or another."

I thought of the Major's threat to get someone else to teach Amanda. "I think he's done that already," I commented.

"Just remember, if it gets worse, you can come to me," Victor said. I was grateful for his concern, and leaned forward to brush his forehead with my lips. Concern seemed a quality in short supply here at Darkwater Farms.

"I think it's time I got back," I said, and he rose, pulled me with him. I climbed into the pirogue and Victor pushed us out from the tiny island, guided us back along the dark tunnel of water. A wind came up as we rounded a curve, damp and penetrating, and I was glad when we reached the house. Victor brushed a hand across my back, the gesture more quickly intimate than words, and strode away. I went into my room, walked the few steps to Amanda's door and checked on her; she was asleep on the bed. I returned, closed the French doors, undressed and fell into bed. I went to sleep wondering about Victor, about the depth of his vibrant sensuousness, unlike that of any man I'd ever met before. I wondered why the Major had never mentioned him, why he never spoke of him at all. Obviously, there was a strain in their relationship. One more veiled part of Darkwater Farms. I slept finally, wanting to speed the new day nearer.

When I woke, I dressed and went down to the kitchen again to bring Amanda her breakfast. I'd just reached the study door when I heard Sami's voice, dark and low, and then Marie Opatu's. "I watched yesterday," he said. "She might do it. She might have her ready to ride Saladin."

"Nothing you can do. You stay clear," Marie said.

"No. He'll get his way again. No," Sami said. I heard Marie's voice full of tired anger then.

"Why don't you leave here, go away someplace?" she said.

"Why don't you?" Sami threw back. I heard the uneven sound of his limping walk and stepped inside the study door until the sound vanished down the hall. The exchange had been bitter, filled with unstated accusations and ominousness. I waited a moment, then stepped into the kitchen; Marie had on another gaily-designed kerchief. She turned from a plate of biscuits and I pretended I hadn't seen the residue of pain in her eyes.

"Good morning," I said brightly. "Biscuits. Wonderful." The woman nodded, put two plates on a tray with butter, coffee, the biscuits and fresh peaches.

"The Major asked where you were at dinner last night," she said casually, so casually that I caught the warning in it. "I told him what you'd said about spending more time with her," Marie said evenly. I nodded understanding, took the tray and brought it to Amanda. The girl was dressed and as I breakfasted with her I thought Marie's casual-seeming words had been anything but casual. She had told me that she suspected my reasons for closeting myself with Amanda and that the Major would be equally suspicious. I prepared answers as I finished the coffee and then left with Amanda for the stables. I had her watch as I saddled a deep-brown gelding; I saw that she kept her eyes on everything I did. With Amanda beside me, I led the gelding to the far corral where we'd worked with the old mare; I held the halter as she mounted. Amanda took the reins as I stepped away and I felt my lips draw tight, instantly certain I'd made a mistake in not using the old mare this morning. Amanda was nervous, much more nervous than I'd realized. Her mute, silent, expressionless mask was deceiving; dammit, I swore inwardly. The gelding was a lively, very alert horse, not spooky but quick to react, and smart. Her control of him was almost zero and I knew it at once. He balked, came close to bucking once or twice and when he began to bore, I had her dismount, and I swung into the saddle myself.

Like most horses, he was aware of his rider at once. He tried a few of the things he'd done with Amanda, received a few sharp kicks and a snap of the bit and quickly realized his tricks weren't working. He stopped and I let him canter around the ring a few times to shake out some more energy and then I put Amanda back in the saddle. He didn't play games with her this time but it was afternoon before she settled down, her nervousness staying with her, and by then she had wilted.

I refused to be discouraged. Each step forward with Amanda was apt to be accompanied by such after effects. But it showed me, painfully, how far away she was from coping with Saladin as a rider. I took her back to her room, she dragged her feet in a tiredness that was as much inner as outer, I was sure. But as we passed the living room she kept her eyes open, even though she stared straight ahead and I was grateful for small signs again. I took her ice tea and a sandwich and went back outside to hunt down Paul. The Major stood by the exercise ring, clipping angry words at two of the local hands.

"That fence was to be fixed yesterday. Any more excuses and you'll be looking for another place to work," I heard him say. "Now get inside and pick up those tools I left for you." I watched the men, sullen faced, walk into the side door of the house, and I wondered for a moment about the photo. Anyone could have found it in the desk, the Major had said. Sami remained my choice but I saw that I couldn't rule out others. Major Jeffries strode toward me, his remarks abrupt as usual.

"I'm told you intend spending dinnertimes with Amanda," he said. "Any special reason?"

"I need more of her confidence. I think that's the only way to get it," I lied. His eyes tried to see through me, and I wondered if he did.

"All right," he said after a moment, and he strode away again. I went on past the first exercise ring. The red cab of the pickup truck appeared and Clay sprang out around it, a small, black physician's bag in his hand.

"Hi," he said cheerfully.

"Hello, Clay," I returned, his pleasant, open face suddenly very welcome. "What brings you here today?"

"Getting blood samples for analysis. Preventive medicine," he said. "But I was hoping to see you. There's a *fais do-do* a week from Saturday. I thought you might like to go."

"There's a what?" I questioned.

He laughed. "A *fais do-do*, that's Cajun for a dance, a hoedown, actually. I thought you'd enjoy it and we could have that second talk you promised me. You've probably been stockpiling questions, anyway."

I had to laugh. I hadn't been stockpiling, not consciously, yet I had thought of a few matters he might answer. "With all those good reasons how could I say anything but yes," I replied, and he nodded in satisfaction. He started to go on, then looked at me with a faintly quizzical glance.

"I take it you've met Victor by now," he said. Something in his tone made me wary at once.

"Yes, of course," I said.

"Victor sometimes plays at affairs," Clay said blandly. "If that won't bother you."

I suddenly felt implications buzzing around me like invisible wasps. "Why should that bother me?" I asked with far more haughtiness than the question deserved. Clay's small smile told me that he'd caught the revelation in my tone. *Damn him*, I swore inwardly. He was entirely too perceptive.

"No reason, I guess," Clay said affably. "It's just that Victor Jeffries has a reputation for his acquisitive ways."

"Thank you. I'll remember that," I said stiffly, unable to stop myself and furious at how transparent I was being. Clay's smile continued to be infuriatingly pleasant.

"I'll pick you up that Saturday, about eight," he said; he walked on toward the barns and I fumed silently. He had no reason to assume I'd had anything but the most proper and casual relationship with Victor Jeffries. Did I resent his being so accurate? I joined Paul. The remainder of the day followed the pattern I'd begun to set with the farm manager, absorbing the feel and flow of his running the operation. It was what I'd really come here for and I took in every little detail that I could. Yet, as the day ended, I found myself looking forward to working with Amanda again. I brought dinner into her room, a thick fish chowder; she was sitting in the wing chair sullenly. She ate as I sat down with a bowl opposite her.

When dinner was finished, I put aside the plates, stretched out in the chair across from her and noted the quick, nervous glances she cast at me. "The riding didn't go as well, today," I said idly. Her eyes stopped their nervous darting, stayed with me.

"You were nervous, very tight." Her eyes continued to hold me, round, light-blue saucers. "It'll get worse unless you start remembering," I said. "You've got to stop shutting out yesterday."

She began to shake her head violently again. "Yes, Amanda, you've got to remember. You've got to stop blocking out the past," I said gently. She continued to shake her head and now she folded her arms across her breasts, rocked back and forth on the edge of the chair. I leaned forward.

"It happened, Amanda. It happened and now it's over and you have to talk about it," I said. She began to tremble, uncontrollably, almost violently. It was frightening, yet it was a positive sign. That total blocking, that complete, emotionless, impervious withdrawal was being destroyed. The struggle was a revelation of its own. I rose, went to her, and she came forward to put her head against me and I held her as one would a child, until the trembling ceased. It had been enough for this night. As in working with a high-strung colt, this was a tightrope; I had to sense when to press and when to let up. I stepped back and stroked her head for a moment. "Tomorrow, we'll remember more tomorrow," I said. I started to take the dishes and, at the door, saw that Amanda was walking to the bed, pulling off her blouse, starting to undress. I closed the door and left.

Finally, alone in my room, I undressed and lay across the bed, letting the cool night air sweep over my body, suddenly aware of how the session had drained me, also. I kept seeing Amanda's violent trembling as the pain of the past surged against the mental and emotional walls she'd erected. But the struggle was too violent. More than the fact of the mother's suicide was involved, I speculated. Amanda had to have experienced something more, perhaps even seen it happen. Perhaps she had just come into the room when it happened. Good God, I murmured silently. If that were so, it was little wonder the child had gone into an emotional breakdown.

Proper, careful handling at the time might have brought her out of it then but that had obviously not been done. How much had really been done for Amanda, I wondered. Clay had said that the sanatorium was an expensive closet for putting away family skeletons. Had that been Amanda's real treatment—confinement, the shutting away of an embarrassment? Then why parade her now? Once again, it didn't fit. Before closing my eyes, I thought of the exchange I'd listened to between Sami and Marie; bitter, barbed words full of hidden meanings. Everything here full of hidden meanings, I mused. I let sleep drift over me, welcome and embraced at once.

The next morning, Amanda continued to be terribly nervous on the deep-brown gelding, so much so that he almost threw her and I called a break. I took his saddle off, let him run free around the exercise ring, then returned him to the corral where Amanda had waited. She watched as I put his saddle back on him, tightened the girth properly. The brief break had done the gelding more good than Amanda; she continued to lack control of the horse, her nervousness remaining. I worked through the morning and into early afternoon, and she improved some but not nearly enough. Finally, as she slumped in the saddle, I called a halt. Her exhaustion was not simply from the instruction, I knew, but from her inner tension. She stopped at Saladin's stall as we returned to the house, insisted on going inside and, apprehensively, I let her. The stallion came to her and she ran her hands along his sleek, jet coat but her nervousness had stayed with her and the stallion caught it. His ears kept moving back to lie flat, then they'd stand up, and he snorted and moved restlessly. I moved forward into the stall to get Amanda and Saladin came toward me at once, his ears flattening. He tossed his head, blew and his powerful muscles contracted; I moved back. Amanda stayed, leaned her head into his side and he backed, quieted some. I let out a deep breath as she finally moved out of the stall and I swung the gate closed.

I took her to her room and didn't see her again till I brought dinner later that evening. I faced her in the wing chair, watched her cast sullen glances at me. "Was it just your mother's death, Amanda?" I asked almost casually. "Was it just the fact of her death?"

Amanda nodded at once, her head bobbing up and down quickly and she cast quick glances of approval at me. Like a frightened hare, she was leaping into the first hole, the first refuge that offered itself. "You're not telling the truth, Amanda," I said quietly. She stopped nodding, looked at me narrowly. "It was more than that, wasn't it?" I probed. She glared angrily at me but I didn't flinch. "You saw something, didn't you?" I said adamantly.

"No!" She tore the word out, flinging it at me in a half-scream, but in her eyes there was a frantic searching to see if I believed her. I shook my head slowly. *"No,"* she cried out again.

"Yes," I countered quietly. "There's more." Amanda glared at me but I met her fury again and finally she looked away and I saw her start to tremble.

"When you're ready, Amanda," I reached out and pressed my hand into her shoulder. "Tomorrow night, maybe. When you're ready." The trembling stopped and I left her then, sitting quietly in a chair as I closed the door. I decided to go down the hall to the library and find a book to read. The sound of the piano from the music room drifted to me and I crossed to the other side of the house; Victor turned to me as I entered the room.

"I hoped you'd hear," he said, rippling a string of notes across the instrument. "Couldn't get to you last night. Got a sudden call for a gig."

"I didn't expect you to get to me," I said. His deep eyes turned fully to me as he swung from the keyboard, a faintly quizzical light in them.

"Do I detect regrets about the other night?" he asked. "I hope not."

"No, no regrets," I said, sorry I'd been so snappish, but Clay's remark about Victor's acquisitive reputation still clinged. "I guess I'm just not the pleasure for its own sake type. I'm not casual about some things." It was a half-truth but not without sincerity. I knew the aftertaste of casual intimacies and never liked it.

"Who said anything was casual?" Victor asked and his eyes were luminous as he rose to stand in front of me. "You're on edge. Amanda, isn't it?" he asked. "It's not going well."

"I'll get through it," I replied, wanting to say no more yet to anyone.

"Just remember, I'll help in any way I can," he said. "Keep me posted." I nodded, let his lips find mine and enjoyed the electricity instantly there. Any relationship with Victor would be more than casual on the sensuous level alone. I felt small-minded at my reaction to Clay's remark. Why wouldn't someone as pulsatingly magnetic as Victor have a reputation for acquisitions? Yet the word bit in, the term was an irritating one, designed to make me hang back, a subtle attack on the ego. I found myself wondering if Clay had used it purposefully. He was certainly a man who was aware of what he said, and I added another question to those I had for him.

Victor swung back to the piano and I sank down on a short, cushioned love-seat as, in seconds, he lost himself in the music, rippling chords out, turbulent sounds that grew darker, wilder, rolling progressions and fiery glissandos. I sat caught up in his playing. Then he halted abruptly, breathing deeply and heavily as he bent over the piano. He rose, almost whirling around, came to me and took my face in one hand, a sudden roughness in his touch.

"Don't hang in too long," he said, his voice hard, while in the deep, black eyes I saw a kind of anguished concern. He pulled his hand away and strode out of the room, not looking back. I sat quietly, not upset as much as strangely touched. Communication, again, I murmured inwardly; the chemistry we feel is far beyond words, looks or actions. He was concerned about me and that concern seemed to tear at something inside him. I rose in a while, decided to skip the book and walked the hallway to my room. In the darkness, I stood at the French doors, staring out at the deep, heavy-aired oaks and the bayou beyond. The new moon had come up again to tint the ground faintly and, as I watched, I saw a form move, to the right, a figure emerging from the deeper shadows of the trees. The slow, slightly halting gait was unmistakable and I watched Sami cross the grass, turn, then move toward the house. I shrank back along the edge of the French doors, watched as he came closer, then turned myself and headed for the window of Amanda's room. I moved again to keep him in my line of vision, saw him pause at the window, step close to it and peer in. He stayed for a few minutes, then went on in his halting gait, down along the side of the house, disappearing into the darkness.

Was it his practice to go about peering into windows, I wondered? Was he, as I'd first wondered, a quiet voyeur, harmless and pitiful? I grimaced. Pitiful, perhaps, but not harmless. No one with the brooding hatred in his eyes was harmless. I undressed and went to bed, not unhappy to get a few extra hours of sleep.

The following day, and the days that came after it, went on in the pattern I'd established, the mornings and early afternoons spent working with Amanda, the late afternoons with Paul, and the evenings given over to Amanda in the privacy of her room. Paul asked no questions. Perhaps because he didn't need to ask. He had ample chance to see me working the girl in the corral. The Major continued to stop me and throw peremptory questions about Amanda at me, most of which I answered with cold honesty. Amanda had reached a plateau on which she stayed, showing no progress, either in her handling of the gelding or her unblocking, though I said nothing of the latter to Major Jeffries. She was nervous, tense, erratic with the horse and stubborn with me. It was no better in the evenings when I tried to help her talk.

The two things were intertwined and both seemed at a standstill. More importantly, the days were rushing on and I realized that the County Fair was but two weeks away. Unless something unexpected happened, Amanda was in no way ready to ride Saladin. Her daily visits to the stallion were the only times when her nervous, tense erraticism seemed to drop away; then she withdrew into that protective cocoon of her own, able to respond only to Saladin.

Even that communication was flawed. My worst fears were confirmed one morning when Saladin stood loose in the large exercise ring as I passed with Amanda. The sight of him there, not in his usual place, upset her at once. I felt her body tense next to mine and she insisted on rushing into the ring. The horse saw her, trotted over to her and then raced off again, repeated the process three times before halting for her to touch him. She put her hands on him but I saw the lines of tension in her face, her lips moving nervously, and the stallion backed away, his ears twitching. That calm, special communication was not there, or very little of it was, and Amanda herself backed away finally, retreating to the gate and I pulled her outside. I had mental pictures of her atop Saladin that morning and closed my eyes to shut them out. Then, strangely, at the end of the day, when Saladin was in his box stall again, that mysterious, very real communication was unmistakably there again as she leaned her face against the stallion and he stood still as a carving. Seeing him running free in the exercise ring had struck at something in her rapport with the horse. Because he was really freer than she, I wondered? Because he was actually less a prisoner? But when she saw him imprisoned in the box stall, the kinship reestablished itself again. What would happen when she tried to ride him? What sparks could be set off, I groaned to myself.

The volatile possibilities were etched even more clearly now, and everything still interlocked. If Amanda couldn't be brought at least partly out of her withdrawal, she'd never be able to control the stallion in an unconfined situation. It pushed me into pressing her a few evenings after that when I'd cleared away the dinner trays. She had sat sullenly, refusing to respond even with the breakthrough of a single word we had been able to achieve earlier. I hesitated, fought with myself and decided to plunge.

"It happened in the living room, didn't it, Amanda?" I said. "And you were there."

Her lips parted and her eyes widened as though she'd been slapped across the cheek. "You saw it, didn't you, Amanda?" I pressed.

"No!" The single word uttered again, not a word but a cry of anguish torn from her very innards. In it's strangled, gasping denial lay an admission.

"Yes, Amanda, yes. You saw it happen," I repeated. Amanda had risen, her hands outstretched rigidly, her fingers almost like claws, the veins in her delicate neck pulsating and then, with another gasped cry, she flung herself on the bed and sobbed, her shoulders quivering with each anguished sob. With a shame-faced excitement, I suddenly realized that for the first time, Amanda's sobs were audible, normal, vocal sounds, heartbreaking yet another step forward for all their anguish. The sobbing, the anguish was outside instead of inside and I felt sadly satisfied. I went to her, stroked her blond hair, and waited until her sobs began to trail away. Finally, she half-lifted herself to look up at me; her tear-streaked face was grave, her eyes round and searching.

"No more now, Amanda," I said. "No more remembering for tonight. The rest will come. We'll look back together. And tomorrow, you'll do well on the gelding. I know it."

She said nothing but something flickered deep in her round eyes, a concession behind emotions still fiercely guarded, a tiny awakening. "Sleep well," I said. As I pulled the door closed after me, a big figure stepped out of the shadows in the hall, the eagle's countenance was darkened with rage.

"How dare you?" Major Jeffries thundered. "How dare you probe into Amanda's past?"

I stepped back, suddenly frightened at the fury of the big man in front of me, and tried to gather myself. He had obviously been listening outside the door.

"You little busybody," he hissed. "Poking into things that are none of your concern."

"No, I'm trying to help Amanda," I protested. "I was right from the start. She can't ride Saladin the way she is. Anything could happen."

"She and the horse get along. I've seen it," he snapped.

"You haven't seen the things I've seen," I returned, finding anger rising up to dispel my initial fright. "It's too dangerous. She could be badly hurt, killed."

The man's lips curled into a sneer. "You were hired to teach her to ride. That's all, nothing else. You've no business poking into her past," he shouted.

"It all hangs together. You can't separate it. She must be in control of herself to be in control of Saladin," I flung back, trying to answer with convincing arguments when I knew that rational decisions had little to do with the man's fury.

"You see to her riding and nothing else," he threw back and I felt anger and stubbornness spiraling inside me at his total disregard for Amanda.

"I'll see to it my way," I retorted. "Amanda has made progress, more progress than she has in ten years, it seems. You heard her just now. You ought to be overjoyed."

"Nothing but her riding concerns you," he said, his intense eyes blue circles of fire. I felt myself digging in.

I said, "I'll do it my way; I'll do whatever I think she needs."

He pointed a long, spear-like finger at me and suddenly there was more than fury in his voice; I felt danger, cold, shadowed danger. "Amanda is my daughter. I know what's best for her. I'll decide what should be done with her. Stop meddling, stop prying into her or you'll be sorry," the man warned. He spun on his heel and stalked down the hall and I realized that I was trembling in barely contained rage. I wanted to strike out at his icy, merciless face, that face as void of human feeling as an animal's when seizing its prey. The man was a monster. He seemed oblivious to the meaning of what he had overheard, that his daughter could unblock, could return to the world after all these years. He cared only about one thing, to parade her before the community at the show. No, that's not enough, not enough, I muttered inwardly. There was a terrible darkness behind his obsession. I felt it just under his unyielding, singular insistence.

I opened the door to Amanda's room and felt my lips press downward as I saw her cringing near the window, pressed against the wall. She had to have heard his angry shouts.

"It's all right, Amanda. It's all right," I murmured, going over to her, taking her back to the bed. "Go to sleep. Tomorrow will be a wonderful day." She lay down and her hand reached out, rested against my leg and she closed her eyes. I stayed until she seemed to relax and I saw her draw her legs up into a fetal position. I turned away, walked from the room, the sign of regression stabbing at me. Outside, in the dark hallway, my voice a strained whisper, I stared down the length of the house.

"Damn you, damn you and your self-centered obsession," I swore into the dimness. Had his rage and his shouting ruined everything I'd managed to achieve? Had those painful, halting advances been sent fleeing back into the dark of her tormented mind? I went into my room, thoughts churning as I undressed, lay across the bed. How much damage had his rage done tonight? How much had it done to Amanda a long time ago? The thought shimmered, hung in the darkness before me. Had Major Robert Jeffries driven his wife to suicide? Perhaps the entire affair had been the poor woman's flight, her last gesture of total retaliation. Had he driven her to it? Had Amanda known the truth in the instinctive wisdom with which children know such things?

The questions spawned more. Had he been happy to shut the child away rather than face her accusing stares? Had he done nothing about her shattered emotions out of cowardice? The questions whirled and swirled and came back again to the present, the question that burned today. Why this obsession to have Amanda ride Saladin at the show? Why, after all these years, bring her forward in front of the community? The local hands had seen me working with her. Word would already be spread far and wide; many would come to the show just to see for themselves. Why was that important? Why now, after all these years? Not to feed his ego. Not just to still wagging tongues. I refused that once again. His reasons lay in that shattering time when a woman killed herself and a little girl withdrew from the world.

Robert Jeffries had planned carefully for this time, sought me out, arranged every last detail, anticipated my every reaction. But his rage as I probed into the past, freeing Amanda from her emotional prison, had held the edge of fear in it. The past threatened him in some way and I had to find out why and how. Time was racing and Amanda's progress was painfully slow. If I couldn't have her ready to ride Saladin, I had to find a way to stop Robert Jeffries from his obsession. He was consumed by an uncaring, unfeeling madness. Only the truth would be a weapon against his driving pursuit. I'd keep trying to pull yesterday from Amanda but I didn't dare wait for her to explode with the truth, not any longer. I had to find another way to learn why it was so important that Amanda ride the stallion, after all these years, and why nothing else mattered.

I had to know for Amanda, for her safety now, and for her chance at tomorrow. I felt uneasiness stabbing at me then. Perhaps knowing was not for Amanda. Realization doesn't always explode as a sudden light. Often it's like a blade emerging slowly from a scabbard. I suddenly had a dawning suspicion that *my* tomorrows might depend on finding the truth every bit as much as Amanda's. I'd been brought here for a purpose, I was a vital part of his plans. Could he just let go when it was over? Would he? Did he ever just let go of anyone?

I felt tiredness dulling my mind, closing down on the thoughts that chased each other. I turned over and slept with a new inner crystallization of purpose.

CHAPTER SIX

I brought a breakfast tray into Amanda with apprehension and was encouraged to see that she had dressed already. I searched her eyes; what would have been discouraging in someone else was hopeful with Amanda. The dull, staring, withdrawn blankness had been replaced by a darting, fearful nervousness but it was at least active and a kind of life. She ate in silence and I thought about my decision to probe for the truth as quickly and as purposefully as I could. I wondered about asking Paul Agee again. He'd shut out questions abruptly once but since then we'd developed a working rapport. I discarded the idea as I finished my coffee. Uneasiness is mother to distrust. Paul was, after all, a part of Darkwater Farms and everyone here seemed a captive of the Major in some way. Marie Opatu and her brooding son; even Victor, with his concern and empathy, held an inner turbulence just beneath that sensuous magnetism. No, I'd ask nothing of anyone here now. Possibly, later, Victor, if I needed help.

Amanda and I went to the stables where she watched again as I saddled the gelding. She held his head as I put the bridle on and then we walked to the far corral. Big Red Honey Island watched us pass with his head lowered, the massive width of his huge horns taking up half the length of the gate. As soon as Amanda mounted the gelding in the corral, I saw trouble at once. She did almost everything wrong. The gelding didn't try any tricks with her this morning but he reacted to her mistakes. I tried short, fifteen-minute sessions with breaks in between but it didn't help any. Amanda seemed to be trying, yet that very conscious effort became a kind of barrier to her.

I clung to my patience, worked with her, and suddenly saw a tall, ramrod figure standing by the corral fence, his bald head catching the sun like a reflector. The Major watched, his fierce eyes following her every move, missing nothing. Then I saw a white-suited figure standing back near the stables, watching from a distance. Doctor Percy Thedeaux's face wore an almost worried expression. No, not worried so much as anxiously concerned. I turned back to work with Amanda; she wheeled the gelding to see the Major standing at the fence rail. Her nervousness became even greater, her erratic lack of control increasing. Finally I went over to where Major Jeffries stood.

"Your standing here isn't helping any," I said sharply. His eyes stayed on Amanda as he answered me.

"She'll get used to it," he said coldly. His eyes narrowed, watched as Amanda managed to wheel the gelding in a circle. "That gelding's no good with her. Get her on the stallion," he bit out.

The shock wave went through me as though I'd been slapped. I finally found my voice. "You're mad," I shot back. He continued not to look at me, his piercing eyes still on Amanda.

"You've got the basics into her. That's enough. She can ride Saladin," he growled.

"Good God, man, just look at her out there," I protested.

"She's got a thing with that big bastard. That'll make the difference," he returned.

"No," I said. "There is something but it's completely unpredictable; it's not enough. She has to be able to control him."

As if in support of my words, I heard the gelding snort. I spun around to see Amanda trying to hold him as he began whirling. "No, let him go around," I shouted at her, starting towards her. "Let him go, then bring him up." She seemed beyond it and then, suddenly, by accident, luck or somehow remembering her lessons, she did the right thing, let him come completely around, then sent him forward and managed a semblance of control. I reached her, took the gelding by the bridle and looked up to see the perspiration staining Amanda's blouse. "Easy, now, easy," I said, soothing horse and rider. Amanda's lips were drawn tight, her eyes darting nervously back and forth. I shot an angry glance at Major Jeffries.

"Keep on with it," he clipped out, as he turned and strode away. The ramrod figure walked to where Clay's father stood, then disappeared beyond the box stall with him. Amanda relaxed a little after he left, but not enough. Her work was uneven, not at all good and I bore down on her, then realized that didn't help. Finally, seeing that she'd had more than enough, I called a halt, feeling unhappily like a drillmaster. I led the gelding back to his stall, untacked him and found one of the local hands nearby.

"He needs a rub-down," I said and the man nodded. Amanda pulled to go to Saladin and I went with her to the box stall. She leaned against the half-gate to the stall and the tenseness in her came through her obvious tiredness. Saladin was in a corner of the stall by the grain manger and his head went up as she came to the gate. He watched her but made no move to come over. Looking on, I suddenly had the distinct feeling that there was a waiting and a searching taking place before me, stallion and girl looking to sense something; a sign, a reassurance, a message? Finally Amanda turned away and I was not at all certain that the searching had been rewarded on either part. I returned to her room with her and she took off her perspiration-wet blouse and lay down on the bed, her girlish breasts rising and falling with deep breaths. She shook her head when I mentioned something to eat; I left her alone, and walked out to my little blue car. I slid behind the wheel and drove from Darkwater Farms, hurrying along the narrow roads.

I'd already formed some thoughts, too loosely organized to call a plan; they started with the fact of the suicide itself. It had taken place here and there had to be a record of it. Perhaps there had even been an inquest, though I doubted that. Still, the official records might hold something. Little locks open big doors. I needed something that would serve as a starting point, that might help me reach Amanda. Or, hopefully, the official records would provide a clue to the Major's obsession. I kept a heavy foot on the gas pedal and slowed as I moved into Santal's wide main street, passing four boys in a stripped-down mustang that had been almost made into a dune buggy. I pulled into the narrow lot alongside the square building and hurried inside. The Post Office took up the front part of the interior and a hand-lettered sign directed me to a short corridor in the rear of the building where a closed door with tinted glass bore the words: County Records Office.

I found myself facing a long counter and, behind it, rows of file cabinets. A man rose from a small, metal desk behind the counter and came forward. He had rimless glasses on a face that somehow managed to look pinched despite its roundness. His eyes, pale and watery, wore the officiousness of bureaucrats of minor importance. "Yes?" he asked, giving the solitary word an air of imperiousness that was destroyed by the whine of his voice.

"I'd like to examine some county records of about ten years ago," I began. "Specifically, the records on the death of Mrs. Edith Wentley Jeffries."

I watched the pale, watery eyes take on surprise, then instantly become uncomfortable. "Why would you want to see that?" he asked.

"I'm doing some research on the history and background of the Wentley family. That would, unfortunately, be a part of it," I said. His attitude changed to one of dubious stiffness.

"Well, I don't know, really," he muttered.

"The county records are a matter of public record, I believe," I said with asperity. The man's stiffness turned to sputtering at once.

"Why, yes, yes, of course," he murmured. I pressed, unbending.

"Then may I see the official records on Edith Wentley Jeffries, please," I insisted. The man's lips pulled back and his eyes blinked nervously.

"Well, now, that's ten years ago. They … ah … they aren't in our active files," he stammered, discomfort sitting on his every word again. He was lieing, I was certain. Not all that much happened in this county. The file cabinets behind him were large enough to carry fifty years of records, I estimated.

"What does that mean?" I said firmly, coldly.

"Just that they'll have to be taken out of back files. That will take some time and searching. I couldn't do it today any longer," he said groping. Lies, I murmured inwardly.

"When can I see them?" I pressed.

"Tomorrow," he said, licking his lips. "Tomorrow afternoon. That'll give me time to dig them out." His tongue ran across his lips again. I looked past him, beyond the rows of file cabinets to the rear of the room. Three windows, two open from the bottom. I paused a moment, my mind clicking off inner certainties and next steps at once. The man waited for my reply, his lips twitching anxiously.

"Tomorrow afternoon, then. I'll be back. I do want to go over those records," I said severely. He nodded and I walked from the room. I let the door remain open as I hurried out through the Post Office-front of the building. He'd have to come around the counter, close the door, then return back around the counter to his desk, all valuable seconds to me as I stepped outside and raced around to the back of the building. I rushed to the half-open windows, positive of what the nervous little man would do. Under the first window, I felt a grim satisfaction as I heard his voice after a moment.

"Hello, I'd like to speak to Major Jeffries, please," he said, nervousness still very much in his voice. The little weasel, I murmured to myself. "Yes, Ben Hibbell at the County Records office. I'll wait. It's important." My lips pressed into each other. Ben Hibbell was one more person with strings to Major Robert Jeffries, it seemed.

"Yes, hello, Major, Ben Hibbell here," he said then. "A young woman was just here. She wanted to see the official records on Mrs. Jeffries. She said she was doing a history of the Wentley family." He paused. "Yes, dark-haired, round cheeks, very pretty, that's right." I sniffed disdainfully as he went on. "Yes, I put her off but they are public records and she'll be back. What? Yes, of course, that's why I called. I know you don't want anyone stirring up old memories." The obsequiousness of his voice was sickening now; he fell silent a moment, then came on again. "That's right, they would consist of the medical report, the death certificate and the records of the probate proceedings. Yes. Yes, I see. Mislaid someplace; I understand. I can't put my hands on them. All right." Another pause and then, "Yes, I suppose they could be mislaid for a week or two. Yes, Sir, I'll appreciate that. Thank you. I'll handle it."

I heard the sound of the phone being put down and walked to the car and backed out onto the street. A grim anger had begun to churn inside me. The man was an octopus with tentacles that reached everywhere. The records must reveal something. Most official records were bare recitations of fact and these were probably the same, but he was afraid I'd pick up something from them. I drove slowly down the rest of Santal, trying to form plans. I had almost reached the end of town when I heard the horn behind me, insistent. Through the rear-view mirror I saw the red cab of the pick-up truck and Clay waving out at me. I pulled over and Clay did too; he got out, and came over to the car. We were only a few yards from his place. I opened the door and stepped out.

"What brings you into town?" he asked amiably.

"Just out for a ride," I said. Clay's eyes appraised me.

"You seem preoccupied," he remarked. "Trouble back at the ranch?" He smiled.

"Maybe. Things are going too slow with Amanda, I'm afraid," I said.

"Pressure from the Major?" he asked.

"Yes," I almost snapped. "He's hung up on this thing. He's afraid of something."

Clay frowned. "Afraid of something? Such as?" he asked.

"I don't know. Why don't you ask your father? He was there again today. He and the Major seem quite close," I said and was instantly sorry I sounded almost acid. Clay didn't respond in kind.

"They've known each other a lifetime," he said quietly.

"I'm sorry. I'm on edge," I apologized. "I suppose he has friends as well as the people he owns. Which is Paul Agee?"

"Paul? Maybe some of both. He's got a deep streak of loyalty in him. Some people are more loyal than others, you know. Just like animals." Clay paused a moment. "Paul was in a bad way some years ago, as I hear it, heavily in debt to gamblers. But he had an outstanding brood mare the Major had tried to buy. This was in southwest Texas. Some of the gamblers tried to collect out of Paul's hide and in the fight, one of them was killed. Paul was up for murder. In his way, the Major got him out of jail and out of there, even though the original charge is still on the books."

"And he got the mare as well as Paul," I said. I sniffed disapprovingly. The original charge was still open, a sword held over Paul Agee's head.

"I can read what you're thinking," Clay said, "and I suppose you're right in a way. But he also straightened Paul out, gave him a new life here."

I shrugged. "It was still self-serving," I returned. Clay glanced at his watch.

"I've some clients due in a few minutes. I'd be finished in an hour if you can wait," he said hopefully.

"No, I've got to get back," I replied. His affable face took on an expression of resignation.

"I'll pick you up Saturday about nine?" he said, and I nodded, ashamed that I'd not really thought much about the *fais do-do.*

"You're a nice person, Clay," I said, suddenly very much aware of it.

"Absolutely super," he smiled, waved and returned to the pick-up. I got back into the car, made a wide turn and started back through town. I looked hard and long at the square building as I passed it and went on, ticking off plans in more detail. It was nearly dark when I returned to the house and parked the car nearby instead of in the shed. I was going up the corridor to my room when Marie started into Amanda's room with a tray. She turned as she heard me come up, my frown question enough.

"The Major's orders," she said apologetically. "No more dinners with Miss Amanda. You're to spend time with her only in the riding ring." She shrugged helplessly at me.

"I see," I answered through hardly moving lips. I followed her into the room, waited as she left the tray. Amanda sat in the wing chair, her eyes watching me as I went to her.

"We won't stop," I said. "Not now, not after you've come this far. I'll come to you, late, after everybody's asleep and we'll keep on remembering."

She said nothing but I saw a flicker of agreement. Or I thought I did. I hoped so. I left, then, angry stubbornness seething inside me. He wouldn't get his way, I vowed silently. I wouldn't let him.

In my room, I changed into dark slacks and a deep-blue blouse, before going down to the dining room. The table was set for two and Major Jeffries was pouring a white wine into both his and my glasses. Marie served dinner; spicy, delicious *boudin* with rice and fried *gratons* on the side. The Major ate in silence until the meal was almost over. The strained air at the table bothered me at first but I shook it off. I was more apprehensive about my plans for later in the evening. Besides, I enjoyed being one ahead in his little game for a change, knowing that he didn't suspect I'd listened to his orders on the phone to Ben Hibbell. He finished his wine, then fastened his penetrating eyes on me.

"Do you know classical Greek Mythology, Miss Forester?" he asked.

"Some," His face could have been cast stone.

"In Greek Mythology, as you probably know, Pandora was the first woman on earth, created by Hephaestus at the order of Zeus, as a vengeance on Prometheus and mankind. She was blessed with every charm, but also disobedience and curiousity. Zeus sent her to marry Epimetheus, brother of Prometheus, and gave her a box as a wedding gift. It was a very beautiful box but Pandora was told she must never open it. She disobeyed, opened the box and all the evils which have afflicted mankind ever since flew out," he said.

He rose abruptly, turned and stalked from the room, not even glancing back. The message had hardly been subtle, yet, for a moment, I wondered if he'd been trying to say something more. I shook away the thought, then concluded it had been just another attempt to warn and frighten. I rose, went out into the dark and had made my way to the car when Victor's tall, thin figure appeared with a warm smile. "Hello," he said softly, his hand closing around my arm. "Going out on the town?"

"Just feel like getting away by myself," I said.

"I heard all the shouting last night. He thinks you're prying into Amanda, it seems," Victor said.

"I want her in control of herself before she gets on Saladin," I answered. He leaned forward, brushed my forehead with his lips.

"I'm worried about you. I wish you'd just quit," he said.

"Thanks for worrying over me, but aren't you concerned about Amanda? Doesn't anyone here think about her?" I exclaimed, unable to hold back irritation.

"I am thinking about her," Victor said calmly. "Without you, I don't think my father would go through with it."

I made a face. I couldn't imagine Robert Jeffries bluffing. "He'd go on, especially now," I said and then, suddenly, a question pushed itself forward without my wanting to ask it, "Why? Why is this so damn important to him?"

I saw Victor's eyes narrow. "To stop gossip. To show people she isn't what they keep saying. His damn ego," Victor said.

"No," I said, shaking my head. I refused to accept that from Victor or from anyone else.

"That's what makes it so terrible. It'll all be an act, a lie, a masquerade. Amanda will still be what she is," Victor added. "She was disturbed long before mother's death."

Clay's words flashed before me. "How do you know that?" I questioned.

"The therapists at the sanatorium said that was no doubt the case," Victor shrugged and I felt better immediately. The therapists were caretakers, I sniffed inwardly. I'd come close enough to Amanda to have more faith than that in her.

"Maybe and maybe not." I opened the car door and got in behind the wheel. Victor's hand brushed my cheek gently. "Just be careful," he said, stepping away and I snapped the ignition on, waved to him and drove off. I headed down the dark night toward Santal, certan that Victor was concerned for me and equally certain that he, too, was all wrong about his father's ego. Robert Jeffries feared my opening up the past. He didn't want me to look at the official, public records because he feared what I might pick up. Perhaps that wasn't ego as much as dark reason. I swung onto the road to town, too fast, skirting oaks and skidding around corners, slowing only as I reached the town. It was mostly dark; only the ice-cream parlor, the bowling alley and the dance hall were lit. I slid the car carefully into the parking area at the side of the square, white building, now a rectangle of gray in the darkness. I drove carefully back beyond the side lot, turned and drew up close to the rear of the building. I shut off the engine, sat listening for a moment, then got out.

Santal was a quiet, back country town and I'd counted on a certain casualness of behavior. I was pleased to see I'd been right. The windows in the back of the structure were still half open. Climbing onto the fender of the car, I could reach the sill with ease. I searched my trunk for the powerful road lantern I carried there. With the light in hand, I climbed up on the fender again, slipped my shoes off and pulled up onto the sill, got a firm grip on it and swung a leg over, then another. Seated on the sill, I turned the light on, then dropped down to the floor inside the building, landing lightly on the balls of my feet. Keeping the light low, I moved into the first row of cabinets. I was five years too early and I moved down into the next row. I was still much too early and I skipped three rows, and swept the drawers of the fourth with the light. Nine-teen-sixty-six: the drawers were alphabetized under the year.

Excitement suddenly gripping me, I moved along the rows of drawers, shining the light up and down each cabinet until I found the drawer I wanted—I—J. I began to go through large, manila folders of varying thicknesses. It was almost at the very end of the drawer, a folder of medium fatness and I yanked it out, took it to the rear of the room and knelt down on the floor with it, keeping the light low to avoid any reflection against the windows.

I began to go through the papers: documents, certificates, attestations, medical reports, the first group all dealing with the suicide itself. First, I read the Police reports of the call, their flat, short-phrased recitation of facts, then I came to a statement by Marie Opatu. I settled down, my back against the file cabinet, and read it carefully.

Statement: Marie Opatu
Domestic, employed in household of victim.

I was in my room, in bed, when I heard the shot. I threw on a robe and ran down to the living room. Mrs. Jeffries was on the floor. A gun, a pistol, was right next to her. She was bleeding terrible. Major Jeffries was there, in a corner of the room, holding Amanda (daughter). She was screaming. The Major told me to call the doctor and he took Amanda away. I called Doc Thedeaux and waited in the hall.

Signature: *Marie Opatu*

I put the statement aside and went on to the next document, the death certificate signed by Doctor Percy Thedeaux. I read again, slowly, carefully.

Death Certificate: Edith Wentley Jeffries
Location: Darkwater Farms, Hackberry, Louisiana
Cause of death: Suicide; gun shot.
The victim was dead when I arrived on the scene. The bullet, retrieved and filed, #77357, .38 caliber revolver cartridge, entered the head through the left malar at an upward angle, continued on through the Sphenofrontal suture and shattering the left parietal as it exited. Powder burns on skin indicate revolver was fired almost directly against face. Laboratory analysis of revolver showed cleaning oil fluid on weapon. Analysis of scrapings of victim's hands established traces of cleaning oil on both hands. Death by suicide.

Signature: *Doctor Percy Thedeaux*

I paused for a moment to wonder why traces of the cleaning fluid from the outside of the gun had been on both of the woman's hands. Probably, she had moved the weapon from hand to hand as she anguished over her decision, I decided. I went on through a Sheriff's Deposition, then a Deputy's statement and then came to the statement taken down from Major Robert Jeffries. I read it slowly, carefully. It tied in with the statement by Marie Opatu in all the essential details. He had heard the shot and raced to the living room from his study, nearby. He'd gotten there first, a few moments before his daughter, Amanda, ran into the room, he said, and went on to corroborate Marie's deposition. I frowned, went back to where he said he'd gotten to the scene first, before Amanda. That would mean Amanda hadn't seen the actual shooting. She had come upon it afterward, when he was there. I'd seen Amanda's eyes, her face, her body as she'd risen from the chair when I'd pressed her about the shooting. *You saw it happen,* I'd said, and her reaction had been a violent, anguished admission, a reaction that meant but one thing.

I looked at the Major's statement again. That part of it, at least, was a lie. Amanda's tortured eyes had told me that. Had he simply wanted to spare her more grief, more questioning, more pain? The rest of the papers were of little importance, one a statement taken from Victor. He had been asleep in another part of the house and hadn't come onto the scene until the Police were almost ready to leave. I shifted the light, went on to the second group of papers in the folder, feeling disappointed. I'd found nothing that really helped in any way, certainly nothing for Major Jeffries to be concerned about.

The second group of documents were copies of the will, filed in probate, of Mrs. Edith Wentley Jeffries. I scanned the formal phrases, reducing human hopes and fears into dry, legal paragraphs, when suddenly I stopped at a sentence, went back over it again. "Edith Wentley Jeffries, being owner of Darkwater Farms," I read, frowning, pausing to take in the meaning of the line. Amanda's mother had been the actual owner of Darkwater Farms, then. I returned to the document, "being owner of Darkwater Farms, hereby bequeaths all land, buildings, livestock and all other real property and assets that are part of Darkwater Farms, to her daughter, Amanda, aforesaid Darkwater Farms to be held in trust for her until her eighteenth birthday. Further, said property, livestock and any and all other assets, are to be administered for the aforementioned Amanda Jeffries by Robert Jeffries until she has reached age eighteen. Further, a sum of monies specified herein below, is set aside for this purpose. An additional sum of monies as specified herein below, is hereby set aside for the care, education and raising of Victor and Amanda Jeffries, such monies to be used by Robert Jeffries in this task."

I lowered the document, excitement coursing through me. Amanda was to inherit everything at eighteen ... now. Her mother, for whatever the reasons, had made that decision. But the woman hadn't, of course, envisioned what the suicide would do to the girl. She had obviously felt that Amanda would weather the shock. Or, more likely, she hadn't really thought about that aspect of it at all. Suicide was such a self-consuming, aberrant inner struggle of itself.

I brought my eyes back to the will, read on and the next clause that followed seemed to rise up from the document to sweep over me.

"In the event that, through accident, injury, disease or death, Amanda Jeffries is unable to assume, govern or otherwise inherit aforesaid estate, all properties and assets thereto will become the property of Robert Jeffries."

I felt a grimness settling over me like a shroud, grimness and a kind of shock, almost a disbelief at the thoughts that whirled through my head. I wanted to push them aside but I couldn't. If Amanda were mentally incapable, her fitness to inherit the estate could be brought into the courts. The proposition would be argued that she was, indeed, unfit to govern herself and so the estate should be awarded to the next in line, Major Robert Jeffries, and he would continue to provide care and treatment as he had in the past ten years. She had, after all, spent most of her life in a sanatorium. There would be logic, direct evidence and expert testimony, and yet a court challenge to a will was always tricky business. What if a doctor, a psychiatrist, came up with an expert opinion that Amanda could recover? What if the court decided to let the will stand, with Amanda as sole inheritor, and merely appoint the Major as administrator? The thoughts that raged inside me refused to be pushed aside now. It would all be so much simpler if Amanda were dead.

I shuddered at the word but the truth lay in front of me, stark and shattering. Were Amanda killed, or fatally injured, in a bad riding accident, Darkwater Farms would belong to the Major. It would be all so neat and so above suspicion. Hundreds at the show would see her riding Saladin, making progress in her recovery from her long confinement. It would appear that Major Jeffries was working hard and successfully with his daughter. The accident, when it happened, would go unquestioned. And there would be an accident if Amanda continued to ride Saladin in her present state. She might manage a few times, but one day there would be an explosion, of her agitation and the stallion's untamed wildness, the wrong thing done at the wrong moment, and tragedy would result. Without Amanda in control of herself and the horse, it was but a matter of time.

I felt my lips draw back in distaste. I had been brought here to put the girl into a saddle of death, to prepare her for a fatal accident that was bound to come. I'd been hired to teach her enough to ride the stallion at the show, that was all he needed of me. He had only to sit back and wait after that. Training Amanda to ride was, in actuality, abetting in murder, a clever, carefully planned murder that could only be seen as an accident.

My stomach held a cold stone inside it. I was even more deeply entrapped, now. If I ran now, Amanda was certainly doomed. He'd go through with it, put her on Saladin in some way, parade her before the people at the show. The fatal accident would come sooner, rather than later, then. No, I murmured inwardly, I couldn't flee, abandon her. I had to stay and try to teach her all that I could, as hard as I could, and continue to try to free her of the past. I had to run on two tracks at once, and hope that at least one worked.

Slowly, I put the papers back into the folder. It was plain, now, why he hadn't wanted me to see the official county records. He knew I'd see the shape of his obsession. I rose, slipped the folder back into the file and, using a chair, climbed up to the window and wriggled through it, dropped to the top of the fender outside. Sliding off it, I got behind the wheel and nosed the car out into the Main street of the town, now almost a deserted thorough-fare, only the lights of the dance hall blinking lazily. I drove back to Darkwater Farms, the night insects accompanying me with slurred sounds. The house was dark when I parked the car in the shed, but I knew that the penetrating eagle's eyes could be watch-ing, waiting. I went to my room, stretched out on the bed and waited in the darkness. I let a half-hour go by, then rose and opened the door, listened in the hall. There was no sound and I crept to Amanda's room, entered, saw that there was enough moonlight coming into the room to make turning on the light unnecessary. Amanda sat up and I saw that she hadn't been asleep; her eyes were round, focusing on me instantly. Time seemed to press even more heavily now that I'd read the file folder. I had to keep on; I sat down beside her and spoke harsh words in a soft voice.

"You saw it happen, Amanda. Say it. Say the words," I asked. The words were important, perhaps vital. They would be a psychological crack in outer as well as inner barriers. "You saw it happen, didn't you?" I said. Amanda stared at me, made no attempt to deny what her eyes revealed. "You want to make believe you didn't see anything. That's what you've been doing all these years, blocking it out of your mind as though it never hap-pened. But it did happen. You did see it. You can't keep blocking it out. You must face it, Amanda, you've got to face reality."

Her hands began to dig into the edge of the bed, turning and twisting into the sheet, and her eyes darted back and forth fear-fully. "Say it, Amanda, say it," I pressed. Her body grew rigid and her hands spread out, claw-like fingers now. "Stop blocking yourself in," I urged.

"*No!*" The single refusal again, once more torn out of inner anguish. Reality had been dammed up too many years. The block refused to give way yet. Amanda was shaking, her entire body consumed with violent trembling. I put my hands on her shoulders, pressed and held them there until the trembling began to subside.

"It'll come, Amanda," I soothed. "You'll say it. You'll face it. Soon." She lay back, curled up on the bed and I rose. It was enough for tonight, progress so slow it seemed no progress at all. Yet I knew better. Just as the solitary words she had managed to utter had been a break in the wall, blocks chipped away, the rest would shatter, I was certain. Only time was the chief enemy now, time and mistakes. I had to take care not to push too hard.

I left, returned to my room, undressed and lay across the bed, both drained and excited. I knew, now, the reasons for the Major's mad pursuit. Amanda had to be seen riding Saladin in public; the image was integral to his plan. As always, he had prepared with absolute thoroughness. I thought again as I lay in the dark about the story of Pandora. He'd failed to make his point. Finding out the truth behind his obsession was not opening a box of unknown evils. It wasn't loosing unsuspected troubles on the world. The truth was a singularly pointed finger. His little tale didn't fit. He had merely attempted to frighten me. I let my eyes close and slept still churning thoughts.

The morning came quickly enough and I swung from bed, dressed and hurried to the kitchen where the breakfast trays waited. I took them to Amanda's room, passed Sami and ignored his brooding glance. Amanda was dressed and in her eyes, once again, I was sure I saw tiny pinpoints of new vitality. She finished the morning meal quickly, and went with me to saddle the gelding. The day began with promise; Amanda was less nervous and the gelding responded. She worked hard, obeyed instructions well and I decided to move forward with her, let her trot the gelding. She tried and grew nervous at once but I stayed with her, taught her how to keep her weight forward, to post to the trot. I kept at it, finally stepped back and watched as she trotted the gelding around the edges of the corral. She was doing well when I saw her suddenly yank back on the reins, her mouth open and her eyes looking behind me. She swung, almost jumping down from the saddle and I turned to see Major Jeffries at the gate of the corral, leading Saladin, bridled and saddled. The Major wore his gray hounds-tooth jacket and, Doctor Thedeaux stood a dozen yards behind him. Amanda was racing toward the gate and I broke into a run, reaching it just as she did. Her eyes were on the horse, a tremendous kaleidoscope of emotions mirrored in them; shock, anger, protectiveness, possessiveness. She reached out, tried to snatch the reins from her father's hands and he pulled back. She half fell against the gate of the corral. I pushed myself partially between her and the gate, and glared up at the Major.

"What are you doing?" I hissed, fury spiraling inside me. Amanda grabbed for the horse's reins again and he pulled back once more. I heard her breathe in gasped sounds of turmoil. It was plain that she didn't want him holding the stallion.

"What do you think this is doing for her?" I flung at him. He turned to the girl.

"She's going to ride Saladin, to take him out alone," he said. "She wants to ride Saladin. Isn't that so, Amanda?"

Amanda made another unsuccessful grab for the reins and her face twisted in tension, her lips working, though no sound came from them. Major Jeffries smiled at his daughter, the smile cold, taunting. "Yes, Amanda wants to ride Saladin," he repeated. Little clusters of perspiration appeared on the girl's forehead.

"She's not ready," I said. "She's not at all ready. Why are you doing this?" I cried out at his cold face.

"Because you're holding back on her. She's learned more than you want to admit," he said, suddenly turning on me.

"No, I'm not holding back. She's not ready for that stallion. I know what I'm talking about," I shouted back.

"She's getting on him now," he said.

I shook my head. "She's not ready," I insisted. "It's too dangerous."

"I have to see for myself," he said. "She's riding him now."

"No. It won't prove anything. It's not time yet," I refused. Silently, I cursed his need to know. He wanted to satisfy himself his plans were coming along.

"She rides," the man growled.

"No."

Almost in disbelief, I saw him reach into his jacket and bring out a huge revolver, heavy and long-barrelled. He raised it alongside the stallion's head. The horse tried to back away but the man held him firmly. The revolver pointed directly at the horse's forehead.

"She rides now or I pull this trigger," Major Jeffries rasped. "Your choice, Miss Forester."

"You wouldn't," I gasped, then realized how wrong I was, not from the sound of the hammer being pulled back on the gun but from the icy flame of his eyes.

"Now," he growled. "Let her on now or I'll shoot." He looked at me for an instant and there was no hollow bluff in him. I could only look at the stallion, at the magnificent, wild beauty of him. I felt my answer gathering inside me. I could not see him destroyed. I could not sacrifice that beauty. There was no victory in that. As I stepped back, I wondered how often we are faced with choices that lie so far beyond our conscious decisions that they are no choices at all but simply the only answers we can give. To destroy that magnificent creature, even to call the Major's bluff knowing that I might lose, was beyond me and Robert Jeffries knew it—and I hated him for knowing that. Amanda brushed past me, pushed the corral gate open and he flung the reins at her. She caught them, pulled herself to the black stallion. I saw his ears moving nervously back and forth, his sensitivity quickly catching the tension in the air. Amanda mounted and Saladin backed, half-reared. Major Jeffries gave a shout and the stallion roared away, at a full gallop almost at once. He raced down the roadway, toward the flat land and the woods beyond where I'd ridden him. I saw Amanda bent far over in the saddle, not riding him so much as clinging to him and then he was out of sight and I turned to the ramrod figure standing next to me, fury sweeping aside caution.

"You won't get away with it," I said. "I won't let you." He peered through me.

"I won't get away with what?" he growled, his eyes searching, perhaps the faintest tint of alarm in them.

"Amanda," I said, turning away quickly, retreating by being cryptic, afraid I'd said too much. But inside, I meant every word. I wouldn't let him make me into a partner in murder by accident. I leaned against the fence. Doctor Thedeaux's face was grave, worried. I uttered a small, silent prayer that somehow Amanda would retain enough of what I'd taught her to stay on the stallion. She wouldn't bring him under control, I knew, but perhaps he would come down to meet her distraught and limited abilities, the magic of that special bond working between them. I found myself pacing back and forth, tying the gelding to a fence rail, casting glances at Major Jeffries who stayed unmoving, a statue of flesh and blood.

I heard the horse before he came into sight, the sound of a steady trot beating against the earth. He rounded the bend and Amanda was still in the saddle, her hair disheveled, her eyes round and staring. The horse came up the corral and the Major reached, caught hold of the bridle. I ran forward as Amanda began to dismount, half-caught her as she slid to the ground. I felt her body trembling. Saladin backed, blew, half-reared and the Major had to go with him, give him more rein. Paul Agee came over to take the horse, his face unsmiling, his eyes meeting mine for an instant. I held Amanda's arm, turned to face the Major and met his stony stare.

"It doesn't mean anything," I slid at him, my voice tight. "Nothing happened this time. She was lucky. It doesn't mean anything. She's not ready for him.

"No more hanging back, Miss Forester," he bit out. He swung around, handed the horse to Paul and stalked away, joining Clay's father; the two men walked off together. Amanda seemed drained of blood, her face chalk-white. I led her back to her room where she slumped down into the wing chair. I searched her eyes for that new, tiny spark I had seen in them but it was gone, the expressionless stare back in its place. Did she know, with some instinctual sense, that she was being made to flirt with disaster, I wondered? Had she sensed, on top of the stallion, the precarious limits of her bond to the magnificent wildness of him? I put a hand on her shoulder.

"Tonight, late, we'll try remembering again," I said softly. There was nothing, not even a flicker from her eyes and once again I silently flung curses at her father. Damn the monstrousness of the man, I swore as I left the room.

The afternoon moved swiftly and later I went to the kitchen to get something for a throat as dry as a desert. Sami entered just as I finished my ice tea, accusation in him as he stopped in front of me.

"I saw just now," he said.

"You, too? Everybody was there, it seems," I bit out.

"The Major won again," Sami said, vitriol in his voice.

"He didn't *win* anything. It turned out all right, a matter of luck," I retorted. I felt my temper, already shredded, tearing further. I was tired of his brooding, hating eyes, his sullen face. "Is that all you care about?" I snapped. "Whether he gets what he wants or not?"

"Without you, he couldn't win. Only you could have taught her that much," he said doggedly, his compliments really spears. They stabbed deeply, echoing inner misgivings of my own. If I hadn't come, would the Major have had to alter his scheme? The Major had thought as much himself, his seeking me out having been a kind of proof of it. I met the boy's gaze again, and grew angry at his singular hatred.

"You don't care about the girl at all, do you?" I cast out.

"She means nothing to me," Sami admitted coldly. "Only he is important."

"You hate him so, why don't you leave?" I thrust, echoing the exchange Marie had flung at him.

"Leave? With this leg?" he almost snarled. "Who would have me? What work could I do? I can't even move fast enough to trap the nutria."

Words that were cloaking something else, I felt certain. "Self-pity," I snapped. "You're full of self-pity. Your leg isn't that bad. You could do plenty of things. But you'd rather hate than help yourself."

His face, contorted, became a mask of viciousness. "A lot you know," he shouted. "You should never have come here. You should never have agreed to take his money and do his work. You're the real trouble here." The onslaught took me aback with its savagery, more full of venom than I'd expected, even given the barbs I'd flung at him.

"Get out of my kitchen. Get away from her," Marie Opatu said from the doorway. "You've no right to talk like that."

"I've a right, all the right I need," Sami flung back and the woman stepped forward, chin lifted high, staring down his angry eyes. She stopped directly in front of him; he spun, almost brushed me as he made for the door and I couldn't help thinking that his spirit limped more than his body. But he made one thing crystal clear. My connection with the Major, willing or unwilling, made me a party to his hate, as much a target of his venom as the Major. Perhaps more so, I reflected.

Marie Opatu's embarrassment, and a defiant protectiveness, mingled in her face; I decided to make no further comment on the incident. Besides, I'd had enough emotional buffeting for one day. I left the kitchen and these undercurrents, too deep for me to fathom now. In the hallway Victor appeared, his smile welcoming again.

"Rough day?" he said, catching the weariness in my face at once. Apparently he'd been one of the few not watching the events of the afternoon. I nodded.

"Full of surprises," I said. His face showed sympathy.

"I wish I could stay to help," he said, "but I've a late-night gig on this evening. I'm leaving in a few minutes."

"I think I'd just as soon be by myself, anyway," I said. He stepped closer, brushed the back of his hand across my cheek.

"Don't let it get to you," he said. I nodded, grimly, and went on, conscious of his look following me with concern. I went to my room and lay across the bed until blackness surrounded me. It was a blanket that covered only physical things, and the events of the day insisted on moving in front of me like an unwelcome reel of film. Major Jeffries has pushed and, despite his smugness, had been terribly lucky. Had he truly thought I was holding back, I wondered? It was quite possible, I realized. He was suspicious of me, now, of everything I did. Or had he some other, arcane reason for pressing Amanda to ride Saladin today? Had he needed reassurance that his scheme could work? He was a man of hidden motives and cleverly disguised plans. Had today been one more such move?

Suddenly restless, I pushed away further useless speculation, looked at my watch and saw that I'd toyed with my thoughts far longer than I'd realized. I went outside, an overwhelming sense of uneasiness on me. I had learned Major Jeffries' hidden motives and yet today's incidents hadn't properly fitted in with anything. I moved out into the night, the wind sudden and surprising as I stepped beyond the corner of the house. It grabbed at my hair, pulling it out, tossing it wildly and I smoothed a hand over my head. The willows rustled with the sound of the wind and the moon was a fitful light peering out from behind swift moving clouds. I walked to the dark ribbon that was the bayou, stood at the edge of the water and inhaled the night-blooming jasmine. The bayou seemed a cloaked peacefulness that pulled at me, a dark refuge suddenly terribly attractive. I found the slender pirogue a few yards away, the paddle inside it. I stepped into the craft and pushed off from the bank. A gust of wind pulled at me, sent the pirogue half-turning and I dipped the paddle into the water, straightened the boat and sat silently, letting it drift out into mid-stream.

In the other-world mysteriousness of the bayou, the oppressiveness of the house and all the inwardly-turned hatreds that were a part of it were closeted away. The silent, secret, ominousness of the dark waters seemed to gather me in, making me a part of that eerie world. I paddled around a cypress that rose from the water, a twisted dark shape that seemed to bend toward me. A sudden funnel of wind caught the pirogue, sent it into a half-spin and I corrected the turn with short strokes of the paddle. Wind moved along the banks, bending tall grasses with a strange, swooshing sound. It whirled around me again, played with my hair and, idly, I wondered how the wind could sweep along so and the air itself could remain heavy and sweet with jasmine. I paddled on, paused as, to my right, two orange-yellow circles appeared, then two more nearby. Magically, as I looked out across the dark waters, I saw two more appear suddenly, then others. I seemed to be passing through a circle of 'gators and I stroked the pirogue faster, saw yet another quartet of the unblinking yellow circles just ahead of me and slowed down. The bayou was alive with them; the more motion I made in the water, the more surfaced to watch.

I let the craft drift again and suddenly, almost at my side, I heard the sound of the water in a quick swirling. I glanced down in time to see the upward arc of a cottonmouth as he lifted himself from the water, then dove down again. I felt myself shudder and lean toward the other side of the pirogue; the craft dipped at once. I straightened instantly, let a deep breath escape. It had been a foolish, unthinking notion, coming out here, I told myself angrily. I was a stranger in a strange world here, not at all prepared for this stygian scene. I began to turn the pirogue and felt the wind again, strong against my face and yet sweeping along just above the bayou, hardly rippling the water's surface at all. It spun my hair into my eyes and I shook my head to toss it aside. I heard the sound, then, soft at first, next growing louder, afterward softening again. Sitting motionless in the pirogue, I listened, frowning; the undulating sound was not unlike that of a woman sobbing with her face muffled against a pillow. It grew stronger again, seemed to come closer; I felt a sharp gust of wind and saw the branches of the oaks and cypresses bending—and I knew the sound for what it was, the wind sobbing its way through the closely-packed branches, pushing through the denseness of the foliage.

I felt myself tense, remembering Marie Opatu as she had spoken to me that night by the corral. *When the wind cries, there is death. When the wind cries, old man death is hunting.* I felt a shiver go through me. The wind was indeed crying, now, the sound growing louder, an uneven, wailing cry. Superstitions, old wives' tales, country lore, I told myself. It didn't help. I dipped the paddle into the water, swung the pirogue further around. I'd just completed the swing when a shot split the night, a sharp, single interruption of the wind's cry. I felt the pirogue shudder, and looked down at the hole that appeared as if by magic near the bow. I was transfixed by the water as it poured through the hole into the boat. Only a big-bore gun could make a hole like that. I was unwilling to accept what I saw. When the wind cries, I whispered silently, and I was the one sought by death.

I scanned the shore, trying to peer into the blackness of the night. I saw only the shapes of the trees that lined the bank like so many twisted sentinels. Automatically, I made myself smaller, bent forward, waited. But no second shot followed to explode the night. There was only the soft sound of the water pouring through the hole into the boat. The bow of the pirogue was settling rapidly, and I hastened to try to paddle, succeeded only in swinging the stern of the craft around as the water-filled bow acted like an anchor. I was sitting in the water now, and the craft was filling fast. There'd be no paddling it to shore; I half-rose to swing over the side and into the water. The bayou was warm, and I clung with one hand to the gunwale of the boat. I was about to strike out for the shore, when two orange-yellow eyes appeared to my right, then two more, and another pair after that, I saw others surface behind me; I treaded water, and stayed beside the pirogue which was now almost full of water. I saw one pair of the orange-yellow eyes move, glide magically across the water toward me, then stop, motionless. There was a sound close by in the water and I saw an undulating shape swim silently past.

I felt my stomach contracting. The alligators would move in on me when I started to swim, a normal reaction more than sheer viciousness. Only the results to me would be the same. They'd snap their huge jaws around this new, strange object that moved through their waters. The venomous vipers would react more quickly if I bumped one as I swam—and more fatally. I glanced at the pirogue. Fear, as much as necessity, can be the mother of invention. I swung in the water, put both hands along the edge of the pirogue, pushing down on it and half-lifting myself up at the same time. The craft came over on its side, water cascading from it, poised in mid-air and heeled half-over. I pulled and pressed again at the edge of it and it flipped the rest of the way. As it came down, I ducked under the water, pushed sideways and came up alongside the overturned craft, putting both hands against it.

I glanced around; the eyes that had stayed so motionless were all moving now, in widening circles that brought them closer to me, back and forth in the water. Pulling the pirogue over had sent water rippling out and the 'gators had responded at once to this sudden disturbance. The water moccasins that infested the bayou were no doubt reacting, too. I used both hands, and pulled myself onto the overturned pirogue to lie flat on top of it, my arms drawn in close to my sides. The overturned hull was slippery but flat and wide enough, and I stayed motionless there, my head inclined to one side. I could see the 'gators coming in close, their thick, gnarled snouts rising higher in the water as they circled the overturned pirogue. I lay still on top of the hardly-moving craft and the wind still cried through the trees. Slowly, excruciatingly slowly, the 'gators grew calmer, the orange-yellow eyes moving away from the pirogue, some disappearing beneath the water completely, others resuming their motionless vigil.

I continued to wait, and finally, very slowly, I lowered my arms over the upended sides of the craft, and dipped my hands into the water. I began to paddle with both hands, pushing the boat quietly through the water. The inert, overturned craft was unresponsive but again slowly, it began to move toward the shore. I pushed the water with my hands, using very faint, still motions, inching the boat along, pausing every few moments to scan the dots of orange-yellow eyes for movement. At every little sound from the water, I pulled my hands out and waited, paddling again when I felt confident no moccasins were near. Finally, I neared the shore and paused, my wrists aching. I rested a moment and realized how still it had become. The wind had stopped crying through the oaks and cypresses. A deep sigh of relief escaped me and almost at once I grew angry. How could I embrace old folk's stories so quickly, I chastised myself.

I scanned the bank only a few yards away now. Nothing moved. Had the marksman waited to see the results of his shot, I wondered? Was he still lurking nearby? Or had he hurried away immediately, taking no chances of anyone seeing him, certain of what would happen? My lips tightening, I returned my hands to the water and pushed the remaining distance to the bank. The overturned craft bumped against the soil and I saw the quick movement of a snake as it sprang from the bank into the water, an arrow uncoiled, disappearing instantly. Grasping one of the low bushes along the bank, I pulled the boat around, swung a leg over onto the soil and crawled ashore. The pirogue slowly moved along the bank, bumping its way downstream. I sat for a moment, drawing deep breaths, drinking in being alive. I wasn't afraid now of another shot. I rose, feeling soggy, sloshing as I walked, and made my way alongside the bayou until the gray hulk of the house finally came into sight. I left the edge of the water, then, crossed to where the French doors to my room waited invitingly. Stepping inside, I pulled them closed, and latched them.

I climbed out of my wet clothes, showered, washing off the warm water of the bayou and, then, fell across the bed and let relief flood over me.

I lay still and, for the first time since the solitary shot had exploded the still of the bayou, I had a chance to reconstruct what had happened. The marksman hadn't missed. I was certain of that. I hadn't been his target. That would have caused problems when I'd been found, questions, investigations. It had been more cleverly planned than that. The night creatures of the bayou were to administer the actual *coup de grâce,* a term quite appropriate here in Cajun country, I reflected. There would be no investigation that way, no sticky questions to answer. There'd be only solemn acknowledgement that a foolish young woman had gone out alone on the unfamiliar bayou. She had struck something sharp, put a hole in the pirogue and then gone thrashing about in the water. Disturbed and curious, the 'gators and water moccasins had done the rest, simply reacting as was their natural manner, with monstrous jaws and teeth that ripped apart bodies, or the sharp, swift fangs of the *congo*. A tragic accident, I murmured grimly.

Who had the night-shrouded marksman been? One name sprang up at once, of course. Major Robert Jeffries was partial to murder by accident. He apparently took great care to prepare the right kind of accidents. Mine hardly required that kind of careful preparation. In fact, I grimaced, I'd set myself up for it. He had only to see me go out in the pirogue and take advantage of what I'd given him, a marvelous opportunity, better than any he could plan himself. But why, I questioned in the darkness. Because he feared I might somehow find a way to those records and put together his scheme? Was that what he didn't want to chance? Or had it been the events of the afternoon? Had he thought that Amanda was ready to ride the stallion, that she'd been taught enough for him to take it from here? Did he fear my interferences if I stayed around? Did he fear I'd keep Amanda from riding Saladin? Was my role here at an end, of no further use to him, now? Was I not only dispensable but potentially dangerous now?

I let the thoughts revolve, and then one more leaped onto the carousel in my mind. Was it really because of my work with Amanda? Or was he afraid I'd come too close to something still hidden? I thought of his deposition to the sheriff wherein he had said he'd reached his wife, first, that Amanda had only come along later. Amanda had seen it happen, though. I was certain of that, now. Seen her mother kill herself, I murmured silently. But he had told the police differently. I still wondered why.

I reined in on the circling horses of the carousel. They were running away with me and I couldn't afford that. I had been thinking only about Major Jeffries; I couldn't afford the luxury of being wrong, either. What if the marksman had been someone else? The deep, brooding eyes of Sami swam in front of me at once. He blamed me for making the Major's wishes possible. I was in the center of his circle of hate, very much in the center. I saw the savagery of his face when I exchanged words with him earlier in the day, the absolute venom in his eyes. Had he steamed, simmered like a kettle since then, seen me go out in the pirogue and decided to act? Was Sami the one who'd leaped at the opportunity? In one stroke, he'd have been rid of me here and disrupted the Major's plans, he would have thought. It was all too possible, I decided. Sami couldn't be ruled out at all. He was perhaps not a harmless voyeur at all.

But whoever the marksman had been, the attempt had failed and I still wondered if that much was known. I felt exhaustion starting to dull my thoughts and I settled on one promise to myself. I'd make no pretense of what I thought in the morning and I'd confront the Major with it. I'd watch his every expression, scan his tiniest reaction. I sighed, had enough strength left to wince at my own naivete. I would be like watching a stone for a sign. But I had to try.

Before I dropped off to sleep, pulling a sheet over my nakedness, I thought about Amanda. I hadn't the strength left to go in to her, to try to work with her tonight. It'd have to wait for tomorrow. My eyes closed and I slept in seconds.

CHAPTER SEVEN

The morning was gray, with heavy air. Tonight was the *fais do-do* and I didn't feel at all like merry-making. Yet I did want to talk more to Clay. I'd phone him later, I decided, as I went down to the kitchen. The trays were ready with jam and biscuits, but the coffee was still brewing; I stepped outside and scanned the sky. It was unrelievedly gray. Sami came down the path alongside the corrals. He stopped as he saw me in the doorway, stared at me for a long second, then walked on. Surprise, I wondered, or was he still stinging from the barbs I'd flung at him yesterday? I heard footsteps from behind me inside the house; the Major was disappearing into the study. Anger stormed up inside me at once and I followed him into the room. He turned to look at me with surprise. I took a deep breath.

"Someone tried to kill me last night," I said, with studied casualness; his eyes barely flickered. "And very cleverly, too," I added.

"What are you talking about, Miss Forester?" he asked icily.

"I went out in the pirogue by myself," I began, and, recounted all that had happened and wondered if I were talking to someone who knew precisely all about what I was saying. When I finished, he stared at me coldly, his eyes twin lumps of blue ice.

"No one tried to kill you, Miss Forester," he bit out after a moment."

"I'm not making this up," I snapped.

"Perhaps not, but you're being paranoid," he said. "I'll tell you what happened. The pirogue was hit by a stray shot."

"A stray shot? From whom?" I frowned.

"The bayous wind back and forth, paralleling each other. Sometimes, trappers steal out to bag a 'gator, a blue goose or even a heron at night, illegally. Someone shot, missed and the bullet went into the pirogue. A high-powered rifle can carry a tremendous distance."

"No. The sound was too close," I said.

"Sound can fool you on the bayous. It only sounded close," he said calmly.

"Just one shot?" I demanded skeptically. "One shot that just happened to hit my pirogue?"

He shrugged. "He'd no doubt been out hunting some while. It was probably his last shot," the man said. I sniffed disdainfully, unwilling to accept the reasonableness of the explanation. "Why should anyone want to kill you, Miss Forester?" Major Jeffries asked quietly.

"I don't know. I thought maybe you'd have some ideas," I snapped. His expression still didn't flicker.

"Sorry," he said "It was just one of those things. It's happened before, a stray shot in the night. You were lucky it hit the boat."

He turned, walked behind the desk and sat down, began opening letters. I'd been dismissed as an over-imaginative child and I strode from the room. I wanted to reject his explanation out of hand but found myself unable to do so. I swore at my father for having raised me to be both fair-minded and rational at all times. The explanation was not without rationality, was even quite plausible. Was he right, I wondered? Was I being paranoid? I refused that angrily. The shot had been close, I told myself. It was no nearly spent bullet that had shattered the hole in the pirogue. And yet, I couldn't be certain. Swearing under my breath, I stepped into the kitchen to find Marie there now, the coffee on the trays. I made myself sound casual, suddenly seeing an opportunity for information.

"I'm sorry about some of the things I said yesterday to Sami," I apologized. "I shouldn't have said them."

The woman's eyes were tired. "Hurting and being wrong aren't the same," she said softly. "You were right."

I chose my words carefully. "Did he say anything more last night about it? Later in the evening, I mean?" I asked.

"Didn't see him afterwards," the woman said. "He went off by himself like he always does."

I kept my face stiff, took the trays and hurried away, the answer I'd wanted tucked inside me. I'd try to find out where Major Jeffries had been last night, I vowed silently. I opened the door to Amanda' s room; she hadn't dressed and she looked up at me. In surprise, I saw angry resentment in her eyes. I ignored it, put the tray down beside her.

"It might rain," I said. "Let's hurry and get some time in before it does." She shook her head vigorously back and forth.

"What does that mean?" I asked. Her eyes glared up at me and she shook her head again. "'You don't want to have a lesson?" I tried. She nodded, and looked at me with pointed anger too obvious to ignore. 'Are you angry at me, Amanda?" I asked.

She sat unmoving, looking down, her stillness my answer. "Why?" I asked. "What is it?" She made no move and continued to stare down at the floor and then, suddenly, taken aback, I had a thought. "Are you angry because I didn't come in to see you last night?" I queried. She continued to stare away sullenly and I suddenly realized that her anger was an excitingly wonderful sign. She wanted me to work with her, to help her reach back into yesterday, to help her unblock. Despite her pain and anguish and refusals, she wanted that, her anger now was proof of it. I put my hands on her shoulders.

"I'm sorry about last night. I was too tired. I want to remember with you. It won't happen again, I promise." She lifted her head, looked up at me and I saw her eyes searching mine, seeking her own assurances. I thought I saw them soften ever so slightly.

"Eat your breakfast," I said gently. "I'll come back later. Maybe we can have a lesson then." I watched her take the tray and I finished my coffee and left, secretly excited, Amanda suddenly a source of renewed hope. Leaving the tray in the kitchen, I stepped outside and walked down past the corrals, past the bull who stood with his little eyes glaring out of his box stall. I spied Paul Agee with Major Jeffries by the barn. The big man towered over Paul, stood very close to him in earnest conversation and I saw Paul nod, his face stiff. I turned away, strolled to the exercise ring and watched three of the local hands riding the saddlers. I watched as long as I could, and finally turned away, unable to stand anymore of their heavy-handed horsemanship. Walking back to the barns again, I saw Paul was alone, now, watching a flock of calves being let out. I came up beside him and his eyes flicked at me, hard and cold. I felt surprise.

"You've something to ask me," Paul said crisply.

"There was something. You know about it already?" I questioned and his eyes met mine.

"The Major figured you'd come around asking," the small man answered. "He was with me last night, going over the month's books."

"Is that what he told you to tell me?" I returned brusquely. Paul Agee's face remained hard.

"That's the way it was," he replied stiffly. I turned my back on him and strode away, disappointment churning along with anger inside me, Clay's story about Paul very much with me. The man was in the pay and in the hands of Major Jeffries. Perhaps more deeply than anyone realized, I muttered silently. Was he telling the truth? Or had he been ordered to give that story to me and to anyone who asked? Thoughts leap-frogged over each other. What if Major Jeffries' rational explanation were really correct? My lips drew back in a gesture of distaste. All I really knew was that I could accept nothing and reject nothing. Not now, not yet. I'd started into the house when I saw Victor at the car shed and I headed toward him. He straightened up from the open hood of the little Fiat as I neared, put a wrench on the fender of the car and reached out to grasp my hand. He saw the trouble in my face at once.

"What's up?" he asked. I hesitated. Victor had offered words of caution already.

"What would you say if I told you someone tried to kill me last night and make it appear an accident?" I blurted out. He stared at me and I could see his thoughts revolving.

"Go on," he said, and I told him what had happened.

"Your father doesn't agree with me," I said as I finished and recounted the Major's explanation. Victor sighed, almost wearily, when I ended the explanation.

"In this case, I think he's probably right," Victor remarked. "Why would anyone want to kill you?" he questioned. *Your father might well want to*, I answered silently, wanted to voice the words, but I held them back. I was unwilling to tell Victor his father was scheming to arrange a murder and, moreover, I realized, all the certainties I'd put together were not evidence. Knowing was not proving, not to Victor, not to the police, not to me.

"I don't know," I answered lamely, holding out the uncertainty for him to see. But inside, I was all too sure of Major Jeffries' plans for Amanda, those motives that seemed crystal clear once I'd read that will. I glanced at Victor, met his eyes and the question fell from my lips of itself, bursting free.

"Why don't you and your father talk at all, Victor?" I asked.

"We're having a feud. It's too long a story for now," he said and his smile was slow, almost dreamy. "I guess we're just both stubborn," he added. He put his arms around me, pulled me close and I felt the warm sensuousness of him against my breasts. His face had grown serious. "Get out of here," he said. "Leave, just get away. I'll help you."

"I thought you said your father's explanation might be right," I questioned.

"Yes, I'd say it probably is right but I'm thinking about other things. The strain is beginning to show on you. You've let yourself become too involved with Amanda. It's no good for you," he said.

"Maybe not, but I can't leave now, not till after the show. That's only a few days away. I want to see Amanda through that day safely, at least," I replied.

"And then?"

"We'll see," I said. I hadn't thought about that yet and didn't intend to try now. He leaned forward, his lips finding mine, sweet and hard, soft and strong and I was suddenly wishing it were another place and another time. He pulled back, finally, his eyes grave.

"Take care, and call me whenever you need me," he said. I nodded and walked back to the house, grateful for one ally in a place of twisted allegiances and strange obsessions. The day continued to remain gray, without rain, and I went inside to phone Clay.

"Hi, Clay. I'm glad I got you in," I began. "Would you be angry if we didn't go to the *fais do-do,* tonight? I don't feel much like dancing, but I would like to sit quietly and talk to you."

"That's sweetening the bitter pill," he answered, and I laughed. "Sure, I'm not much of a dance partner, anyway. I'll pick you up."

"Thanks. I'll be ready," I said gratefully, put the phone down and went to the window, peered at the sky again. The rain still stayed in the clouds, and I went to Amanda. She was dressed, sitting near the window. "There's time for a lesson," I said. "You must work more if you want to ride Saladin again."

Her eyes blinked slowly and she rose like a recalcitrant child, suddenly obedient, went with me and I saddled a horse for myself as well as the gelding. I rode with her, gave her lessons from horseback and we worked till dusk. The lesson had gone exceedingly well, and, returning with her to her room, I realized that the session had, in an oblique way, reinforced my fears.

Amanda's moods were still totally unpredictable and that held the seeds of her danger on the stallion. One mistake, one wrong move, and that special bond could shatter in tragedy.

In her room, I faced her, put my hands on her shoulders. "I must go out for a while tonight, but I'll be back and I'll come in to see you then, I promise," I said. She stared at me, then nodded slowly, and I hurried to my room and pulled off clothes that were sticking to me, heavy with perspiration. I showered and rested across the bed in my bra and panties, letting my mind go over all that had happened once again. When I called a halt to sorting and resorting, I was left with two conclusions. I was no longer certain that last night's shot had been an attempt on my life. I was certain, however, of the Major's plans for Amanda. I had automatically connected the two, yet I had to admit they weren't necessarily part of the same web. I had to be more careful, I chastised myself. I couldn't afford errors, wasting worry and energy in the wrong direction.

I rested a while longer, then rose and dressed. I was still feeling edgy, unable to shake the night before, as Clay arrived. As we drove away, I saw that Victor's little Fiat was not in the car shed. "I suspect you were right about Victor playing at the dance, tonight," I remarked.

"Yes, he usually fills in at them," Clay said. "I'd forgotten about mentioning that. You remember everything said to you?"

"Some things," I replied. "Certain words especially. Acquisitiveness is one of them."

"Ouch," Clay winced. I didn't feel like letting him off the hook.

"It's an unusual word. You meant something by it. A kind of warning, wasn't it?" I said.

"Warning is too strong a word," he smiled. "Jealousy is better."

"My ego would like to believe that. My intelligence refuses," I answered.

"Always listen to your ego," he said and his smile was bland, too bland.

"What were you trying to tell me?" I pressed. "Not that Victor Jeffries attracts and conquers easily, not something that obvious."

Clay's smile took on a faint edge. "That is obvious, isn't it," he said.

"So what were you trying to say?" I insisted.

"Just that Victor Jeffries has been involved in a few nasty scenes with young ladies," Clay Thedeaux said. "Things didn't go right with the relationships and he became more than unpleasant, it seems. He has a nasty temper, I've heard. That magnetic quality has another side, or maybe it's all of a part."

"Meaning?"

"Highly charged, compelling people are very often highly charged in all areas of their existence," Clay said with clinical abstraction.

"Thanks for being concerned," I said, feeling slightly ashamed at my annoyance at him for the remark, annoyance that was more at being understood than at anything else. Clay pulled into a small, unprepossessing little roadhouse that turned out to have a lovely back terrace overlooking the bayous. He ordered drinks, a mint julep for himself and I had a Tom Collins. I had a sudden, overwhelming desire to tell Clay what I had learned in the county records. His quiet steadiness reached out with the lure of security, but I decided it wasn't time, not until I had a few more things to add to what I'd concluded. I could safely go into the rest, though, and was suddenly terribly interested in his reaction.

"I had an unnerving experience last night," I began, quickly recounting all that had happened. I finished with what Major Jeffries had said to explain it away. Clay listened without interruption.

"You don't believe the Major's interpretation," he remarked.

"I don't know. I'm not sure," I said.

"Why would anyone want to see you killed?" Clay queried.

"I've been working hard with Amanda. The Major was furious at me for that. I've been making headway with her, maybe too much so," I replied. Clay's lips pursed.

"You're making dark and dire hints, Gail," he said. "Are you saying Major Jeffries could want to see you killed?"

I had to back away or reveal more than I was ready to, yet. "I'm saying that Darkwater is a place of hatreds and secrecies and that anything is possible. Take Sami. He's full of loathing for the Major. What keeps him there? Why does he hate so?"

"I've heard a lot of stories. In time, fact separates itself from fiction," Clay said.

"Such as?"

"Sami's deformity was due to an injury at childbirth. It seems Marie Opatu waited for the Major to take her to Passerelle for the baby to be born. My father had a clinic there, then. But the Major didn't come to take her for hours and hours. When he did, the birth was imminent. Rushing her to Passerelle, the car skidded into a tree just as she was giving birth."

"And the child was injured as a result," I finished. "Sami learned of it as he grew up and blames the Major for the way he is."

"That's the story as I've sifted it down," Clay nodded. I fitted pieces silently. The story made them come together, Sami's hatred a primal force, the Major keeping him there out of guilt and out of debt to his mother.

"But Marie, she doesn't hate the Major," I queried.

"I've heard that Marie Opatu was always more than a housekeeper to Major Jeffries," Clay commented. The answer made still more pieces fit, words I'd heard flung back and forth suddenly taking on meaning beyond anger; *Why don't you leave here? Why don't you?* One stayed to be a living reminder of guilt and blame, the other because she could do nothing else and be true to herself. It fitted, I grimaced inwardly, it fitted.

"Has your father told you about these things?" I asked Clay.

"My father keeps his own privacies," Clay said. "I was only a young boy when these things happened and then I was sent away to boarding school and later to college. I only spent summers here until I returned to practice."

I decided it was time to get away from the subject of Darkwater Farms. "Do you intend to stay on here to practice?" I asked. He surprised me with his answer.

"No," he said. "I want to do more work with finely-bred animals. I think their inbreeding opens them to a set of problems much closer to those of man. I'd like someday to develop a line of parallel causes, symptoms and cures."

"And out here?"

"It's pretty much routine cattle treatment. Except for the Major's stock, equine treatment is mostly with working horses and just as routine."

"What do you get mostly?"

"In the horses? Thrush. It seems to be endemic here. I suspect it has something to do with the dampness in so much of the ground here. I get a lot of mud fever, too."

He went on to tell me more of his work, his daily routines and I listened, eager to plunge into a world that was my love and in which I felt most at home. It also pushed aside all other things, for a little while, at least. When I glanced at my watch, later, I was surprised at how long I'd escaped into Clay's world. Amanda flew into my thoughts at once. I didn't want her tightening up, thinking I was breaking my promise to her again. "I have to get back," I said. "But it was fun, just what I needed tonight."

"Then we can do it again, I hope," Clay said and I nodded willingly. Clay Thedeaux had none of Victor's throbbing excitement but a quiet, comforting charm was part of him. We drove back through the warm night, and had just reached the house when, pulling to a halt, he turned to appraise me.

"You've hurried back to see Amanda," he said and my hesitation gave the lie then to anything I could say. I stayed silent.

"Even though Major Jeffries is furious at you for that," Clay echoed. I pressed my lips tight, shrugged. "Have you gone too far with her to stop?" he asked.

"Yes," I said. "There are things I'm not ready to talk about yet. I've got to help her unblock all the way."

His eyes were serious. "You're hanging everything on an assumption," he said. I frowned. "The assumption that unblocking will solve her problems," he went on. "It might not. Blocking is, after all, one way of coping with something too painful to face. Take that away and there's no telling what you might have."

I thought about the Major's story of Pandora's box, different words presented in different ways but the point very much the same. It came to the same with me, anyway, the Major's attempts to frighten me and Clay's cautious, conservative approach. I had to go on. There was no other way, certainly not for Amanda, and perhaps not for me. I pressed Clay's hand, opened the door and stepped from the car.

"Thanks for caring," I said. "I'll be in touch." Unsmiling, he watched me as I went into the house. I heard him turn the car and then the sound of tires moving back along the dirt road. I went to my room, and closed the door, unwilling to trust the darkness of the house. Too many eyes could wait and watch in its inky refuge. Once in my room, I went outside through the French doors and around to the window of Amanda's room, raising it softly, and climbing over the low sill into the room. She was seated on the bed in a short nightgown and the moon, strong and clear again, gave enough light inside the room. I sat down beside her and began to coax her into responses. I expected resistance. It had to be there, a part of moving forward. I brought her back to where we'd been the last time, then urged her forward, refusing to accept her denials or her attempts at avoidance. Finally, I stabbed hard.

"You know you saw it happen. You admitted it inside your-self last time. Now bring it out, say it out loud. You were there. You saw it happen right before your eyes," I demanded.

The word came out as a torn half-whisper. "Yes," she breathed, and then, repeating the solitary word, *"Yes."* She began to shake, to tremble violently then and I held her until she grew calmer. She leaned away from me, fell back onto the bed and lay on her side, looking up at me. I felt like a mountain climber who has reached a plateau, drained but satisfied. It had been a break-through, her recognition given voice. The next step was to help her say what she had seen, that further step in the march to face reality. But not now. There'd been enough for tonight. I patted her head and she lay on her side, her eyes starting to close in exhaustion, her step forward so small yet so tremendous. I used the window to leave her, lowering it after me. Outside, I felt too excited for sleep. I walked along the house, crossed the front to the other side and down past the stables. I saw the corral, empty, moonlight giv-ing it a faint glow of silver-blue light. I ducked under the fence, walked to the center of it and stared up at the near-full moon. I thought of how few days I had left before the show. Time enough, I grimaced? A wave of discouragement swept over me, anger fol-lowing in its tracks. I wanted to hold time back and knew only helplessness. The moon looked down with serenity and the night was soft and still. Nature was mocking the churning moods of mere man. It was a night for love, not for thinking of ways to prevent murder by accident. I drew a deep breath, and tried to let the quiet of the night release the restlessness inside me, let my eyes draw a lazy circle around the misty edges of the moon.

It was not the sound that made me suddenly stop breath-ing, a tiny, creaking noise I hardly even heard, but the presence that swept over me. I saw nothing yet the presence, the force was overpowering. I could think only of Clay's words about how little we knew of and understood the mysteries of communication, because the presence of danger filled the night, surrounded me with its power. I felt raw, brute force and yet I'd seen nothing, heard nothing to make this a conscious awareness. Not moving, I turned my head enough to look behind me. The huge form stood silently at the far end of the corral and, as I watched, moved slowly, head down, sniffing the ground.

Words of realization sifted through my mind as though they were abstract statements. The bull was in the corral with me. The tiny creaking noise had been the gate as he came out of the attached pen. He had been let out into the corral. He had been let out on purpose. The staccato truths tumbled after each other and I felt the trickle of perspiration coursing down between my breasts. The brute hatred of the bull permeated the night now, and, still rooted in place, I watched the black bulk of him move in a half-circle round the edge of the corral. He halted, lifted his head, pawed the ground with one foot. He sensed too. He had merely not focused in on me, yet, but he knew someone was there. I could almost feel his senses gathering themselves and I thanked God that bulls were not keen of nose. I watched as he stopped pawing, paced a few steps, then swung his head toward the corral fence.

I took a step backward, froze at once as his head swung around, lowered. I could feel the hate-filled little eyes peering across the darkness and prayed for a cloud to cover the moon. No cloud came and I stayed motionless. The bull moved toward me now, slowly, directly, and I heard him grunt. He became more than a huge, black bulk in the night as he neared, his horns standing out now, twin curved spears. He kept moving forward and suddenly I saw him break into a cautious trot. He had focused on the object in the corral but he wasn't certain what it was yet. I shot a wild glance around the corral. I was almost in dead-center; I grimaced at the phrase. I had no chance in a straight run. I'd never reach the fences alive. I looked at the bull. He had halted, directly in front of me, a dozen yards away. His little eyes were evaluating the object in front of him, a message trickling to his brain. Suddenly the connection exploded inside him.

I saw him lower his head, heard the bellow and watched as he gathered himself. I forced myself to stand unmoving and then he charged and I could feel the ground tremble. Fighting down panic, I waited in place for a few seconds longer, stared at the tremendous animal barrelling at me and then I leaped, sideways, a diving leap. I felt the rush of air as he thundered past me and then I hit the ground, rolled and came up on my feet. He had skidded to a halt, was turning and I was glad for the half-light of the moon. It took him a moment longer than usual to find me. I backed, glanced behind me at the corral rails. Too far yet, I saw, much too far, and I had to force myself not to turn and flee in headlong panic. The ground trembled again as he roared at me and once more I held my position till the last moment, then dove away. But this time I felt his horn tear through the back of my shirt as he hooked to the left with his head. I rolled across the ground, came up again to see that he had halted his charge in a shorter distance and was coming around again, a roaring bellow filling the night.

The rails were still too far away, but I was no bullfighter. I'd been lucky twice. I could be lucky a few times but no more. My legs were already trembling and nerves would make me mis-calculate. Once would be enough, I knew. I turned and ran this time, looked back at the immense head thundering up behind me. I cut to the left and then to the right and dove again through the air. He had followed my first cut, hooking savagely with his horn and once again he pushed hooves into the ground and halted, spun around, came at me this time just as I was getting up. I flung myself to the left again and felt my leg kicked sideways as his foreleg collided with it. The pain wasn't what snapped in my mind. I saw only that my margin of life was growing smaller with each pass. It was a contest I could only lose. I rose, glanced desperately at the rails. They were closer, yet not close enough. I wondered if I oughtn't simply to run for them. He would have me in a few moments, anyway.

I'd half-started to turn to run when I heard a sound, hooves, unmistakably, but not the thunderous stamp of the bull. I turned and saw the shining black horse running around the corral.

The bull ceased his occupation with me, swinging around now as this new object diverted his attention. Saladin was trotting in a circle and the bull turning slowly to watch him, starting to gather himself again. I called out to the horse. "Saladin," I screamed, and I broke into a run. The stallion halted, ears up at once, snorted. He began a slow trot, not directly at me but crossing my path. I streaked toward him, heard the roaring bellow behind me. The bull had focused himself again and was charging. The stallion passed close and I leaped, caught hold of his mane, pulled myself up, and vaulted atop him. He halted, half-reared, and I brought a hand down hard on his rump and kicked with my heels. He leaped forward and I saw the bull brush past only inches behind, head down, the huge horns sweeping out to rip and tear.

The stallion would, in some ways, be an easier target for the bull, I knew. I kicked hard again, yelled and Saladin leaped forward. I brought him into a full gallop as the bull came after us. This time I held a straight line, and my lips pulled back as I realized how high the corral rails actually were. I went up with him, cried out as he cleared with his forelegs, felt his hindlegs hit against the top rail, but he was over and I clung to his smooth back as he landed, almost went off but managed to stay. I heard the tremendous, shuddering crash behind me as the bull, in fury, smashed into the fence rails. Using his mane, I wheeled the stallion around, and looked back at the glowering bulk of the bull as he stood with head lowered, pawing the ground. I felt my breath escape in a long gasping sound and I walked the horse along the path between the exercise rings to the stable. Keeping one hand on his mane, I walked him into the open door of the stable before I dismounted and led him into the box stall. Shutting the half-gate, I leaned against it for a long moment, and fought off the desire simply to collapse onto the floor. My legs quivered, the reaction not wholly one of muscle and flesh.

I refused to do anything now but return to my room, closing my mind off until I had made my way back to the French windows and shut them behind me. I undressed slowly, almost as if in a dream, sank down across the bed and let the air blow over my body, still soaked with perspiration. Facts insisted on being heard, silent voices that spoke more loudly than any scream. I was alive but I wasn't supposed to be. Once more, an accident had been arranged for me. I would have been found in the morning, gored and stomped to death. The reconstruction would have been simple. I'd gone out to the bull, either let him out of the pen with a foolish notion that I could handle him, or he'd managed to get out himself. After all, I wouldn't have been the first one he'd attacked. A tragically stupid mistake on my part, everyone would conclude. Except one person.

The bull had been released, an opportunity once again seen and acted on. Last night's incident had been no stray shot from a distant trapper, I murmured silently. Any doubts I had entertained were wiped away now. Someone was trying to kill me, and make it appear an accident. Once again, as last night, I thought about Major Robert Jeffries and his plans for Amanda, that certain accident being engineered. All one mind at work? I questioned. Yet something else bothered me now, and I thought of the photo that had been slipped under Amanda's door to shatter her. Perhaps I'd served my purpose in the Major's eyes now, but I hadn't then. Someone wanted Amanda beyond my reaching her, someone who'd decided to see that I reached no one any longer. Who? The question leaped up, mocking reason. The Major, suddenly afraid? Sami, hating, pushing his hate to new lengths? Or both, working at cross-purposes that happened to focus on me? The thought was frighteningly possible.

I paused, forcing myself to go on. Was I limiting my palette of killers to too few? Was Paul Agee's loyalty more than loyalty, I wondered? Did he have reasons and motives I could not suspect, even entertain? Was that why he'd told me not to want to know too much? It seemed unlikely, yet I couldn't afford to exclude anyone here, now. Twice, I'd been marked for death, pushed close to its cold hands. There was evil here, a deep, dark evil that waited to erupt in death. But there was one thing more, a silent friend.

Someone had sent the stallion into the corral. Someone had come on the scene, realized there was but one chance for me to get out of the corral alive. That someone had acted and then melted away, unwilling to step forward. Fear, of course, I concluded. Fear of the Major? Of his wrath? My thoughts continued to pursue little side paths, chasing down every possibility. Perhaps it wasn't fear at all but something else; conscience? I pondered. The conjecture hung before me and I let it build itself, following it along as it unfolded. Sami had let the killer bull out of the pen, it went. He had seen his opportunity, taken it and then disappeared, certain of the results. But Marie Opatu, on one of her night walks behind the corrals, had come on the scene. She knew who had done it at once and, driven by conscience, had to act. She'd let Saladin out into the corral and then, when she saw my escape, hurried away. She could do no less. To come forward would have said too much.

The speculation closed itself down, one more possibility among so many others. Paul could have come onto the scene, let Saladin out and disappeared, unwilling to face the Major's fury. The speculations were too endless and I closed my eyes. I would build only on facts and the answers would come in time. I'd been marked for death. I had to walk with caution, move with care. The thought held me, the wisdom of it suddenly more appealing. But not alone, I told myself. I'd flee with Amanda. She was too close to returning to a sane, normal tomorrow to be left here. I closed off my spiraling thoughts, and let exhaustion overcome me.

CHAPTER EIGHT

The show was only two days away. That was the fact I woke with, pushing at me with alarm. As I showered, I thought of the feasibility of fleeing with Amanda now, and set it aside for further exploration. It was short-lived; when I went down to get breakfast, the Major was in the kitchen. "Amanda's taking breakfast with us in the living room," he said. "Marie's gone to fetch her."

I made no answer. It was obvious that the man intended to watch her, and me, with increased surveillance. To flee now, before the meet, might well be impossible. I'd hang in until the show was over. He would have made his gesture, then, paraded her for all to see. He would relax some after that, the first giant step in his scheme a *fait accompli.* I'd been the key in making it come about. I'd do everything I could to see that the rest of his plans failed.

Amanda came down to the room with Marie, her eyes meeting mine in silent greeting and as soon as breakfast was finished we were in the corral. I'd saddled up another horse, one more difficult, edgy with a touch of stall courage. She did well and I noticed the Major paused at the corral with unaccustomed frequency, watching. I kept her at it all day and only her obvious exhaustion prevented him from having her take dinner with us. I washed and changed in my room, rested a half-hour at the close of the day and finally went down to dinner. Major Jeffries was there, serving wine with the impervious formality he could assume. I was happy for the way the day had gone but the night when I had faced death at the ends of those sharp horns was still very much with me. I'd forced myself not to glare at everyone with open suspicion and now I wondered if I were going through a macabre charade, sipping wine with the man who had twice tried to kill me.

"The show grounds are only two miles east of here. You'll ride there with Amanda," Major Jeffries said. "It'll be a good warm-up for her."

"Will you be riding along?" I asked pointedly.

"No, I'll be at the meet to see some people earlier. Paul will go along with you," he said. The answer was equally pointed, I realized, no chances taken. When dinner ended, I went outside just in time to see Victor come around a corner of the house, heading for the car shed. He came over to me.

"Want to go for a drive for an hour or so," he asked. "It's a nice night."

The idea appealed at once. I had to wait till later to go to Amanda, anyway, and getting away from the oppressiveness, the presence of danger, was more than a welcome idea. I went with him to the car shed, and swung into the low seat of the little Fiat. "I've been having engine problems and I wanted to test her out again," Victor said as he swung the car down the road. He found tiny back roads I'd never even seen, some hardly more than cow-paths and, not unlike the bayous, little trails of otherworldliness. I let my head rest on the back of the seat but I couldn't really relax. A silent, invisible spectre rode with me. I wanted to tell Victor everything, to tell him there was no doubt about someone trying to kill me and that his father was at the top of the list. Yet I held back. There seemed little love between them and yet the Major was his father. I couldn't call him a murderer, not yet. If I were right, Victor would learn the truth himself in time. He'd have to face that bitter knowledge in his own way then. It would be a terrible enough cross to bear. I wouldn't hurry it. I felt only a tremendous surge of sympathy for the handsome, magnetic man beside me, so full of his own turbulence. When Victor stopped the car on top of a tiny rise in a narrow path where the moon touched the bushes with silver, I turned to meet his lips as they pressed down on mine.

It was but one more way of shutting out everything else, a wonderful refuge for at least a little while. Victor's pure animal magnetism and my own inner tensions exploded together, and I gasped with pleasure at his touch, answering his every hungering caress with my own. But even now, plunged into ecstacy, I suddenly recoiled, wanting and yet not wanting. Shuddering with desire and pleasure, I finally pulled away, aware only that I was swept by a strange kind of disloyalty, with Victor as its central point. I felt that I oughn't to be here, making love to him while I saw his father as a scheming, ruthless man bent on arranging murders. It simply wasn't right. I was never one for conventional moralizing but this was different, a matter of personal integrity. I forced myself back as his hands cupped my breasts.

"No, no more now," I breathed. "There's something I've got to know first." I saw his dark eyes frowning at me and I turned to pull him against me. "It's not you, good God, no," I said. "Just go along with me, please, until I can tell you more."

His eyes continued to hold a dark anger in their depths. "I don't like Amanda coming between us," he said.

"It's not Amanda, not directly," I returned.

"Helping her is a dead-end street, anyway," he said. "You'll find out."

"No, you haven't seen the things I have with her," I answered. He shrugged, turned, switched the ignition on and rolled the car down from the rise. I sat silently beside him as he headed back to Darkwater Farms, unable to explain more and all too aware of his resentment. We were nearing the house, perhaps a mile further to go, when the engine coughed, died away and the car rolled to a stop.

"Dammit," Victor swore as he swung from the car. He opened the hood, bent over the engine, then had me sit behind the wheel and turn the ignition on at his commands. The car half-started then failed. He took a big wrench from the dashboard compartment, bent low over the open hood and I could hear him cursing. He yelled at me to try the ignition again. I did and the engine only sputtered and died away. "Goddamn car," I heard Victor explode. "Once more," he yelled savagely at me. I obeyed with the same results and, almost in disbelief, I saw him straighten, lift his arm and bring the wrench down on the engine with a tremendous blow. He struck again and again in a wild fury as I stared at the sight and heard the sounds of metal breaking, wires tearing; he pounded away with the wrench, knocking off gaskets, connections, anything that would break. All the turbulence inside him seemed to be erupting, spewing out as he raged and I remembered Clay's words about his temper. Finally, abruptly, he halted, threw the wrench into the engine.

"We walk," he said curtly to me and I climbed from the car, fell in step beside him as he headed down the road. I looked up at the sensuous handsomeness of his face.

"Why, Victor?" I asked gently. His glance at me was fiercely sharp and then, suddenly, his smile flashed, captivating, full of boyish warmth, totally at odds with what I'd just seen.

"It's good to explode once in a while," he grinned at me. "It cleans inside and outside." He smiled again at me. "Besides, I hate being crossed, even by inanimate objects," he said and now his eyes were twinkling. I could only marvel at the abruptness of the change. He did, indeed, seemed cleansed of tension. The walk wasn't long or hard and when we reached the house, he faced me, boyish sheepishness in his eyes. "I'll make the walk up to you," he said. Turning, he left at once, saying not another word and, I felt, ashamed of the childishness of his behavior with the car. I went to my room, lay down, a feeling of disappointment hanging over me like a pall. The evening hadn't gone right, not even those moments pressed hard against Victor's exciting warmth. My fault, I knew. I was too tense, too on edge, and Victor, with that pure sensitivity that was his, had picked it up at once, become part of it in his own way. I lay quietly, letting time tick away until at last I went to Amanda, taking the path through the window once again.

She was waiting, sitting cross-legged on the bed in her nightgown and I sank down beside her. The break-through of last evening hadn't backfired, I was relieved to see; her eyes met mine in a quiet understanding that was welcome. The session began well until suddenly the blocking rose up, stone-wall-like. She refused to go beyond a certain point.

"You saw it happen, Amanda," I prodded.

"Yes," she said.

"Say it again," I insisted.

"I saw it happen," she said, the sentence clear, the words spoken without being torn out of her.

"What did you see happen?" I pressed, and she refused to respond. "You must say it out loud, Amanda. You must break through another block."

She shook her head and stayed mute. There was no time for slow, painstaking therapy left. "You saw your mother commit suicide," I threw out brutally. "Say it out loud. Put it in words. Bring it out of yourself."

"No." The word came out gasped. "No."

"You saw your mother kill herself," I returned, bearing down hard and watched her flinch at the words. "Face it, say it, Amanda. Admit it out loud."

She shook her head vigorously, refused to answer in words and I saw her shoulders tremble. I retreated. Perhaps I demanded too much too soon. Last night she had given voice to having seen the act. Perhaps that was all I could expect now. I stood up, put a hand on her blond hair.

"I understand," I said gently. She looked up at me and I saw anger flash in her eyes.

"No," she bit out tightly and I frowned in surprise.

"I don't understand?" I asked and she nodded agreement quickly. "Then tell me, make me understand," I said. She turned away, stretched herself out on the bed and I knew it signified she would say nothing further. "Tomorrow, then," I said, patted her shoulder and turned to the window. Before clambering out, I searched the darkness with my eyes. Fear usually speaks quickly. I saw no movement, no shadows not usually there, and I swung from the room and hurried to my own, closed and latched the French doors. I went to bed and slept quickly, my body exercising its own wisdom.

The next morning, I had Amanda in the exercise ring early, wanting more room than the small end corral afforded. I watched Major Jeffries appear with Clay's father, stand back and watch, then detach himself from the doctor and move closer. "You're not putting her on Saladin before the show?" he questioned.

"No," I snapped.

"She should be on him. She's ridden him already," he countered. I fastened the man with an angry glance.

"I don't try my luck. I won't have her on him for one moment longer than necessary," I said.

"Dammit, she and that horse understand each other," the man rasped.

"Yes, a kind of understanding. It will only go so far. I won't push it," I returned. He pressed his mouth tight, grunted and strode back to where Doctor Thedeaux waited. I turned back to Amanda, made this the longest session ever and at the end of the day she was drained. But she had done well. I allowed myself hope that tomorrow would go well. I didn't worry about the ride inside the show ring, anymore. The Major would have that moment he so desperately wanted. It was all he planned for the following days that I feared.

I took Amanda to her room, waited as she fell across the bed in utter exhaustion. She'd sleep well and be refreshed in the morning, I noted approvingly. Leaving her, I went to my room, changed into fresh slacks and a white cotton blouse with a large yellow flower embroidered across the front of it. I found only one plate at the dinner table, Marie waiting to serve me.

"The Major's taking his dinner in the study while he does some work," the woman explained. I nodded, watched her as she served a cold aspic with shrimp and ham.

"I heard that the bull got out of his pen the other night," I said casually, my eyes searching her face.

"He's bad, that one, a real killer," the woman remarked. I met her eyes and could see nothing in them, looked away and she left me alone in the big room. Was she the one who'd come to my aid, I wondered again? I owed someone my life. And someone undying enmity. It was later, when I'd finished dinner, that I went outside and almost bumped into Paul as he crossed to his quarters over the stables. He paused gravely.

"She'll ride tomorrow. You'll be finished here then," the small, wiry man said.

"Just about," I answered. I gazed down along the corrals, returned with idle curiosity to Paul. "I heard that the bull got loose the other night. How'd that come about?" I asked.

"Somebody didn't latch the gate right," he said and I grunted silently, once again hearing the sound, the slow, tiny creaking of the gate being carefully pushed open. The bull would have sent it flying open with a blow of his huge head.

"It's luck no one was in the corral," I commented, looking hard at him.

"Very lucky," he grunted and walked away. I watched him until he went up the outside steps to his place, and turned away knowing no more than when I'd begun, still wondering if he were friend or enemy, a weak man with a conscience or a weak man without a conscience. I went back into the house, to the music room, found a book on musical influences in Louisiana and sat down with it. I read for little more than an hour; the book was well written.

I'd just stopped to rub my eyes when a scream shattered the silence. It hung in the air, a cry of pure terror, Amanda's voice, and I leaped up, knocking the book aside as I raced for the door. It had come from her room and now she screamed again and then there was silence. I raced to the other side of the house, rounded the corner to the hallway to see Major Jeffries just emerging from the study, starting for her room. I passed him, reached the door first, and tore it open as he came up behind me. The room was empty and looking at the window at once, saw it standing open and ran to it. I peered into the night outside. Major Jeffries came up beside me.

"Did you see which way she went?" he asked, and I shook my head. I heard others, turned to see Marie Opatu in the doorway, then Victor appearing, his face filled with anxiety. I heard Sami's limping step coming down the hallway.

"She could have gone in any direction," Major Jeffries exclaimed and suddenly I knew where she'd gone.

"No, not anywhere," I murmured, swinging over the window sill and dropping to the ground. I raced alongside the house toward the stables. I ran as fast as my legs would carry me, knowing the others would follow. I'd just reached the stables when I saw the thundering form streak from the back door, at a full gallop in seconds, the slim, blond-haired figure clinging to him without saddle or bridle. I saw the light go on in Paul's quarters as I raced into the nearest stall, threw a rope halter over one of the saddlers and vaulted onto his back. I spurred the horse out of the stable, sent him into a gallop at once but knew I'd catch the big stallion only if he halted or circled. I only hoped to get close enough behind him to keep on his trail. I had the saddler going full out, bent low over him, using my legs, glad my father had taught me to ride bareback as a little girl. I kept him racing, strained my ears, and caught the sound of the stallion ahead of me. I flew around a bend in the road, cut out across the flat land toward a line of trees, barely able to glimpse the black form in the distance. I was falling back, I realized, just as I heard the sudden whinny, then the bellow and the wild snorting. I charged on, saw Saladin first, standing by the form of the girl on the ground. He reared up as I galloped to the scene, then trotted away into the trees and I leaped from the horse, knelt down beside Amanda.

The nightgown she had on was streaked and torn but there was no blood on her head anywhere. She hadn't slammed into a tree branch, nor had she been thrown hard. Most likely she'd just fallen from him, unable to hang on any longer. Bareback riding is its own technique, a matter of practice. I lifted her head and she moaned, opened her eyes and I propped her up in a sitting position. I heard the sound of horses coming up, and looked up from Amanda to see Major Jeffries and Paul Agee.

"Is she hurt?" the Major rasped as he swung from the saddle.

"Not physically, except for the wind knocked out of her," I said. "You two had better go get the stallion."

The man grimaced, climbed back into the saddle and rode off with Paul Agee following him. I helped Amanda to her feet, used a flat rock nearby to help her get a leg over the saddler and then swung on behind her. "Are you all right?" I asked. There was no answer. I leaned forward, put a finger on her chin, turned her face toward me and my stomach knotted. The blank, expressionless stare I'd first seen on Amanda held her face again. Her eyes stared dully at me and I sat back, let her look away. I wheeled the horse, headed back to the stables. Once there, I left the horse hitched for Paul to put away, and led Amanda back to her room, passing Marie as she held the door open for me. Alone with Amanda in her room, I watched her sink down on the edge of the bed.

"What happened, Amanda?" I asked. "What was it that made you scream?" Her eyes stared at me, not even flickering. "What made you scream and run away?" I tried again. There was no reply, no sign of understanding. "Something frightened you terribly. What was it?" I prodded but she only stared into space. I heard the door open; Major Jeffries stood there, his eyes focused on the girl.

"We brought Saladin back," he said, not looking at me. He was staring at Amanda.

"What was it?" I tried once more. She made no move and I turned away, swept by a terrible feeling of defeat. I walked past the man and went into the hallway, moving almost as in a trance, back to the living room. Victor stepped into my path, his face somber.

"What happened? What made her scream? Did she tell you?" he asked.

"No. She's regressed. She's back where she was when I came here," I said. "She's shattered. Something did it to her, something terrified her."

"Did it?" Victor asked solemnly and I frowned at him. "I told you what the therapists said about her," he remarked.

"No," I snapped. "Something happened to shatter her. Just as somebody has tried twice to kill me." I saw Victor's eyes seem to recoil from the statement and then the Major's footsteps came down the hall. Victor backed away.

"We'll talk more about that," he said, hurrying off. I faced Major Jeffries as he came to the living room doorway.

"Amanda won't ride tomorrow," I said, feeling both bitter and perversely triumphant at the same time. I saw the man's sigh of resignation. He had the common-sense to realize the truth when he saw it.

"We'll call her absent when her class comes up tomorrow," he said and I walked away. I went to my room, undressed and lay down in a pair of halter-top pajamas, feeling both defeated and grateful. Certainly not victorious. But at least that first, vital part of the Major's scheme had been ruined. He had needed all those witnesses to attest to her ability to ride before that eventual, tragic accident. But what had shattered Amanda? What had sent her screaming into the night? I was unwilling to accept Victor's implication of her basic disturbance. It hadn't been self-induced, I told myself. There was so much he didn't know about, including that first attempt to shatter her with the photo slipped under her door. I'd been certain that was Sami's doing. Had he found another way to shatter her completely? He had been the last to arrive at her room after the scream. Slowed by his limp? Or by something else? Questions had begun to buzz around my head like angry hornets again and I refused to entertain any more of them. I'd try again tomorrow with Amanda. I refused to believe she had come so far to return completely. I had to know what had sent her racing into the night in terror. Pressing my face into the pillow, I smothered out everything but sleep.

My inner alarm clock woke me early in the morning but when I left my room I saw Marie Opatu just closing the door to Amanda's room. "She's asleep," the woman said. "The Major told me to check on her." I nodded, went down the hall and outside, skipping breakfast. I was just in time to see Major Jeffres riding off on one of the Morgans. I went into the stables, leisurely saddled the brown gelding I'd used in training Amanda and decided to return to the kitchen for coffee. Sami was shuffling out of the room as I entered.

"He ought to be happy today," I said to Marie. "The Major isn't having his way." The woman faced me, her eyes tired.

"You asking me if that's a good or a bad thing?" she questioned almost wearily. "I say it's a bad thing."

"You go along with whatever the Major wants?" I asked, making a statement out of the question.

"Yes," the woman said. "I go along."

"But not with the things Sami does," I prodded.

"Things get twisted, so much sometimes there's no untwisting," she remarked. "People and things."

I turned her words in my mind, something said but unsaid, and I wondered again if she hadn't been the one who'd saved me from the bull. I went back to where I'd left the gelding saddled, swung up onto his back and cantered away. I took the only road east, and finally came in sight of the gaily-colored tents of the County Fair, taking up most of a large, flat field. The Horse Show grounds were at the near end; the small carousels and other amusements for youngsters at the far side. The Horse Show ring had drawn the greatest of the morning crowds, and I rode around the edge of the spectators watching a junior equitation class. I dismounted, found a pole, hitched the gelding to it and got a catalogue. The junior equitation was followed by a Single Harness Horse class, I read, and saw that Amanda had been entered in the class after that, Adult Equitation. I was rifling through the catalogue when I heard the voice at my elbow, looked up to see Clay.

"I heard about last night," he said quietly, noting the question in my eyes. "The Major called my father." His eyes searched my face. "Are you wrestling with mixed emotions?" he asked.

"I guess so," I answered carefully.

"You'll be leaving here soon, I imagine," Clay said. "I'll be sorry about that. I'd like to have seen more of you. Will you drop me a line when you settle? Maybe I'll be able to see you again."

"Of couse," I said, genuinely complimented. Seeing Clay Thedeaux under conditions less strained would be a pleasure, I suddenly realized. We did have a great deal in common.

"Then you'll tell me when you're leaving," Clay said. "I'd like to say goodbye." I smiled, nodded, my agreement symbolic. I'd not be telling anyone when I left. There'd be only Amanda and myself slipping through the darkness, seizing the moment.

The junior equitation ended and the harness class entered the ring to draw Clay's and my attention. Ring attire was very casual, I noticed, but then the meet was really a local show, perhaps on its way to becoming a fully "recognized" show. Proper riding attire would be a must, then. I watched the Single Harness class for a few minutes, trotting the ring to the left, reversing direction on command. An elderly woman driving a maroon harness buggy with vermilion trim and chrome wheels was doing the best job, moving her horse and buggy with snap and perfect control. As the class neared the finish, I scanned the crowd for Major Jeffries, and found the shining pate near the Judge's stand, Clay's father to his left. I kept my eyes on the Major as the harness class ended and the announcer called out the adult equitation. I saw him start toward the Judge's stand, motioning to one of the officials.

The crowd gasped, first, an electric murmur that rippled wave-like through the ringside. Turning, I looked out to the ring and felt my own breath drawn in sharply, my eyes staring at the great, black stallion that entered the ring with the girl on him. I glanced around to see Major Jeffries swing about, astonishment on his face. I felt Clay's eyes on me, looked at him for an instant and shrugged in amazement, moved through the crowd to a corner of the ring where Amanda had to see me as she turned.

Her eyes met mine, flickered, and then she walked Saladin on. The stallion was holding back, brimming over with energy. I counted four more entries, listened to the quiet buzzing among the onlookers as they followed Major Jeffries' daughter with their eyes. The class was called to attention, commands given and I watched with more pride than I'd ever watched any of my pupils before. The demands of the local show were somewhat less severe than at a recognized AHSA show and there was no changing of horse. I watched the individual performances around the ring, the extended trot, gallop and stop and the figure eight at a canter, stopping at each change of lead. The last was a figure eight at trot, changing diagonals on command.

I felt the muscles of my face grow tight. Amanda did well enough, her nervousness visible yet for the most part held in hand. She made mistakes, with movements I'd had no chance to work on enough with her, and once, she flared and the stallion reacted immediately. She backed him, managed to hold him under control and went on with the exercise. She wouldn't win, but she had done better than anyone had a right to expect. Last night she had been terrified, shattered, and she had fought out of whatever had happened to her. She'd pulled herself together, gone to the stables and saddled the stallion. She hadn't gotten the girth tight enough and she'd put on a snaffle bridle with the throat-latch too loose but it all worked well enough. I kept seeing the terrified girl I'd seen last night, her eyes glazed, her emotions plunged into depression. And she was here, riding the stallion and even I could only imagine what that had taken on her part. I wanted to shout for joy, but reality was a chain that strangled. She had refused to stay shattered, had pulled herself out of terror's grip, and in the very act, moved one step closer to death. She had come here and in doing so, had given the Major the very thing he wanted. The bitter irony of it twisted inside me. I wouldn't let death be a reward for courage, I vowed.

The class ended and the crowd erupted in a low, rippling murmur. They were talking more about Amanda's presence in the ring than the class itself, I knew. The judges announced their decision, a young, black-haired man taking the blue, and Amanda was given a white for fourth. I made my way to where I'd hitched the gelding, swung into the saddle and went around to meet Amanda outside the ring at the far end. Her eyes met mine, looked away and she wheeled Saladin around, set off back on the road to Darkwater Farms. I spurred the gelding on and rode alongside her.

"You did well, Amanda," I said. "I'm proud of you." She made no reply and I watched her as we slowly rode back. The strain had been tremendous, I knew, but only she could know the full extent of it and I watched it begin to drain away as we rode. She stared forward and I could see her lips working nervously, her tongue flicking out to wet their dry surfaces. She visibly seemed to shrivel, grow smaller, sag in the saddle and by the time we reached the stables she was hardly holding the reins. I dismounted first, took the bridle of the stallion, led him into the box stall and Amanda dismounted. Hitching the gelding to a post, I went with her to her room. The terrible strain had involved so much more than the appearance in the ring, I knew. That'd been the least of it. The fighting back from her shattered, mute self of the night had been the tremendous effort that had consumed her. She collapsed onto the bed.

"I'll come late tonight, as usual," I whispered, bending over her. She lay motionless, her eyes still staring into space and I left her, returned to the stables, unsaddled the stallion and the gelding, and put the gelding in his stall. I returned to the kitchen; Marie was there. I asked her for coffee and she gave me a cup from a steaming pot on the stove.

"Everything went well," she said. "The Major just came back."

"Wonderfully," I said, hearing the bitterness in the single word. I finished the coffee, went into the hall and saw Victor just coming through from the other wing of the house.

"I heard," he said, his voice tight. "You've done your work well. Better than anyone expected, I guess."

"It means more than just her appearance today," I said. "Don't you understand that? She couldn't have done it if she hadn't made tremendous strides emotionally, personally."

His face remained grave. "You're fooling yourself, Gail," he said. "She'll break again. She'll go off again, just as she did last night."

"Something terrified her last night," I said.

He shook his head. "No. It was just her. She just went off in her own delusions. She did that at the sanatorium, they said."

"No," I snapped back. "Something made her do that last night." Victor was as much a victim of what he'd heard and been told as I had been planned to be, a recipient of second-hand tales and distortions. Distortions on purpose, just as the accidents were on purpose, I mused silently. He shrugged, put a hand on my cheek.

"I'm sorry for you," he said. "You'll find out for yourself." His dark eyes held my somber gaze. "You still think someone tried to kill you?" he asked.

"I'm sure of it," I retorted.

"Then leave, get away from here. Let me help you," he said.

"When it's time. I'll tell you, I promise," I said, still not ready to say more, now. He pressed my hand, hurried away as the Major came out of the study. I walked past the piercing eyes and went to my room, feeling terribly tired and drained and knowing this was but a pale copy of how Amanda felt. I stretched out on the bed and fell asleep as the rest of the day drifted away. I didn't wake until I heard a knocking at the door, swung out of bed to open it and see Marie there with a tray.

"You didn't come to dinner so I fixed you something," the woman said.

"I'm sorry; I fell asleep," I said. "How is Amanda? Has anyone looked in on her?"

"I have. She's been asleep most of the day. I left a tray a while ago for her and it's not touched yet," Marie said. She put my tray down and left and I freshened up, combed my hair and nibbled at the cold chicken and salad, drank the *cafe noir*. I felt on edge, keyed up, the tension of the day, and of the night before, staying with me. I took the tray back to the kitchen and, returning, saw Major Jeffries in the library. I paused in the doorway, wanting to probe the man as much as I could.

"She rode today. My part's finished. What happens, now?" I said laconically.

The eagle head turned to survey me. "I suppose that will depend on how Amanda continues to progress," he answered. "But you're correct about your part being finished. I'll have the balance of your funds drawn in a day or two." He paused for a moment, then went on. "I think it'd be best if you had no more contact with Amanda, now," he said.

"Why?" I snapped.

"She has responded to your work with her. She has perhaps developed an attachment that is going to be severed. I think it best not to prolong that attachment any more than necessary," he said. I almost smiled. The man's attention to every detail was amazing. I turned and strode from the door back to my room. I switched the lamp off, lay in the darkness and waited; the hours dragged maddeningly. But finally, as it neared midnight, I rose and embarked on what would be one of few more stealthy trips to Amanda's room. I went out the French doors and along the house to Amanda's window, halted in instant panic as I saw the window open. Victor's words leaped up at me and I fought them down, shook away the panicked feeling and hurried on along the side of the dark stone house and down to the stables. A sense of relief untwisted my stomach as I saw the gate to the box stall open and eased closer; Amanda was leaning her head against the stallion's ebony, shining coat. Her hands moved along his neck and forequarters, stroking gently and she was talking in murmured words, more words than I'd ever heard her say. I moved closer, trying to catch them. But the stallion caught my presence and his ears snapped upright. His head, half-over Amanda's long, blond hair, seemed to guard and protect her and now he blew, his nostrils flaring in warning. Amanda turned and I moved completely into view.

"Come back with me, Amanda," I said softly. "There's not much time left to talk."

She stared at me a moment, turned to the stallion to stroke his neck again and then moved toward me. I watched him flare his nostrils again, snort and step backwards as the gate swung shut. She went with me around the house, back through the open window of her room and I drew the curtain, lighted the small bedside lamp.

"What made you run last night, Amanda?" I asked. At the question, her eyes filled with fear at once and she slumped onto the edge of the bed. "Was it something you saw?" She made no response. "Was someone here? Did someone frighten you?" I continued and she made no sound, sat withdrawn with round, wary eyes. I kept my voice gentle. "Amanda, you must tell me," I tried again. "Was it something you dreamt? Were you thinking about that time long ago?" She remained silent, immovable.

I sat down beside her. "All right, we'll start with that time when it happened. You saw your mother kill herself," I said harshly. Her eyes flared, stabbed at me, sudden fire in them. She shook her head vigorously. "Amanda, you've admitted that. We've gone past that block," I protested, but she continued to shake her head in heated denial. Frustration swept over me. "But you said so. You broke through that. Don't block it out again. You saw the suicide."

Her lips opened and her face grew strained. "No," she said. I watched her lips work again, her mouth opening and closing as she tried to form words that refused to come out.

"What is it, Amanda? Say it, get it out," I urged; her throat strained, grew tight, the muscles standing out in her neck and suddenly the words exploded, a torn, shredded sound.

"No suicide," she gasped out.

I stared at her and she flung herself face down onto the bed, her body shaking uncontrollably. "Amanda, what do you mean by that?" I asked, hardly able to believe what I'd heard. The words came again, muffled from the face pressed into the bed, almost inaudible. *"No suicide."*

I stared at her shaking form, watched her dig herself down into the bedcovers. "Amanda, you've got to tell me more," I said.

"No. No more," she said and, half-lifting herself, the words came through as a desperate plea for peace. I rose, backed away. I knew the signs by now. There'd be nothing more from her tonight. I went to the window, swung out and closed it behind me, returned to my room and latched the doors, slumping into a chair in a state of dazed shock. The two words rang in my mind like a terrible gong, pounding angrily. *No suicide,* I repeated silently; the impact was shattering. I made my whirling mind halt in its frantic spinning, fought to restore order to it. The deposition I'd read by Major Jeffries came to mind. He'd said he had reached the room first, but I already knew that was a lie. He hadn't been trying to protect Amanda from questions. I felt myself balk. Amanda had been there, she'd seen it happen. I forced myself to confront the ugliness as I'd forced Amanda to confront it. Everything pointed to a suicide, everyone attested to that. Had Amanda witnessed not suicide but murder?

"Oh, my God," I heard myself groan, the horror of it overwhelming. The Major's plans for Amanda, his scheme for murder-by-accident, took on even greater meaning, now, draped in even darker reasons. Amanda, as a little girl of ten, had suffered a complete emotional breakdown at what she had seen and he had shut her away. But for almost ten years he had lived with the fear that one day she could come out of that breakdown. He had finally decided to move, now, to coincide with the time of her inheriting the estate. Carefully, diabolically, he had schemed to make certain that she would never reveal what she had seen that night, that no doctor might someday pronounce her sane. The murder-by-accident would take care of both things in one swift stroke of ultimate betrayal.

I felt sick. It all fitted in so well; with malicious mockery, aspects that didn't fit leaped up at me. I thought of Doctor Thedeaux's medical report, the traces of the revolver's cleaning fluid on Edith Wentley Jeffries' hands and the powder burns against her skin; his medical verification of suicide. Could they be explained in some fashion, or did they really punch holes in everything that Amanda's two words had said? Did they make her words into the ravings of a girl who was really disturbed, subject to deep hallucinations and mental distortions? I sat with the possibility before me, unable to ignore it much as I felt I could. The sound of voices interrupted my thoughts; muffled voices raised in anger. I rose, went to the door and stepped into the hallway. The voices were clearer now, coming from down the hall and I saw a shaft of yellow light from the study. I heard the Major's voice first, and I eased down the hallway.

"Dammit, coming here at this hour. There's no reason for it," I heard him say.

"I couldn't sleep. We've got to talk about this, Robert," I recognized Doctor Thedeaux's voice. "I'm afraid of it," he said.

"Nonsense. They all saw her today. That's just what I wanted. It'll be enough," I heard the Major rasp and I crept closer, to where I could see into the study, pressing myself against the far wall of the corridor.

"No, it's not enough. You can't count on it coming out the way you want," Clay's father said. "I never favored this approach, anyway, you know that."

"It'll work, I tell you," Major Jeffries growled. I saw Doctor Thedeaux shake his head.

"It's too tricky, there are too many chances for it not to turn out the way you want. Then you'll be faced with more problems. You've got to act directly. There's no more time for anything else."

"No," the Major thundered, and I felt cold seizing me. Clay's father was involved. In some way, he and Major Robert Jeffries were in this together and the sickness I'd felt grew more withering inside me.

"What if I won't go along any longer, Robert?" the doctor asked. Major Jeffries strode to a cabinet, unlocked it and took out a steel box. He held it up to the doctor.

"You'll go along, Percy. You'll go along because of what's in here, just as you went along ten years ago because of it," he said.

"I've always hated you for that, Robert," Clay's father said. "I understood you but I never forgave you for it."

"It's called self-preservation, Percy. I do what I have to do for my reasons and you do it for yours," the Major barked, and the other man sighed in defeat, turned and started for the door. I shrank back into the deeper shadows of the hallway as he paused in the door.

"What about Gail Forester?" he asked. "She's suspicious. You said she tried to nose around in the county records. You don't know what she's gotten out of Amanda. Clay tells me she's been working hard with her."

"We'll see about Miss Forester," I heard the Major rasp. I retreated deeper into the dark of the hall; Clay's father left; I waited while the study light went out and Major Jeffries emerged to walk to his quarters in the other side of the house. Plans had formed in my mind already and I retreated to my room, first. I didn't dare go out to the car and bring back my large flashlight, but I found my small purse light in my bag. I went back into the dark corridor and down to the study, pausing every few steps, but the house was still. In the study, I had a piece of luck. In his anger, the Major hadn't relocked the cabinet. I opened it, reached in and pulled the box out, set it on the table.

I beamed the thin little light into it, carefully lifted out a collection of papers and scanned each one by the light. They were mostly medical certificates made out and signed by Doctor Thedeaux, mainly concerning miscarriages, premature births of still-born infants, treatments for stomach pains and signs of pregnancies terminated by injury. But attached to almost each certificate was a handwritten statement, most in but a few lines. I read one clipped to a certificate listing a miscarriage.

> I wanted to get rid of the baby and I went to
> Doc Thedeaux and he helped me do it.
> Louise Touraine.

Each statement was the same, giving the lie to the medical certificate attached. Each of the statements revealed that the certificates signed by Doctor Thedeaux were false medical claims to cover operations that were really abortions. The dates on the papers coincided, went back twenty years. More papers in the box attested to other things that occurred over the years, a medical statement for a father dead of an "accidental gunshot," signed, like all the others, by Doctor Thedeaux, a woman's claim to need two months off because of "stomach troubles," another woman injured at work on a farm while "on the job," and a host of similar medical statements. I put them back into the box and stared at them, their import all too clear. Over his long years here, Doctor Thedeaux had performed abortions for his back-country clients, arranged medical evidence to fit a particular situation, falsely attested to numerous medical reports. Perhaps it had been part of such practice in these places, and perhaps much, even all, had been done with good intent. But somehow, Major Jeffries had amassed the truth and the contents of the box constituted a sword hanging over the doctor's head. It had been used ten years ago to make him sign a medical certificate of suicide when there had been no suicide at all and now, entrapped, he was going along again with the Major's plans. The web of deceit and death had been woven with absolute, chilling efficiency and to top it, working at cross-purposes, someone had wanted the Major's desires thwarted. All of this place truly was a web of personal hatred and intrigue.

I put the box into the cabinet, turned the sliver of light off and made my way back to my room. I undressed, lay across the bed and let the perspiration dry on my body. Major Jeffries had tied everything and everyone into place. After I left, when Amanda was urged to ride Saladin again, and perhaps again, Doctor Thedeaux would be on hand to sign the medical certificate after the tragic accident. I felt utterly drained, too tired to take in any more. I let sleep press down upon me, but not before one final realization. I would have to find a way out of here tomorrow night. I didn't dare risk staying any longer, not for myself and not for Amanda. The web had too many strands. I finally slept, putting off practical plans for the morning. Amanda's words drifted through my almost-asleep mind ... *no suicide* ... I shuddered and slept.

CHAPTER NINE

had spent the night tossing and turning, falling into a sound sleep just before dawn and I woke late, showered and dressed quickly in slacks and a blouse. I opened the French doors and stepped outside to be met by a hot breeze and air that lay heavily over the ground. The oaks moved fitfully with the hot wind and the air was as restless as I felt. Only the bayou looked cool and shaded. I moved to Amanda's window, saw her, in slacks and a bra, finishing breakfast. I tapped softly on the window glass and she came at once, raising the window, her eyes round, probing.

"I think I understand everything now, Amanda," I said. "We're going to have to get away from here tonight, just you and I, do you understand?" She nodded. "No one must know," I emphasized and she nodded again. "I'll come for you, about midnight," I said. "You just stay here and wait." Once more she signified understanding and I darted away as I heard a knock at the door of the room. I returned to my own room, went down to the kitchen and had coffee and biscuits. As I breakfasted, I made plans. There was not that much to plan. I'd simply take the car, leave with Amanda in the still of the night and drive like the wind into Texas, across the state line and then swing north. The first practical step presented itself. I'd drive to Santal and fill the gas tank. I had less than a quarter of a tank, now, I remembered.

After draining the coffee, I walked out to the car shed. The local hands were working the saddlers and one of the far corrals held a herd of Black Angus driven in from pasture. Darkwater Farms masked the evil inside it well. Only the squinty-eyed house seemed unwilling to enter the masquerade, still frowning down on me. Victor's little Fiat gone; only the Major's heavy limousine and my own blue compact stood in the car shed. I slid behind the wheel, stepped on the pedal, pumped it for a moment, then switched on the ignition. The engine coughed, turned over and went dead. I pumped the gas pedal again, played with the starter. It whined but the engine refused to cough itself to life. I tried again and only the ignition made a sound. I lifted the hood and stared at the engine, wishing I knew what to look for; saw Paul Agee pass with a bucket of oats.

"It won't start," I complained. He put down the bucket, came over, tried the ignition himself twice, looked at the engine.

"Don't see anything," he thought aloud. He moved around to the back of the car as I stayed by the open hood. "Here's your problem," I heard him call. I scurried around to where he stood, pointing down to a line of fluid that had soaked into the ground. "You've a hole in your fuel line," he said.

I stared down at the irregular line of soaked ground. "There was nothing wrong with it," I murmured, but Paul had taken up his bucket and gone on. I frowned at the wet soil. Fuel lines didn't just develop holes, I told myself, but I knew that they could indeed do just that. But the timing bothered me, the coincidence just too neat. Or was I being ridiculous? Was I seeing shadows that weren't there? My lips drew back in a grimace. Neither the bayou nor the bull had been my imagination, I reminded myself. I'd taken nothing for granted. I knelt down, then crawled half-under the rear of the car, the odor of the gasoline on the ground strong in my nostrils. I saw the hole in the fuel line, a sizeable opening. But there were no rusted, worn edges around it. It was a neat, clean hole made by a puncture, something sharp driven into it. Had I kicked up a sharp rock at high speed while driving? It was entirely possible, I realized grimly.

I'd just started to back out from under the car when, along the inner edge of the rear tire, under the fender, I saw a little rectangular, white object, flat and half-against the tire. I reached for it, pulled it closer. It was one of the little packets in which pills and capsules are given by doctors, two by two by three inches or so in size. I looked at the other side, at the name imprinted across the top of the envelope-packet: Clay Thedeaux, D.V.M.

I pushed myself out from the car, stuffed the little empty packet into my pocket and returned to the house in a kind of delayed shock. In my room, I took it out, laid it on the dresser and stared at it. The little envelope was one more link in what seemed a never-ending chain. Clay would have an instrument sharp enough to puncture the fuel line, of course. Had the little packet fallen out of his pocket as he lay under the car, destroying my chance to flee in the night? I recalled how he had insisted I tell him when I intended leaving. His interest and sincerity had flattered. I grunted bitterly.

Clay, also? In on it like his father, from the beginning? Or was his involvement a later thing? Had his father told him of the contents of the black box? Had he decided to protect his father from what would come to light if Amanda were made to reveal everything? The questions formed their own, inexorable march. He'd suddenly realized that perhaps I'd already learned too much from Amanda. I couldn't be permitted to leave, not even alone. Had Clay fired that shot into the pirogue? He could have let the bull into the corral, also. Certainly he knew his way around Darkwater Farms well enough for that. I stuffed the little envelope back into my pocket and went outside to scan the scene of busy activity. Sami was walking near the stables, Paul Agee stood by the corral with the herd of angus, and Marie Opatu was carrying a sack of flour into the house. One of them was a friend. One had a conscience, no matter what his or her allegiance. One had acted to save my life that night in the corral. But I didn't dare approach any. If I chose the wrong one to confide in, I sealed Amanda's fate and my own. I had only one place to turn to, now; Victor. He'd help me, I knew, and I'd find a way to put off telling him everything I knew until after Amanda and I were safely gone from here.

I went into the house, hesitated to go into the other wing where the Major had his rooms and where I'd never been. I stopped Marie as she passed. "Will you call Victor for me?" I asked. "Tell him it's important that I see him. I'll wait in the music room." The woman's eyes searched me briefly and I kept my face masked; in a moment, she went into the far end of the house. I paced the music room as I waited. Almost a half-hour had gone by when Victor appeared, barefoot, in slacks and a shirt hanging open to the waist, his dark, compelling handsomeness accentuated by the tattered earthiness of his clothes.

"I was taking a shower," he explained, coming to me, putting his hands on my shoulders, warmly, strongly. He pressed and I half-winced; his laughter was quick, as embracing as the arms that pulled me against him.

"You said you'd help me," I murmured into his chest. "I've got to get out of here, tonight, with Amanda." He pulled back and stared down at me. "I can't go into all of it now, Victor; just trust me, believe in me. I must get away from here tonight with her. Will you help me?"

I saw his lips tighten. "Tonight, it has to be tonight?" he asked and I nodded. "I've got a job tonight, with another musician, a banjo player," he said and I felt my heart sink. "But I'll be back by eleven. It's an early gig." My heart soared at once.

"I wouldn't want to try to leave before midnight," I said.

"All right," he agreed. "I'll be back by then." I reached up, brushed his lips with mine.

"I'll explain everything later," I promised. His hand moved across my cheek.

"Why didn't you leave when I told you to leave, long ago?" he asked softly, almost idly. "Why didn't you listen to me? You'd have been safe and away from here."

"Maybe I knew too much but not enough then," I said. "It's unimportant, now. The only thing that counts is getting away from here tonight with Amanda. My car's been fixed so it won't work and you wrecked yours. How can we do it?"

He smiled. "You leave that to me. I'll follow along the bayous, first, probably," he said. "Tonight, midnight." He left the room, silent on bare feet and I allowed a deep sigh of relief to escape me. I started back to my room, and heard my name called as I passed the study; I went in to where Major Jeffries sat behind his desk.

"Your check will be ready in the morning," he said.

"Thank you," I replied; he clearly dismissed me. I turned away, marveling at the ice of the man, everything carried down to the last detail, all the proprieties observed, every i dotted and every t crossed. Why, he'd just paid the girl for her work with Amanda, people would say after my accident. I went to my room, sprawled in a chair and let myself wonder what had been planned for me, this time. One thing was certain. The hole punched in my fuel line was proof that the weavers of the web had grown fearful. They were uncertain of how much I knew, or how much I could put together and had decided to act. I toyed with speculations about the shape of death by accident. Perhaps I was supposed to be driven to a train station in an adjoining county. A car accident would be easy enough to arrange, the driver prepared and poised to leap to safety at the last moment. Or perhaps the Major would be sympathetic about my broken fuel line, call in someone from Santal to have it replaced. Meanwhile, I'd have to stay on a day or two more; additional time to prepare my accident. It would be said that I was impatient, did something foolish that ended in tragedy. Would Clay take me out someplace, I wondered, and felt a wave of depression sweep over me.

I cut off further macabre games and began to pack my things, pulling my bags from the closet. I'd finished packing when I realized how stupid I'd been. I couldn't be lugging suitcases along tonight. I'd have to flee with only as much as was necessary, only that which I could cram into my big, leather shoulder bag. I spent the rest of the afternoon unpacking, choosing those things I could get into the shoulder bag. Finally finished, I put my other things neatly in a corner of the closet. I fully intended calling for them, and for my car, once Amanda was in the proper hands. It was evening when I went to the kitchen, told Marie I wasn't hungry but that I'd take a sandwich and some milk. She fixed the snack for me and I took it to my room. I had nothing to fear yet, I reasoned, but I latched the French doors and finished my snack. I slipped down the hall to Amanda for a moment, opened the door to her room to see her sitting by the window. She turned and I put a finger to my lips. "Tonight," I whispered and her eyes flickered understanding. I returned to my room, put the bolt on the door and lay down on the bed. I forced myself to relax, and store up energy. It would be a long night; I set my alarm clock for eleven, and managed to sleep.

The sounds didn't come first. A sudden, icy fear seized me in a terrible grip, and I snapped awake, sitting up instantly. Shivering, though the room was hot, I peered into the darkness and only then did I hear the sounds, voices, distant, a shout and then the pounding of hoof-beats. I shot from the bed, swore at the extra moments it took to unlock the bolt on the door and raced into the hallway. Marie was half-way down the corridor, beyond her; Sami standing against one wall, fright and consternation showed on her face.

"What is it? What's going on?" I asked.

"Miss Amanda, she's gone," the woman said, and the icy hands of fear gripped me again.

"What do you mean—run away?" I almost shouted.

"I guess so," the woman answered. "Doc Thedeaux came by. He and the Major went to her room to see her. Next thing I know the Major came running down here yelling that she was gone."

I spun, crashed open the door to Amanda's room. I saw the chair on its side, first, then the bedcovers half-pulled from the bed, and the open window. The small lamp near the bed lay overturned, also. The struggle had been brief and silent but there had been a struggle and I turned to Marie as she appeared in the doorway. "You only saw the Major run back?" I asked.

"Yes. He said Doc Thedeaux had gone out the window looking for her. The Major ran to the stables to saddle two horses; Sami saw him," the woman said.

I turned to the room again. Amanda hadn't fled, run away into the night. She'd been taken away, dragged from the room, perhaps gagged with an ether-soaked rag. Doctor Thedeaux had probably taken her out the window while Major Jeffries ran to get the horses, shouting the alarm, setting up Marie and Sami as witnesses; everything in place again. Something had triggered them into action, or perhaps they'd found a sudden opportunity to arrange an accident. Amanda hadn't run away by herself.

I brushed past Marie as she just managed to step aside, and ran down the hallway, aware again of Sami standing against the wall. His brooding eyes were filled more with wonder and fear than hate, for a change. I raced out of the house and the wind struck at me at once, almost a physical blow, a hot, strong wind that had blown up in the night. I stared out into the darkness, past the corrals, the exercise rings, the road beyond and the land that became only so much blackness. A moon touched the tops of the trees when it peered from behind scudding clouds.

They could have gone anywhere, in any direction, once they were beyond the corrals. Finding them would be pure luck. I wouldn't even know which way to begin. If Victor were here, we could set off in different directions and perhaps be lucky. But he wouldn't be back for another hour at least. The accident would have taken place by then. I wanted to sink down to the ground, helplessness sweeping over me in sickening waves. The wind gusted sharply, swirled around me and I tasted despair and defeat, longing to shout out in rage. Suddenly I heard an angry bellow from the stables and then the sharp, unmistakable sound of a horse kicking hard against its stall.

I turned, frozen in space for an instant, and then I was runnng, racing again, toward the stables, skidding into the first door, snatching a snaffle bit and bridle from a hook as I sped by. There'd be no time for anything else; I heard the angry snort again, the sound of hooves cracking against wood. I swung the gate of the box stall open and rushed in. The stallion's eyes were wild, turned back so I could see the whites of them. Only my own desperation made me go into the stall with him. But the huge stallion held Amanda's life; in him lay her one chance for survival. I knew it and, more than I could know, he was aware of it; he stood still as I threw on the bridle and vaulted atop his back. I'd just chanced to seize the reins when he hurtled from the stall, at a full gallop, and we went into the night.

I clung to him, letting him race on, hoping for that extra sense beyond the ordinary senses, that magic of strange, mysterious communication that performs strange and wondrous miracles. Heightened instincts, psychic communication, sensitivities we neither understood nor believed in properly, I didn't know what or which, only that the stallion knew she was in danger. Perhaps it was a kind of love, with depths we couldn't yet comprehend, a feeling of one creature for another that transcended and broke through all the barriers of reason and intellect. As I clung to the back of the speeding stallion I suddenly wondered if that wasn't simply what love is, a special bond, a touching of depths that go beyond rational, reasoned explanation. Perhaps man was a diluted creature now, unable to understand or touch the singular purities of that special bond.

"Find her, Saladin, find her," I cried, shaking away my thoughts. The big stallion hurtled on, suddenly veered toward the line of trees that were the woods. I did nothing to stop him; nothing would have, anyway. Another sound began to mingle with the staccato thunder of his hooves, an undulating sound, growing in power, and I heard the trees to my left bend with it. It rose, fell, crying, sobbing; I knew that sound, and heard the words once more... *when the wind cries.* The wind was crying, wailing, now; as death sought a victim. "Find her, find her, Saladin," I whispered in anguish.

The stallion, a jet streak through the night, hurdled a sudden hedge with winged hooves, then a small stream, soaring through the air. The tremendous power of the animal vibrated under me as he raced along the edge of the trees and suddenly veered, almost into them. I saw the horse, first standing just under an overhanging oak, then the white-suited form crumpled nearby. I yanked on Saladin, managed to wheel him around and finally he halted, impatiently stamping the ground. I slid down and ran to the still form of Doctor Thedeaux. The top of his head was streaked with blood from a deep gash along the temple, but he was still alive. Had they fought, I wondered? Had he, in a last moment of conscience, tried to stop the Major? Or had he simply struck his head against a low branch?

I heard him groan, saw his eyes lift, half open. "Where are they?" I asked, leaning closer to his bloodied head. "The Major, which way did he go with Amanda?"

The man tried to form words with his lips. "No," I heard him half-whisper. "You don't... understand," he managed.

"I understand," I said almost savagely. "Which way did he go?" The man tried to talk again, fell back; his breathing was labored, his eyes closed. I rose. I couldn't stay with him. I heard Saladin beat a tattoo on the ground with his hooves and turned, pulled myself onto his back again. He wheeled, twice, halted, half-reared and shook his head in the air; then his ears lay back and he bolted forward as if propelled out of a cannon. The wind howled and cried now, hot and thick, a wind from the depths of hades. The sobbing sound matched the sobbing inside me, as I felt time running out, Saladin veered again, thundered on and I knew I'd never ridden so fast on any horse.

I saw the tall silhouette of marsh grass and then the moon touching the flat, watery land to the right. Saladin slowed suddenly, almost stopped, pranced, tossed his head and blew. Then he bolted again, this time sharply to the left. I felt the thin water on my legs as he raced through soft ground. A knot of low trees appeared directly in front of me and he shifted, raced around them and then the vast marsh lay before me. Saladin slowed again, veered, raced along the edge and then, at the marsh, I saw a horse standing quietly. To the left two figures loomed, one holding a long, thin silhouette—a rifle.

Saladin bolted forward just as the shot rang out and one of the figures staggered, fell back and crumpled to the ground. The moon glinted on the bald pate of Major Robert Jeffries. Saladin came to a halt. Amanda lay on the ground at the edge of the marsh. The figure with the rifle turned and Victor's dark handsomeness looked up at me as I leaped down from the stallion. I felt almost weak with the relief that swept over me as I started toward him.

"Oh, God, how did you know?" I asked.

He stepped toward me and then I saw flashing red spots in front of my eyes, my face exploding in sharp, sudden pain. I felt myself go down, the ground damp and soft under me. I lay there, shook my head and gazed up at Victor, unable to comprehend anything but that I'd been struck by something. I reached my hand out to him.

"Stupid, meddling little bitch," he snarled. He kicked me then, his shoe catching me in the ribs, the pain stabbing deep. I couldn't believe what I felt or heard. He moved after me, as I half-rolled on the ground, swung again with his hand and the blow smashed across my forehead. I fell backwards, fighting off pain again.

"Victor, stop," I heard my voice cry out. But he came after me again, kicking out once more. I rolled, avoided the kick, tried to scramble to my feet. I could not accept what was happening. It was beyond my understanding. Victor rushed at me as I regained my feet.

"She wouldn't listen to me. None of you listen," I heard him shout. He swung and his blow struck sharp pain into my upraised arm; I tried to duck away. It was no use. He was a man berserk. His right fist smashed into the small of my back as I half-turned and I felt searing agony shoot up through my body. I fell forward, to my knees, and rolled away from another kick. On my back, I caught sight of Victor turning, reaching to where Amanda's form lay. He pulled her half-up.

"Bitches, all of you just bitches," he shouted. He flung her limp form away. The rest happened with such fury and raw wildness that I could only lie there, unable to move, to look away.

Victor had raised the rifle toward Amanda's form when a bellowing, blowing sound of rage ripped the air; Saladin reared upward. Victor started to whirl around, but the stallion came down with his forelegs striking out. One hoof smashed down on Victor's arm to send the rifle skittering out of his grasp; the other ripped a line of red along his leg. Victor dove away, hit the ground, rolled, and tried to dive forward again for the rifle. Saladin moved with instant fury, coming down again with his hooves, and Victor screamed in pain as one struck his hand. Victor twisted; he started to leap up, a gleaming knifeblade in his hand. He rushed at the horse but Saladin had reared into the air again, coming down with his forelegs flailing, kicking. One thunderous hoof struck Victor full in the chest as he rushed forward with the knife. I heard the sound of his gasping breath as he staggered, and fell backwards. Then the stallion was over him, coming down again and again with his hooves. I could hear bones shattering, agonized cries and then more dull, thudding sounds.

I snapped out of my stunned trance, pulled myself up and ran around to the horse's head. I jumped up, seized the bridle and yanked down hard. He tossed his head, reared and I flew into the air. But I refused to let go. He came down, backed, lowered his head and dragged me along the ground. I managed to regain an upright position, clinging to the reins, got a hand onto the bridle, pulled hard and forced his head around.

I heard myself talking to him; soothing words, whispered entreaties, pulled out of automatic reaction rather than conscious thought. I took hold of both reins, turned him in a circle and led him around to where Amanda lay. I knelt down beside her, holding the reins. She was alive and she seemed unhurt though unconscious. The stallion lowered his head, pressed his soft nose down on her, held it there, nuzzling her face, her neck. Then she stirred, slowly opening her eyes, and I pulled her to a sitting position. She reached up to find Saladin's muzzle, held it there and I saw her glance at the scene of horror around her.

I rose, looked around myself in shock and felt dizzy. I was unable to put it into any sort of focus. Only Victor's raging fury stayed with me, still incomprehensible, terrorizing; the pain of his blows was more inside than outside now. There had to be answers somewhere in this night of terror that had suddenly turned my world upside-down.

I focused again on Amanda. She was on her knees now, her hands against the stallion's lowered head. Then we heard the sound of a galloping horse and turned to see Paul Agee on a chestnut saddler racing up to us.

"I heard the shot," he said as he jumped from his saddle. "It took me a few minutes to zero in on it." He surveyed the scene, then strode to where Major Jeffries lay, kneeling down beside the man, resting his head on his chest. "He's still breathing," Paul said. "Help get him on my horse. Maybe there's a chance yet."

I stepped closer as he half-lifted the big man. I got under his arms and Paul took his legs. Half-dragging him, we got the Major to the chestnut mare and Paul, putting his shoulders under the limp form, managed to place him across the saddle. Paul swung up just behind the dangling form.

"I don't understand, not any of it," I said helplessly. "Doc Thedeaux's back by the woods. He's hurt, too."

Paul Agee shook his head at me. "I don't have any answers either. We don't have time to talk. I'm getting the Major back and taking the car. There's a hospital in Beaumont. You see what you can do for Doc Thedeaux," he said.

He wheeled the horse, rode off at a canter and changed into a gallop as he disappeared into the night. I turned, looked down at Victor's form. He lay motionless, a crushed, crumpled shape, redness staining every part of him.

"Leave him," I heard Amanda say and I turned to her. There was a calm, contained quality in her eyes I'd never seen there before. I'd hoped to see it one day, but not for these reasons.

"What did it all mean, Amanda?" I asked.

"Later," she said, turning, pulling herself onto Saladin. I went to the horse standing nearby, the one the Major had ridden. Or perhaps Victor had ridden him here. I swung into the saddle and headed back to the line of woods where I'd found Doctor Thedeaux. The white-suited form still lay there; I dismounted, and wiped some of the blood from the wound with a kerchief. The gash in his temple could have been a bullet, I realized, as I looked closely at it, a shot that just missed being fatal. He was still breathing, and Amanda came up to help me lift him into the saddle. Then I heard the sound of the pick-up truck roaring across the ground, the headlights illuminating the scene by bits and pieces.

The truck skidded to a halt and Clay leaped out, knelt down by his father and examined the wound. He picked the older man up and laid him in the back of the truck, applied antiseptic and a bandage. Then he used smelling salts. Doctor Thedeaux opened his eyes. "You stay right here, Pop," Clay said. "We'll be back at the house in no time. You'll be all right."

He started into the cab of the pick-up, then paused briefly, his eyes meeting mine. "Paul Agee called me before he took off," he said. "He knew only that something had come to a head."

"Is that all you know?" I asked.

"Hell, I scarcely know that," he shot back, clambering into the truck. I watched it roar off, a small cloud of dust rising into the night after it. Slowly, I turned away, pulled myself into the saddle and waited as Amanda swung onto Saladin. She rode beside me in silence; finally we reached Darkwater Farms. She stabled Saladin as I put the chestnut into a stall. I faced her then in front of the stallion's stall.

"He found you," I said. "He saved you. Somehow, he knew." She nodded, unsmiling, her eyes round, flicking to the stallion. "Tell me, Amanda, tell me, now," I said. I watched as she drew a deep breath and slowly formed her words, each one an effort.

"Victor killed mother," she said. "I saw it, all of it." Amanda shuddered and, inside myself, I echoed the movement. "I reached the living room as mother tried to wrestle the gun away from him. She had crossed him. Victor always went into a rage when he was crossed. They fought for the gun and he got it away from her." I thought of the words on the death certificate... *traces of cleaning oil on both hands of victim*. Of course, she had used both hands in struggling for the gun, I bit out silently. Amanda went on. "He shot her then, on purpose, deliberately."

Waves of horror buffeted me as I envisioned the scene as Amanda must have seen it. "I don't remember much of anything after that," she said. "I didn't want to."

I reached out, touched her cheek. "Tonight, it was Victor who took you out of your room," I said.

"Yes," she said. "He surprised me, hit me with something and I blacked out."

"And the other night, when you ran off on Saladin?" I asked. "Victor, again?"

She nodded. "He opened my door, stood there with a pistol in his hand and laughed at me. I could only see mother again—as he shot her. I ran, out the window and down to Saladin."

I grimaced. Victor had almost had his victory that night, his attempt had been very close to successful. He'd expected Amanda would do just what she'd done, in terror and blind fright. I felt another wave buffeting me, this time of guilt. Amanda had given me the core of it, the truth that lay at the very center; there was much that began to fit now, but so much that still didn't fit. However, the picture had changed, in shape, in content and in color. Major Jeffries had laid plans; part of them had been his obsession that Amanda ride Saladin so that everyone could see her. But those plans were suddenly not what I'd concluded they were. I had indeed opened a Pandora's box.

Amanda was standing motionless in front of me and I reached out to her. "Do you want me to stay with you?" I asked.

"No, I'll be all right, now," she said. "It's over, now, all over."

"It's over and it means a new beginning," I said as I walked to the house with her. "You've a new life ahead of you, now, Amanda."

She nodded, looked almost dreamily at me. "Here," she said softly. "I think I'll stay here. It's what mother always wanted for me."

"Then stay here," I said and watched her walk the hall to her room, her head held high. I went to the phone and called the Thedeaux home. Clay's voice answered. I wanted to know about Doc Thedeaux and all the other pieces that still didn't fit.

"He's asleep. I gave him a sedative. The bullet only grazed his scalp," Clay said. "Ten years ago it wouldn't have even slowed him down."

"Did he say anything to you about all that's happened tonight?" I asked.

"Yes. He spoke to me as I dressed the wound. I can come over now, if you like."

"Please," I said and put the phone down.

I went into the bathroom, freshened up and then walked outside into the night, to sit on the bottom rail of one of the corrals. I waited. Waiting had never gone on so long.

Finally, I heard the sound of the little pick-up approaching, then saw lights prowling the darkness in front of it. Clay rolled to a stop, climbed out and came over to ease himself down beside me. I spoke before he had a chance to begin; there was something I had to tell him.

"I saw the contents of that box the Major has," I said. Clay gazed at me, slowly nodded, pursed his lips.

"Dad told me about that box," he said quietly. "The Major was never a trustful man. He went to great lengths to insure his secrets would be kept."

"Blackmail, I think, is the name for that," I said.

"Not completely, not in the true use of the term. He never used the things he gathered to force Dad to do anything, only to make sure he wouldn't ever tell certain things. It was a form of blackmail, I guess. Yet they remained good friends. Dad's done a lot of things that shaded the law in all his years here in the back country. I dare say every country doctor has; in Dad's case it was all done for the best interests of the people involved."

"Yes, I'm sure of that," I said. "Amanda told me about Victor and her mother, and I know about the will," I said.

"It seems that the Major thought Victor would grow out of his problems, all the time knowing better deep down inside himself," Clay went on. "Dad said that he was too proud to do anything about Victor as the boy grew up and the changes he'd hoped for didn't happen. The tragedy with Amanda's mother was a closed book, beyond repairing. He had shielded the boy from that indictment, but finally he had to face the truth, that Victor was a child of madness, a truly schizoid personality, a dangerous person. Yet the Major still clung to the hope that he could keep that danger somehow contained here at Darkwater Farms. Then something happened which made him realize that that was impossible." Clay paused and I waited. "When Amanda turned eighteen, Victor got a lawyer out of the county and filed a claim for the estate, using the fact that Amanda was insane, incapable of inheriting the estate as a normal person, and pointing out the years she had been confined."

"The will provides that the Major inherit the estate if Amanda were incapable," I said.

"That's true, but, as Dad told me, Victor wanted to press the suit in court to have Amanda legally removed. The court would, then, award the estate as per the provisions of the will, to the Major. All Victor had to do, then, was to get rid of the Major and the estate would become his. When his original suit was filed, Major Jeffries realized what he was going to do—he really feared Victor then."

"Why didn't he go to the authorities about Victor?" I asked.

"How?" Clay rejoined. "Admit that the suicide had been murder? Admit to being an accessory to his wife's murder after ten years, dragging my father in with him?" Clay shook his head. "No, the Major decided that the first thing he had to do was to prove that Amanda was fit to inherit the estate, that she was capable, not beyond helping and improving."

"The fastest way was to show her riding Saladin in front of everyone in the community," I almost gasped.

"Exactly," Clay said. "He could call countless witnesses before the court. It would be enough to destroy the suit claiming her unfit. That was to be his first step. The next would be to get Amanda away someplace where she'd be safe and then wait for the next time Victor erupted. Instead of covering up then, he'd move to have him confined, put away."

"And Amanda?" I asked.

"Dad said that the Major had uncertainties about her mental health. He was open, willing to wait and see. Of course, he felt he could say nothing to anyone until after the show, after she'd proven herself. So her riding Saladin at the meet was an obsession, more of one than anyone suspected. Except my father."

"I read everything wrong," I said quietly. "Oh, God, how terribly wrong."

"I don't know that you could have seen it any differently than you did," Clay said. I shook my head, unwilling to accept his kindness, feeling wrapped in guilt.

"I even suspected you," I said, drawing the little pill envelope out of my pocket. "I found this on the wheel of my car where the fuel-line had been punctured."

Clay half-laughed. "I keep dropping those things all over. I probably lost that one here and the wind just blew it to the wrong spot at the wrong time."

"I think I was at the wrong place at the wrong time," I murmured, as I felt his hand turn my face.

"No, just the opposite. Amanda responded to you and you had faith in her. You and the stallion touched her, reached her, each in your own way. It was a good thing. If she hadn't ridden, if you hadn't come to teach her enough, the Major's plans would have failed and Victor would have been successful. But, more important, Amanda would have failed, too."

"It's the one really bright light in all of it," I said, reflecting with a note of pride I allowed myself. "Amanda was worth all of it, I guess. I'm glad for her, so terribly glad."

The sound of a car approaching cut into our conversation and Clay's arm went around me as Paul Agee drove up in the old Lincoln limousine. He got out, tired, his face strained. "They think he'll live," Paul said. "It'll be tight but they think he'll make it. I've called the Police to pick up Victor's body."

He strode into the house and I turned again to Clay. All that had happened came into place at last, starting with the closed road when I first came here. Victor had put up the pole, hoped I'd plunge into the bayou; it would all have been over before it started. He'd been the one who slipped the photo under Amanda's door, another attempt to drive her into a complete mental collapse. He'd released the bull while I was in the corral, and shot the pirogue out from under me. Only one thing still remained unexplained. "Someone let Saladin out into the corral to save me that night. Someone here had to know, or to suspect Victor," I said.

"Only one person," Clay said. "Don't you know?" I followed his glance to the lighted window of Amanda's room and suddenly I felt warm and dense, happy and guilty. Of course, I realized now. Amanda had come down, seen the bull in the corral with me. She hadn't improved enough yet to step forward but she had rushed to Saladin, let him into the corral and then slipped away unseen.

"What now?" Clay's question broke into my musing.

"Get my car fixed, pack and leave in a day or two," I said.

"Where?"

"I've friends in Kentucky. They want me to ride for them and they'll help me start a breeding farm of my own."

"A veterinarian in the family would certainly be a help to anyone starting a breeding farm," Clay remarked.

"Yes, it certainly would," I said. "Aren't you going to stay here?"

"Not for long. I'd like Kentucky," he said, almost idly. "We could explore deeper into this business of communication between living creatures." His eyes held mine, a faint smile in their depths. "We might even explore that special communication called love," he said. "There's clearly more strength and more mystery in it than we know."

"I think we're exploring a little of it right now," I said as his lips moved toward mine. He pressed against my mouth, warmly and tenderly, exploring. Finally he pulled back.

"Let's explore it more," he said. "For a long time, a lifetime."

"Yes, let's do that," I said.

The wind had stopped crying. There'd be a new day soon. I leaned against Clay. It was a good feeling and I promised myself not to let it go. His hand pressed tight around my waist. Communication, I reflected; so many parts to it, so much more than mere words. He didn't even have to say he loved me. I knew it. The words would come, of course. But they would only be an affirmation. We stayed there and watched the night slide into tomorrow.

GLOSSARY

AHSA — The American Horse Show Association, arbiter and regulating body of all official, recognized horse shows in the United States.

Boudin — A pork dish of the Cajun country made with rice and hot spices.

Boring — When a horse lowers his head, bends his neck until his chin is almost touching his chest, making it extremely difficult to control him with the bit.

Curry-comb — A rubberized, oval grooming tool used to stimulate and cleanse the coat.

Change-of-lead — A horse at canter or gallop always strikes out or "leads" with the legs of one side or the other. The rider's ability to control the horse's leads from one to the other.

Dandy Brush — Grooming tool for removing caked mud and heavy dirt.

Diagonals — At the trot, a horse's feet move alternately in diagonal pairs. The rider rises in the saddle to match this beat. In equitation classes, the rider is asked to post (rise) to either the right or left diagonal.

Equitation Classes — Horse Show classes judged strictly on the ability or horsemanship of the rider.

Gratons — Cracklings in Cajun dialect; crisp, browned pork rind and rendered hog's fat.

Hoof Pick — Tool used in careful cleaning of the horse's feet.

Martingale — A strap attached to the horse to keep him from lifting his head too high.

Quarter Horse — Smallish, short-backed, muscular horses most often used for range work, polo and other strenuous activities, named for the quarter-mile, fast races they ran in Colonial times.

Sweat Scraper — Grooming device used to clean sweat and water from the coat.

Stable Rubber — Tool for giving a high-gloss polish to the horse after basic grooming.

Saddler — A specific breed, very showy riding horse, high-spirited and beautiful to watch. Term is colloquial for this breed, the American Saddle Horse.

Stall Courage — The unruliness shown by a horse kept too long in a stall without being ridden or properly exercised.

Three-Gaited Saddle Horse Class — The horse must demonstrate a walk, trot and canter on command and is judged on performance, quality and manners.

Thrush — An infection of the frog of the horse's foot, that part which is the strong, elastic shock-absorber of the foot, and of vital importance.